What woman wouldn't be affected by Mike Landis?

The years had honed his good looks into white-hot sexuality. He'd always been broad shouldered and muscular, and now he moved with a masculinity that was wickedly attractive.

But she knew about his dangerous side. And his need to prove himself by overcoming any challenge. Seven years ago she'd been that challenge. The daughter of the wealthiest man in town, she was everything the son of the town drunk couldn't have.

She suspected his penchant for challenge had been further honed by his experiences with Special Forces. The framed picture on the wall beside his desk of those haunted, grim-faced soldiers came to mind. Even with his face camouflaged with paint, Mike stood out as the team leader.

Dear Harlequin Intrigue Reader,

This month Harlequin Intrigue has a healthy dose of breathtaking romantic suspense to reignite you after the cold winter days. Kicking things off, Susan Kearney delivers the first title in her brand-new trilogy HEROES INC., based on a specially trained team of sexy agents taking on impossible missions. In *Daddy to the Rescue*, an operative is dispatched to safeguard his ex-wife from the danger that threatens her. Only, now he also has to find the child she claims is his!

Rebecca York returns with the latest installment in her hugely popular 43 LIGHT STREET series. *Phantom Lover* is a supersexy gothic tale of suspense guaranteed to give you all kinds of fantasies…. Also appearing this month is another veteran Harlequin Intrigue author, Patricia Rosemoor, with the next title in her CLUB UNDERCOVER miniseries. In *VIP Protector*, a bodyguard must defend a prominent attorney from a crazed stalker. But can he protect her from long-buried secrets best left hidden?

Finally rounding out the month is the companion title in our MEN ON A MISSION theme promotion, *Tough as Nails*, from debut author Jackie Manning. Here an estranged couple must join forces to solve a deadly mystery, but will their close proximity fuel the flames of passion smoldering between them?

So pick up all four of these thrilling, action-packed stories for a full course of unbelievable excitement!

Sincerely,

Denise O'Sullivan
Senior Editor
Harlequin Intrigue

TOUGH AS NAILS
JACKIE MANNING

HARLEQUIN®

TORONTO • NEW YORK • LONDON
AMSTERDAM • PARIS • SYDNEY • HAMBURG
STOCKHOLM • ATHENS • TOKYO • MILAN • MADRID
PRAGUE • WARSAW • BUDAPEST • AUCKLAND

ISBN 0-373-22708-6

TOUGH AS NAILS

Copyright © 2003 by Jackie Manning

This edition published by arrangement with Harlequin Books S.A.

Visit us at www.eHarlequin.com

Printed in U.S.A.

ABOUT THE AUTHOR

Jackie Manning believes in love at first sight. She and her husband, Tom, were married six weeks to the day after they first met and he proposed, many happy years ago. Home is a 150-year-old colonial in Maine, where they live with their shih tzu and Aussie terrier. When Jackie isn't writing, she's researching and visiting interesting places to write about. She loves to hear from her readers. You can write to her at P.O. Box 1739, Waterville, ME 04963-1739.

Books by Jackie Manning

HARLEQUIN INTRIGUE
708—TOUGH AS NAILS

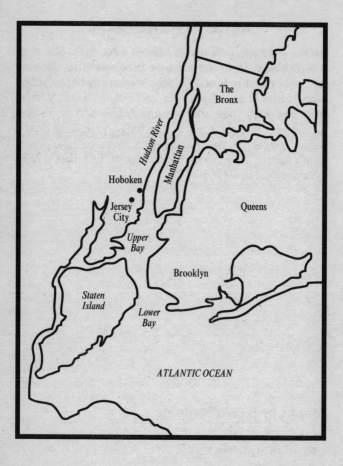

CAST OF CHARACTERS

Michael Landis—A former military man, he now owns a state-of-the-art security company. Little does he know that his ex-wife is about to break in to his heart.

Brianna Kent—She's being stalked by a dangerous man and her only hope is to seek help from her ex-husband. He might be able to protect her from her stalker, but who'll protect her from him?

Lawrence Cunningham—Brianna's colleague seems to have a little more than a professional interest in her.

Simone Twardzak—Brianna's secretary doesn't just answer the phone and schedule appointments.

The Stalker—He's always watching. He's always listening. But soon that won't be enough.

Chapter One

Brianna Kent bolted upright in bed, her chest pounding. Was the noise she heard a dream or was someone prowling around her apartment? Her hand trembled as she brushed back the sweat-dampened hair from her face. Too terrified to turn on the light, she froze, listening. But all she heard was her thudding heartbeat and the terrifying silence of her bedroom.

Nothing would come from huddling with fear in her bed, imagining all sorts of things. She tossed back the covers, swung her feet to the floor and forced her brain to think.

Only a fool would break into a full-security apartment building with burglar-alarm warnings plastered at every window and door. Still, if she didn't check out the noise, she'd be awake until the clock radio blared to life in a few hours.

She slipped into her white terry-cloth bathrobe, then opened the drawer of her bedside table. Taking the 9 mm snub-nosed Beretta from its case, she slipped the weapon into her hip pocket. The revolver hung heavily against her thigh, a grim reminder of the peril that came with her career. But she knew how to deal with threats. Although she hated guns, she'd learned to handle a weapon. The sharpshooter award above the fireplace proved it.

She clutched the lapels of her robe and creaked open the

bedroom door. Peering into the narrow corridor, she was surprised to find the living room at the end of the hall brightly lit.

Damn. How could she have forgotten? Nora was sleeping over before flying out of JFK in the morning. Brianna, herself, had left the light on for her. Feeling like a fool to forget her aunt's visit, she almost laughed with relief. Worry and lack of sleep were playing tricks on her mind.

Tightening the belt of her robe, she headed for the kitchen. Nora was probably unable to sleep and heating a glass of milk.

As Brianna crossed the blue-carpeted living room, her gaze caught the corner of a large envelope peeking out from beneath the front door. Her stomach clenched as recognition brought her to full alert. The manila envelope was identical to the three others that had been slipped under her office door in the last two weeks.

For a moment, she couldn't breathe. *He knows where I live!*

She forced back the fear as her hand found the cold steel inside the pocket of her robe. Something *had* awoken her.

Dear God! Maybe he'd picked the lock and was in her apartment. Her gaze flew to the heavy security chain still attached to the wall.

Get a grip, Brianna. The door is locked from the inside. You and Nora are perfectly safe. And this time, he'd made a mistake. Whoever did this apparently didn't know that security cameras covered the apartment corridors and would have caught him on video.

She dashed to the telephone on the desk. Her hands trembled as she fumbled the receiver from the hook, then tapped in the number for Apartment Security.

After one ring, a man's deep voice answered. "Security. Collins here."

"This is Dr. Kent in apartment 2304. Someone slipped

an anonymous envelope under my door sometime between now and midnight." She paused to steady herself. "I'd like to view the videotape as soon as possible."

After a slight pause, he said, "I'm sorry, Dr. Kent. But our cameras have been down since before midnight. Our maintenance team is still checking the matter."

"Does that mean none of the security cameras in the building were operating?"

"I'm afraid so. But I'll forward your request to the manager, Ed Jenkins. I'll have him call you as soon as he comes in later this morning. Is there anything else I can do for you?"

Her frustration rose, then she realized it was the middle of the night. "N-no, thank you. Tell the manager that I'll stop in to see him on my way to work later this morning."

When she'd hung up, she wondered if she should call the police and leave a message for Lieutenant Jeffries. He'd told her to call him if she received any more envelopes.

She picked up the phone again, then saw Nora staring at her from the hallway.

Her aunt's sharp gaze swept over her. "What's wrong, dear?" Nora hurried toward her, hazel eyes wide behind her gold-framed glasses. "Your face is white as a sheet. Why, you're shaking."

Brianna put the phone back in its cradle and forced a calm she didn't feel. "That was Security. I thought I heard a noise, but everything is fine now."

Nora's thin eyebrows lifted. "I couldn't help overhearing your conversation, dear." Her head turned toward the envelope lying beneath the front door. "You don't know who left this?" Nora scurried toward the door as though she was going to pick up the envelope.

"Don't touch it!" Brianna rushed to her side. "There may be fingerprints"

"Fingerprints?" Nora stared at her. "Brianna, what's

going on? I heard you say the security cameras aren't working?''

"The maintenance crew will have them working in no time.''

Nora glanced back at the envelope lying against the blue carpeting. "Don't you want to see what's inside?''

Brianna shook her head. She didn't have to open the envelope to know what was inside. But she didn't want to worry her aunt, so she kept the thought to herself. "Whatever it is, it's not important. Just someone's idea of a joke, I'm sure.'' She gave Nora what she hoped was an everything's-under-control look. "I'll drop the envelope at the police station on my way to the office this morning.''

Nora's eyes narrowed. "Brianna. What's going on?''

She sighed, knowing full well that her aunt would insist upon knowing everything before either of them would be going back to bed. "Let's go into the kitchen and have some warm milk,'' Brianna said lightly as she put her arm around the older woman.

Nora gasped. Her hand flew to her heart as she glanced at the pocket of Brianna's robe. "You're carrying a gun!''

Brianna looked down at the heavy bulge at her side. "I-I'm sorry to frighten you. When I thought I heard a noise, I…'' She paused, knowing that despite her best intentions to allay Nora's anxiety, her aunt was worried sick.

Brianna shrugged helplessly. "Excuse me while I put away the weapon, then we can talk.''

When she returned to the kitchen, her aunt had poured two glasses of milk, and was standing in front of the microwave oven, her arms folded. For a moment, Brianna was reminded of the many times she'd come home from middle school to find Nora in the kitchen, a plate of fresh-from-the-oven oatmeal cookies and hot cocoa waiting.

Nora had become a fixture in her brother's home after Brianna's mother had died, when Brianna was eight. Nora was someone everyone could count on. Ordinarily, Brianna would have been comforted to have her aunt visit. But until the police found the stalker who was sending the envelopes, Brianna might be endangering her aunt.

Rubbing the tight knot at the base of her neck, Brianna sat on the kitchen stool. She waited until her aunt placed the warm milk in front of her before she spoke.

"In the past two weeks, three envelopes containing photographs of me have been slipped under the door at my office. The first photo was taken in the parking garage across from my office while I was getting into my car."

Nora bit her lip as she listened.

"The second photo arrived a few days later," Brianna continued. "It was a picture of me at a neighborhood restaurant with a dozen friends for Marcie's baby shower. The third photo arrived last Monday. It was taken of a colleague and me having a drink after work." She waved her hands. "Nothing seems connected. Nothing makes any sense."

Nora studied her over her glasses. "Except to the twisted mind who sent them."

Brianna agreed, but she didn't want to alarm Nora any more than she already had.

"You're no match for a stalker," Nora said finally. "I'm afraid for you, dear."

"I've done everything that can be done. I've contacted the police. I know karate, I'm trained with a handgun. My apartment building is one of the most secure in Manhattan."

Nora sniffed. "Not when the security cameras aren't working." She started toward the kitchen door. "This person is fixated on you, Brianna. I've seen this very thing on those crime shows on TV. I'll bet the stalker disabled those video cameras himself!"

Brianna frowned as she watched her aunt. "Nora, where are you going?"

"I'm unpacking my bags." Nora paused and shot a look over her shoulder at Brianna. "Until the police catch the stalker, my place is with you. I'm going to cancel my trip to my sister's—"

"Nora! You'll do nothing of the kind."

Nora glanced at her watch. "I'll call Laura in a few hours. It's only one o'clock now in Denver."

Brianna put her hand on the older woman's arm. "I love you for wanting to help," she said in a soft voice. "But there's nothing you can do. Let's not hear any more about canceling your trip to see Laura."

Nora's eyes glittered behind the gold rims. "I'll go only if you promise me one thing."

Brianna smiled to herself. "Of course, darling. What is it?"

"I want you to call TALON-6. They're a security agency here in the city. I know they can help you."

"TALON-6?"

"Yes, they have an office in midtown. I'd feel so much better if I knew they were looking out for you."

Brianna crossed her arms. "You know these people?"

Nora averted her eyes and fixed her gaze upon her recently manicured nails. "I've carefully followed the owner's career since he was in high school," she added, examining a pearl-lacquered tip.

"One of your former pupils?" She wasn't surprised. Her aunt kept in touch with most of her students. Having no children of her own, Nora had always played surrogate mother to her former math students.

Nora focused on her cuticles. "Yes, he was. I've known him ever since he was in the troubled-youth program, many years ago. I've watched him grow from a defiant teenager into a fine young man who later became—" Nora hesitated and their eyes met "—your ex-husband."

For an instant, Brianna felt as if she'd been kicked in the

stomach. She swallowed hard, trying to catch her breath. "I had no idea Michael was back in the country," she said finally, after an uncomfortable pause. The last she'd heard, he was in Iraq or some such place.

Nora shook her head. "He's been out of Special Forces for over two years now."

Brianna felt a wrench of agony, as if Nora had betrayed her. Immediately, she felt guilty for such pettiness. Her aunt Nora and uncle, the Judge, had been like parents to Michael, and many troubled students like him, long before Brianna had met him.

Her throat tightened, and she glanced to see Nora's compassionate gaze studying her.

"Seven years is a long time," Nora said. "Mike has changed, just as you have."

"Some things don't change."

The words echoed between them, and Brianna could feel what little was left of her self-control unravel. "I'm certain in a city the size of New York we can find someone else who—"

"My dear, please listen—"

"I'm afraid not. The subject is closed."

Her aunt's lips narrowed, her chin lifted. "I had no idea you still have such strong feelings for Mike."

"I don't! How could you say that? Since our divorce, I've had other relationships. I was engaged to Jordan for a year."

Nora's mouth lifted slightly. "Six months."

She glared at her aunt. "Well, it felt like a year."

"Then if you have no emotional baggage where Mike is concerned, you can call him in the morning."

Brianna counted to ten before she spoke. "Maybe Mike won't want to see *me*," she said with more sharpness than she'd have liked.

Mike walked out on our marriage, joined the army with-

out a word. Without any attempt to fight for what had been good between us. The sudden stab of rancor surprised her.

Nora's eyes softened with kindness. "Whoever is sending these pictures is a real threat. You know as well as I do that Mike will see you," she added gently. "And you can trust him to know what to do."

Brianna bristled, unable to stop herself. "I don't want Mike in my life again."

Nora put a hand on her niece's arm. "I'm only asking that you show Mike the photographs. He'll put you in touch with people who can help."

If they didn't agree soon, neither of them would get any sleep. "Very well, Nora. I'll think about it."

Nora pursed her lips. "You looked just like your father just then, when he was a little boy, trying to get out of something." She tilted her chin in challenge. "You either agree to see Mike or I'm canceling my trip."

Brianna groaned. Nora meant well, but she had no idea the real reason behind the failure of her marriage. They were doomed before the ink was dry on the marriage license.

Michael Landis had been her first love, and maybe the only man she would ever love. That fact had become painfully clear while she'd been engaged to Jordan. Poor Jordan. Their relationship never had a chance.

Dear God, she hoped she'd never love someone as she'd loved Mike. Love like that had almost destroyed her.

"I'm not being evasive, Nora. It's...it's... Oh, how could you forget what Mike did? He signed the divorce papers and walked away without so much as a look back. He never even tried to stand up to my father and fight for our marriage, or for me." Hot tears stung her eyes as the pain of those days hit her with the force of a tornado.

Seven years still wasn't long enough to forget the pain.

Nora's lips pressed together. "I know your father never approved of Mike, but—"

"And Dad was right." She fought back the sting of tears. "He always said that Mike would jump ship, just like his mother did."

"You've never heard Mike's side of it."

"Not because I didn't try." Brianna closed her eyes, fighting the flood of memories she thought were buried years ago. "I'm sorry, Nora. I know you're only trying to help." She took a shaky breath. "But I won't contact Mike."

"Then I'm staying with you until the stalker is caught. You shouldn't be alone."

Brianna stared at her aunt. "Be reasonable—"

"You're the one who's not being reasonable." Her aunt folded her arms across her chest in that familiar stubborn gesture. "Either you make an appointment to see Mike, or I'm not leaving the city," Nora repeated.

Exasperated, Brianna shook her head. "Mike considers me the biggest mistake of his life. I'm certain he'll suggest another agency."

Her aunt's eyes twinkled. "Then you have nothing to worry about, do you?" She stood on tiptoe and brushed her lips against Brianna's cheek. "I'll see you in the morning, dear." She was smiling as she hurried down the hall toward the guest room.

Brianna cradled her head in her hands and groaned. Dear God, didn't Nora realize that remaining here with Brianna could be dangerous? Who knew what motive the stalker had for frightening her with these photographs?

She glanced at the chilling reminder—the envelope beneath the door. Who knew what the stalker really wanted? He knew where she worked, where she lived. What was next?

She closed her eyes from the threat of involving Nora in

this. If making an appointment with Mike would get her aunt safely on the plane to Denver, then dammit, she could do it.

MIKE LANDIS SAT at the computer terminal, the telephone receiver wedged between his neck and shoulder. He let out a low whistle as he scrolled down through the wedding pictures that he'd received on e-mail. "For a homely cuss, you've got a sister who's one gorgeous bride," he said to his partner and best buddy, Liam O'Shea. "Did you tell Stacey that I was sorry to miss her wedding?"

On the other end of the line, Mike heard Liam's sigh. "Yeah, but she forgives you. She knew you were watching the shop so her big brother could walk her down the aisle."

Mike smiled, remembering Liam's loud, Irish family in south Boston. Whenever he'd spent time with Liam's mom and six sisters, he felt envy for all that he'd missed from his own childhood. Liam was one lucky guy.

"As if an act of war could keep you from giving Stacey away," Mike said finally.

"I can't believe my baby sister is old enough to be married."

"Seems like only last week when you were running surveillance on her boyfriends."

"Yeah, well…we're getting old, pal. Time we were settling down."

"Uh-oh. Sounds like your matchmaking sisters are working to snare you into the marriage trap." Mike chuckled. "Better hop a plane and escape while you still can."

"Actually, my sister Caitlin had hoped you'd be at the wedding. She'd invited the perfect woman for you. A kindergarten teacher."

Mike groaned. "Thank Caitlin for me, but my tastes run to less-than-perfect women."

"Well, you know Cait. She loves a challenge."

"Hmm." After a short pause, Mike scrolled down to a picture of Liam, his arm around a stunning brunette. "Looks like Cait found someone for you, though. Who is she?"

"She's the kindergarten teacher. I couldn't disappoint my sister, now, could I, ol' buddy?"

"Right, ol' buddy." Mike laughed.

"Say, why don't you and Jake fly down for the weekend. We'll go fishing off the Cape. Mom would love to have you, and Uncle Davy is here with a jug of his homemade wine."

"That's a winning offer, but Jake's in a Miami hospital. He was stung by a jellyfish while wading along a moonlit beach. A beauty queen on each arm, to hear him tell it. He had a nasty reaction to whatever it was the doctors gave him. He won't be back for another week."

Liam swore. "Sure you don't want me back at the office? With Clete and Russell in Saudi, you're all alone."

"Nothing's on the docket till next week. You'll owe me two tickets on the Yankees' first-base line when you finally drag your ugly carcass back to the office."

"You got 'em. In the meantime, I'll just have to play nice with my sisters' girlfriends, all of whom are hot and sexy, I might add."

At the sound of the soft rap at the door, Mike looked up to see his secretary, Bailey, stick her head inside the door. She scowled and waved a file folder at him in a hurry-up gesture.

"Gotta go, Liam. I'll call you later." He hung up and turned toward Bailey.

"You reminded me of your dad just now. Must have been the scowl."

She wrinkled her pug nose and grinned. "What a lovely compliment, Mike. Dad was six foot five, almost three hundred pounds of muscle, and wore size eighteen combat boots.'' She feigned a glare. ''I'm a size four, in case you haven't noticed.''

He grinned. ''You know what I mean. The same red hair. Same freckles. Same sass.''

She rolled her eyes, and he chuckled as she moved to the side of his desk and gazed at the framed picture of the Fifth Special Forces TALON-team that hung on the wall beside the bookcase. Six rugged men, dressed in combat tiger stripes, their faces darkened with camouflage grease, stood at the edge of the Colombian jungle, staring somberly into the camera. The picture was taken just six weeks before Bailey's father, Master Sergeant Stewart Thomas was killed in action. From that time on, the five remaining members of TALON-team vowed to take care of Stu's wife and daughter as their own family.

''Since I've come to work with all of you here at TALON-6,'' Bailey said, her voice tight, ''I've come to realize how lucky Dad was to have you guys in his life.''

''Your dad would be real proud of you, Bailey.''

She nodded, her eyes bright. ''Oh, before I forget,'' she said, her manner suddenly all-business. She put the file folder in front of Mike on the desk. ''You have a client waiting. She refused to fill out the standard office questionnaire. Said it may not be necessary because you might not want to take her case.''

Mike glanced up, curious. ''Funny thing to say. Did she say why?''

Bailey shook her head. ''No. But I'd see her if I were you. She's drop-dead gorgeous with legs a mile long. And she's not wearing a wedding band.''

He cocked an eyebrow. ''Not you, too. I don't need any help with my love life, thank you.''

Bailey grinned. ''Only trying to help. With Clete and Russell out of the country, Liam at Stacey's wedding and

Jake holed up in a Florida hospital, you've got smooth sailing.''

He growled. ''Out of here. Oh, by the way, does Miss America have a name?''

''Yeah. Her name is on the folder in front of your nose. Brianna Kent,'' she said as she stepped out the door.

Brianna Kent? Mike swiveled in his chair and opened the folder. He reached into his T-shirt pocket for a cigarette, then remembered he'd given up the filthy habit over two years ago.

Bailey must have heard the name wrong. He almost clicked on the office intercom for her to recheck the name, but he knew deep down in his gut that this was *his* Brianna. He'd always had a sixth sense where she was concerned.

His phone buzzed and he pressed the lever. He heard Bailey's voice ask, ''Mike, shall I send her in?''

Refuse. Say you're not taking new clients. Mike took a deep breath and braced himself.

Well, if she could face him, then he'd face her, too.
''Send her in.''

Mike rose, shrugged into his jacket and raked his hair back by the time the door swung open and Brianna Kent stepped into his office.

Chapter Two

Tall, willowy, and dressed in a summery, watery-blue silk dress, Brianna looked as he remembered her: warm, sexy and completely off-limits.

"Hello, Michael."

Her smoky contralto was nearly his undoing. For one brief, overwhelming moment, he didn't move. All he wanted was to look at her and absorb every changed detail about her. He knew how her skin felt beneath him. Knew the intimate places she'd loved him to touch, and her sounds of pleasure when he did.

"Brianna." His voice was huskier than he would have liked. Not trusting his voice now, he pointed to one of the leather chairs that faced his desk. She nodded, then eased gracefully into the seat, the motion sending her shoulder-length, silvery-blond hair shimmering in the afternoon light from the window.

His fingers twitched as he remembered brushing that hair until it shone like moonlit waves of satin down her back. When he'd first known her, she wore her waist-length hair parted in the middle and loose. She had looked like what he imagined a storybook princess to be. *His golden princess,* he'd called her, and she'd laugh in that rich, throaty way that always went straight to his heart.

"Thanks for seeing me on such short notice." Her voice

held no hint of emotion, but he noticed her fingers grip the strap on her leather bag.

Her gaze swept his office, more out of politeness than curiosity, he would guess. "Nora told me you were doing very well." She smiled. "I'm glad for you, Michael." Her eyes held his. "And you're looking well."

The proper boarding schools had taught her to be gracious under pressure. He wondered if she really gave a damn how he was doing, business or otherwise. But he let the comment drop. "And so are you." He swallowed. "How is Nora?"

The smile she gave him warmed her eyes. "Nora's fine, thank you. She left this morning for Denver to visit her sister for several weeks." Brianna hesitated, and he couldn't quite believe that his wife—his ex-wife—was really sitting in front of him.

Hell, they were chatting away as though nothing had happened seven years ago. But his palms were damp and his throat felt as if he'd swallowed a basketball.

"I've been back in the city for two years, Brianna. I hardly think you just happened to find yourself in my neighborhood."

"Of course." She fixed those moss-green eyes on him, and he could see reluctance and something else.

"You're right. I'll get to the point." She slipped her handbag strap from her arm and withdrew a large envelope from inside the bag. "I'm a psychologist now, with an office here in the city."

Over the years, he'd kept track of almost everything about her through her aunt. Nora mentioned that Brianna had finished her doctorate, opened her office and became engaged to a London plastic surgeon. Nora also told him when Brianna's engagement had been broken, and he cursed himself for the relief that news had given him.

"Most of my clients are women and teenagers from the city family-violence shelter."

He noticed her hands tremble as she slid the envelope across the desktop toward him. He leaned forward, curious what would bring her to see him.

"Over the past two weeks, I've received four anonymous envelopes, each containing one picture." As she spoke, Mike lifted the flap and pulled out three black-and-white photographs, all eight-by-ten glossies, and laid them across the front of his desk. "There're only three here."

"I left the last one with Lieutenant Jeffries at the local precinct on my way here. It was slipped under my door early this morning." She averted her gaze from the photographs, as though not wanting to face the evidence.

"Did Jeffries say he was running it for prints?"

"Yes, although I doubt if the lab will find any. The other photos were clean, too."

Mike nodded, then studied the pictures. Each one focused on Brianna in full close-up. The first picture showed her in a parking garage as she slid behind the wheel of a Jeep Wrangler hardtop. "Your car?" he asked.

She nodded. "I rent a parking space at a garage across from my office building."

Anyone could have easy access to her car, especially using a zoom lens, and not be seen, Mike thought. The second photo was taken in a crowded restaurant. Brianna was in the center of a circle of women, laughing. On the table, a basket of brightly wrapped gifts hung from the beak of a tall, smiling stork.

"A colleague's baby shower," she said. "That was taken two days before the photo arrived."

Mike's gaze lingered on the next photo: Brianna, drinking wine with a good-looking, dark-haired, bearded guy at a cocktail bar. "Your boyfriend?" He hoped the question sounded motivated by professional rather than personal curiosity.

She shook her head. "No. He's Larry Cunningham, a colleague."

"A psychologist?"

She nodded. "Yes, we share an office suite."

Are you sleeping with him? She looked as if she was ready to bolt from the room, so he didn't ask, but he'd have to know sooner or later.

He put the photograph alongside the others. "The picture Jeffries still has—where was it taken?"

"I'm at the outdoor market near my apartment." She shrugged. "I'm sniffing a cantaloupe." She almost laughed. "Honestly, Michael, I can't see any connection between these pictures, unless he's trying to show me that he knows my schedule."

"Ever consider that the stalker might be a woman?"

Her eyes widened, then her lips pressed in thought. "Possible, but I think unlikely."

He leaned back in his chair and stretched his long legs to the side of his desk. "Why? Do you think you know who's behind this?"

Her mouth tightened. "My first thought is Billie Ray Bennett. He's an ex-con with a history of violence against women. He's angry at me because I helped his girlfriend, my client, finally leave him. She's living in another state, safely away from him, Thank God."

"And Bennett believes you're the reason his girlfriend left him?"

"Exactly." She waved her hand. "Classic denial. It's easier for batterers to believe the problem is with those who help their victims escape than to accept responsibility for their own abusive behavior."

Mike pulled a compact computer from his pocket and

tapped at the keyboard. "Okay, Bennett is a start. Anyone else?"

She took a deep breath and raked her fingers through her hair. "I—I really don't know."

The crack in her confident shell tore a hole deep inside him. He wanted to gather her up, hold her close the way he did all those years ago when she'd awoken in his arms during a lightning storm, terrified and shaking.

But he wasn't her husband anymore. He wasn't the man she chose to keep her safe at night. She needed his professionalism, like any other client. A professional arrangement.

"Do you feel up to filling out some forms?" He was glad his voice sounded neutral.

"Forms?"

"The usual questionnaire. Address, phone number. That sort of thing." He shrugged. "It can wait till later if you'd—"

"Then you'll take my case?" The surprise in her voice was genuine.

He took a deep breath. "I can suggest one of the other TALON-6 partners if you'd rather not work with me."

"I-I'm surprised, that's all."

"Then why did you come?" Damn, he hated the sarcasm in his voice.

"If you want the truth…" Her voice was so low he had to strain to hear her. "Nora refused to leave New York if I didn't make an appointment with you." Her mouth quirked. "I was afraid she might be in danger. You know how stubborn Nora can be."

A family trait, as he remembered. Mike's gaze dropped to the photographs. So Brianna was here only because of her aunt's insistence. He swallowed, unsure how he felt about that.

"I don't think I'll have any problem working with you,

Michael.'' She leaned forward, her voice throaty. ''What's past is past. We have our own lives. I don't foresee any difficulty, do you?''

Foresee any difficulty? Hell, that's all he could see. But dammit, if she could work with him, then he'd sure as hell do his part. ''No. No difficulty.'' He even managed to smile. ''Let me make a few calls while you fill out the questionnaire Bailey gave you.''

He got to his feet as she nodded her understanding. He watched her rise, and when she stood, the sunlight from the window fell across her face and hair. For an instant, she looked as she had the first time he'd seen her, years ago.

He'd been nineteen and caddying at the Cape Hope Country Club. All eyes had turned to her as she led her three male golfing companions from the clubhouse and stepped toward the sunlit tee.

The largest of the men, the senior caddy Mike had seen around the club, had said something clever, and her smoky laughter was his reward.

Mike could only stare, his heart hammering through his veins as she strolled to the first tee, the men in giddy pursuit. Dressed in a sleeveless white T-shirt and shorts that enhanced her sun-bronzed arms and legs, she appeared not to have noticed that she'd captured every male eye on the course.

''She's Brianna Kent, Harrison Kent's daughter,'' Dr. Parker had warned before taking a swing with his driver.

''Harrison Kent? Of Kent Paper Industries?''

''Hmm. The same. You so much as talk to her, and you'll lose more than your job, son.''

How right you were, Doc, Mike thought as he pushed back the thought. He'd lost the job, the woman and his very soul.

After Brianna left his office, a trace of her perfume lingered. Mike shut his eyes against further memories that stirred in his brain.

Damn him, he was a fool to take her on as a client. But she was being stalked. Who knew what kind of crazy might be after her? She needed his help, and no one did his job as well as he did. And regardless of all that happened between them, Brianna knew it, too.

And maybe she was right; the past was past. They both were happy in their own lives. Why the hell not take her on as a client?

Piece of cake.

THE THREE-PAGE TALON-6 client questionnaire had taken Brianna only a few minutes to complete, but she lingered over the last sheet, purposely stalling. She needed time to pull herself together. She needed to calm the feelings that had been stirred up when she'd seen Mike again.

Her fingers still trembled as she noticed her unnaturally scrunched handwriting. If Mike remembered her normal flowing script, he'd know how nervous she was. She hoped he'd think her anxiety was due to the idea that someone was stalking her, not from seeing him again.

She thought she'd prepared herself to see him again. But when their eyes met and he'd flashed that heart-stopping grin, the years tumbled away. Memories of their kisses and being together rocked away that safe harbor she'd built for herself. She'd felt as breathless as when she'd first seen him.

She mentally shook herself. Her nerves were shattered from worry and lack of sleep. That was all. Besides, what woman wouldn't be affected by Mike Landis? He had always possessed that easy charm that made men envy him and women want to throw themselves at him, regardless of the consequences.

The years had honed his good looks into white-hot sexuality. He'd always been broad-shouldered and muscular, but now he moved with a masculinity that was wickedly attractive—that is, if she was interested. And she definitely was not. She'd been around that hairpin curve and had the skid marks to prove it.

No longer was she that naive, overly protected daddy's princess, attracted to the town's bad boy. Now she was a clinical psychologist who knew about life and the sex drives that motivated smart people to make foolish mistakes. She understood his dangerous side, too. His obsessive need to prove himself by overcoming any challenge.

Seven years ago, she'd been that challenge. The daughter of the wealthiest man in town, she was everything the son of the town drunk couldn't have.

She suspected his penchant for danger had been further honed by his experiences with Special Forces. The framed picture hanging on the wall beside his desk of those haunted, grim-faced soldiers came to mind. Even with his face camouflaged with paint, Mike stood out as the team leader.

She felt a tinge of envy. Mike shared something with those men that she had only dreamed of sharing with him as his wife. She knew he would connect with them, need them and trust them in ways he'd never been able to with her.

The cords of her neck throbbed. She closed her eyes and rubbed the back of her head. Damn, why was she putting herself through this torment? She pulled herself up and got to her feet. With the questionnaire in hand, she hurried to the secretary's desk. The sooner she got this over with the better.

MIKE FINISHED his conversation with Police Lieutenant Sam Jeffries, hung up the phone and stared out his office window on the twenty-first floor. Ribbons of bumper-to-bumper traffic crawled along the streets of midtown Manhattan. Millions of people, and one of them held a camera, watching, waiting, stalking Brianna. Waiting for the right moment to…to what?

Dammit, Bria. What have you gotten yourself into?

From what Lieutenant Jeffries had confirmed, the company that installed and serviced the security systems for Brianna's apartment building was highly reputable. Mike recognized the company name and agreed.

The apartment manager had told Mike that the timer on the video cameras had stopped last night at 11:54 p.m. The repair crew had found a timing-delay loop spliced into the building computer system. Whoever had done it required sophisticated know-how and equipment. He doubted this was the work of Billie Ray Bennett, unless the guy worked for the CIA.

Mike took a deep breath and forced himself to concentrate. But the image of how frightened Brianna had looked beneath that cool demeanor kept eating at him. If they'd been friends, he would have pulled her into his arms and promised her that he'd keep her safe.

But they weren't friends. No, she was a client, and she'd made very clear that's *all* she was. Hadn't she said that she didn't foresee any problems working with him?

He rubbed his chin, grudgingly admiring that ability in her. No doubt she'd realized long before she decided to leave him that their marriage had been the worst mistake in her life. On that they could agree.

He glanced at the photographs of Brianna in front of him, forcing his mind onto the case not the woman.

What kind of mind would go to such trouble to stalk her? He took a deep breath and moved back to his desk. If she agreed, he'd begin the case immediately. Once he installed the electronic equipment in her home and office, it wouldn't take long to find the answers. But his experience told him they didn't have much time. Whoever was behind sending her these photographs wouldn't be satisfied for long with only scaring her. More than likely, the stalker already knew that she'd gone to TALON-6.

A rap sounded at his door, then Brianna entered. "Your secretary said it was okay to come in." She handed him the questionnaire before taking a seat.

"I just spoke with Lieutenant Jeffries," Mike said, glancing over her form. "The police lab wouldn't get to the fingerprint results for a while. I took the liberty of asking him to forward the photograph to the crime lab I use. We'll get the results faster." He glanced at her. "That is, if it's okay with you."

"Of course."

"Jeffries will need your written authorization." He pushed the standardized form across his desk at her. "If you'll sign this, I'll fax it right out to him."

"Great." She picked up a pen, glanced over the agreement, then signed her name. When she sat back in her chair, he noticed her fingers were clenched. "I want to make one thing perfectly clear, Michael." Her eyes were wide and serious.

"My coming to you like this is strictly business. If we work together, I don't want…" She ran her tongue along her lower lip. "What I mean is, I don't see any reason to mention the past. I hope we can agree to this."

He felt a spark of anger. She really meant that *she* was able to put the past behind them, but she wasn't so sure about him.

Dammit, if she wanted it all business between them, then that's what she'd get. "The past is forgotten." He waved his hand as though brushing at a fly.

She leaned back and crossed her legs. "Good. Now, I'd like to know what you're planning to do."

He rubbed his thumb along the compact computer on his

desk. "I'm expensive. I use the latest technical equipment, much of which is continually being updated by my team and me. I'll assess your home, your office, then come up with a figure."

"I'm sure you'll be fair."

"Bottom line is that I'll do whatever needs to be done to see that you're protected."

Her gaze leveled with his. "I want to be kept informed of what you plan to do, and approve any actions you take beforehand. Agreed?"

He took a deep breath. She had no idea what she was asking. But he figured she needed to feel in control. "Of course," he said finally. Somehow they'd work out the details. "In the meantime, I'll need a complete list of your clients, plus a—"

"That's confidential information."

He glanced up from his notes to see her eyes snap with challenge. For a moment, he felt a touch of envy for those in her life she defended so staunchly. "Your clients are all suspects, Brianna. I wouldn't be doing my job if I didn't take that approach."

"I know my clients. Almost all are battered women. None of them would be capable of this."

Mike leaned back in his chair. "Sorry, but I'll need to see that list."

She sighed. "If you insist, I'll go over my client list with Dr. Cunningham. He deals more with criminal psychology. I'll have him profile any of my clients whom he believes might be the stalker."

Mike's gaze fell to the bearded man in one of the pictures on his desk. "That Cunningham?" he asked.

"Yes."

"Let me know when you talk with him. I'd like to sit in—"

"Mike, that's impossible. My patients' records are confidential."

He knew enough not to press her, but he'd see those records, with or without her help. He decided to change the subject.

"First, I'll take some measurements of your home and apartment—"

"Why?"

Was she going to challenge his every action? Damn, of course she was! They could never agree on anything.

"TALON-6 needs to know the dimensions and cubic yards of space in each room." He was pleased with the neutral tone in his voice. When she still looked confused, he added, "To determine the range for the audio and special listening devices we may need."

"Oh."

"I'd like to start immediately. I'll schedule a complete debugging surveillance for phones and all vehicles. Do you want to start with your office or apartment?"

"You can't believe my apartment is…bugged. That sounds so dramatic."

"The stalker knows your schedule. These pictures prove he knows when you're going in and out. We can't leave anything to chance."

"Of course. Do what you must."

Mike turned the pages of the questionnaire that Brianna had filled out. "I see you haven't been a recent victim of burglary. You haven't experienced any unusual interference on radios or TVs, at home or at your office. You haven't received any electronic gifts such as alarm clocks, lamps, boom boxes, CD players—"

"That's what I wrote on the form."

Her voice sounded tight. Although she was calm on the outside, he could sense she was wound tighter than a six-day clock. He wished he could make this easy but he couldn't.

"Gifts are an easy way for the stalker to get electronic equipment into your home or office without detection," he said finally. "You're certain you haven't overlooked something?"

She shrugged. "I've received flowers, presents for my birthday. The usual gifts from friends and colleagues. That's all."

"I'll want a list of all gifts you've received in the past twelve months." He frowned at her look of dismay. "It's important or I wouldn't ask."

She brushed her hair from her face. "I'm sorry. I'm not making this any easier for you. I—I guess I'm still in denial."

"It's perfectly natural, Brianna." God help him, but he wanted to take her in his arms and kiss away the worried crease between her eyes.

He forced his attention back to the form. She had checked off that she hadn't had any recent repairs or redecorating done in either her home or office. He had other questions, but they could wait until she was less tense.

"I'll start by having security devices installed in the halls and entranceways to your office and home—"

"But my apartment building already has surveillance cameras. The stalker got around them."

"My devices won't be detected, and they are tamperproof." He glanced at his watch. "Ready to go home for the day? Or would you like to stop off at your office first?"

"Michael, I have clients scheduled until four o'clock. Then I have a mountain of reports to finish. Can't we wait until tomorrow?"

He stood. "You don't have to be at home while the equipment is being installed." He grinned when she shot him another questioning glance. "We'll go to your office. I'll wait for you until you're ready to go home."

She shot him a look of exasperation. "That's not necessary. I'll give you my key, and when you're through with the apartment, you can drop it off with my secretary at the office."

He raised an eyebrow. "You didn't mention on the form that your secretary has access to the keys to your apartment."

She sighed. "Well, my secretary usually doesn't, but sometimes—"

"She either does or she doesn't."

Brianna's eyes snapped. "I forgot. So shoot me." He could see her composure slip away. No doubt she felt it had been a mistake to come here. "I don't need a bodyguard. All I want is to identify the stalker on video so I can press charges against him."

"Brianna, I'm not trying to scare you, but from what the police said, whoever is stalking you has the expertise—"

"Please, I don't need to hear how much danger I'm in, okay?"

"It's okay to be scared."

"I'm not scared."

He studied her. Beneath that stubborn pride she was terrified for her life and she hated that he knew it.

Her mouth tilted at the corners. "Okay, I'm scared." Her eyes snapped green fire. "Satisfied?"

"Nothing wrong with being afraid," he said gently. "It's what you do with your fear that's important." He tucked the compact computer into his jacket pocket and grabbed an attaché case from the bottom desk drawer. "Let's get a taxi and start at your office."

BRIANNA FELT her insides shake when Mike slipped beside her in the back of the taxi. After giving the driver the address of her office building, she leaned back and willed the butterflies in her stomach to go away, to no avail.

Maybe she was entitled to react foolishly where Mike was concerned. She'd known it would be hard to confront all those memories. How silly to have remembered him as that rebellious young daredevil. She glanced at him as he clicked his seat belt into place.

One thing hadn't changed. He'd always been able to see right through her, long before she was aware of her own true feelings. Her thoughts went back to that time so long ago, in that backwater town in Maine. She'd been a college sophomore, spending the summer with her father in Maine. She'd first seen Mike when he'd caddied at the local country club.

Mike had worked for her father, or sort of. Harrison Kent III had been owner of Kent Paper Industries, and Mike had worked there on a hydro-pulper. He lived with his father on Mill Street, the row of company houses the paper-mill employees rented.

She'd been nervous that warm, late-June afternoon when she found out where Mike lived and went to see him. She had planned to ask him if he'd volunteer as lifeguard for the country club's annual children's charity.

She located him in the backyard of one of the typical two-story clapboard houses that were built more than fifty years ago. Mike's jaw dropped when he saw her, then he quickly recovered when he crawled out from under the body of an old-model, yellow Trans Am.

He was naked except for a pair of faded denim shorts. She took a deep breath, trying not to appear unnerved at the sight of him. Serves you right for not calling him before dropping in, she chided herself.

''I was running errands for my aunt and thought I'd stop by.'' Although it was true, the statement sounded lame. The disbelieving look he gave her only increased her nervousness.

He eyed her sideways as he wiped his large, tanned hands on a clean rag. "Don't tell me. You just happened to be in the neighborhood."

Her cheeks flamed with embarrassment. "Why, yes, I was." Her tone sounded defensive. "I just dropped off some proofs for my aunt at the printer's, which is only two blocks from here." She was talking too fast, and she forced herself to be cool.

Her gaze glued to his brilliant blue eyes, although she was aware of his stunning, sun-bronzed torso. She wanted to stare at the fascinating way the black whorls of hair covered his hard muscles and funneled into a dark V past the button of his jeans.

His expression turned cold and flat. "What are you doing here?"

He was obviously upset that she'd come unannounced. If she had a lick of sense, she'd never have come.

"My aunt wanted me to ask you if you'd volunteer at the country club. They need a lifeguard for one weekend a month." Nora hadn't exactly asked her to ask Mike, but Brianna had seen his name at the top of the proposed list of candidates. "The summer program for underprivileged children is in high gear, and—"

"I told your aunt that I'd do it when she asked me last Saturday."

"Oh." Brianna felt like a fool. "I saw your name on the list and…" She took a deep breath to recover. "Nora didn't tell me."

His bottom lip quirked in disbelief. "Your aunt is quite a lady. She and the Judge have done a lot for me, and I owe them, big time." His blue eyes darkened and he lowered his stare to her breasts. She felt caged by his look, and a delicious weakness coursed through her.

"Why did you really cross the tracks to come all the way down to Mill Street, Brianna?"

She stepped back, not wanting to admit the truth, even to herself. "I—I told you." His dark look made her feel like a groupie at a rock concert. "Obviously my aunt either forgot or wanted to confirm that you hadn't changed your mind," she lied. She turned and almost ran toward her car. When she reached the backyard gate, with his long strides he had caught up with her.

Mike folded his arms across his broad chest, biceps bulging. "Tell me why you're here."

"I—I was curious."

"About me?"

"Yes."

"Why? Didn't your country-club friends fill you in on all the details? Did they tell you my old man is a drunken bum? That my mom ran off when I was two? That I'm no good? Didn't they warn you to leave me alone?"

She met his gaze evenly. "I make up my own mind."

"And have you?"

"Yes."

He waited for her to say more. When she didn't, he added, "If you're trying to make your old man angry, I'm not your guy."

"What?"

"You heard me. I'm not about to risk my job at your old man's paper mill just so you can prove to Daddy that you're a big girl. Now that you're eighteen and inherited your mom's money."

He must have noticed her look of surprise. "Oh, yeah. The country-club gossip doesn't limit itself to just Mill Street, Brianna. The Kent family is gossiped about, just like everyone else."

"If you're trying to make me uncomfortable—"

"Nothing like that. I don't care what you've got to prove, just leave me out of it."

"You self-centered jerk. How dare you think I'm interested in you. If you believe for one minute that I'm here to…to…" She watched a muscle clench in his jaw. She was frightened and excited by the sudden change in him.

His gaze dropped to the low neckline of her jade-green sundress. She'd carefully chosen the outfit before coming to see him. She knew the color complemented her golden tan and brought out the green in her changeable eyes. She knew the cut of the bodice accentuated her high breasts and narrow waist.

She went very still as he pulled her into his strong arms. Her breath caught as his mouth, hard at first, covered hers in a hot, openmouthed kiss. She wanted to wrench free, to prove that she was outraged, but instead, her body leaped to life and she felt her outcry melt beneath the heat of his kiss. She opened for him, her body full of sharp, exciting sensations.

Her arms circled his neck as her tongue twinned with his. She'd been kissed before, many times, but nothing like this.

Beneath the thin cotton of her dress, she felt his heart hammer with hers, and she was aware of the hard bulge in his jeans pressing against her.

He wanted her. The thought thrilled and frightened her as she drew him closer.

Just as suddenly, he released her. "That's why you came here." His voice was husky. "And we both know it."

He turned without looking at her and stormed toward the house.

Breathlessly, she stared after him, rigid with anger. Then she dashed to her car, never more humiliated in her life. He'd known why she'd tracked him down long before she'd known, herself. That was a trait of Mike's that had continued to amaze and infuriate her.

But he'd been wrong about one thing—she'd been attracted to him because of who he was, not because her father would disapprove of her dating him. Yet she knew that a part of Mike believed she'd married him to prove to her dad that she had a mind of her own. If she could have convinced Mike, would it have made a difference?

Hell no. She'd never been able to tell Mike anything. Well, as his client, she wasn't about to let him get the upper hand.

"...your reports?" Mike's voice interrupted her thoughts.

"W-what reports?"

From the seat beside her in the taxi, he'd been studying her. His blue eyes were bright with unreadable emotion. "The mountain of reports you said you have to finish. I asked if you can work at home on your reports."

She was aware of his subtle aftershave, spruce or maybe desert sage, and she felt a jolt of feminine response. God, he was so handsome. She fought to remember what he had asked her.

"The reports. Yes. Yes, I'll bring them with me." Her mind felt scattered. Maybe it was a good thing she wouldn't be working late at the office tonight.

She turned her head to glance out the taxi window and was surprised to see the cab pulling to a stop in front of her office building.

Chapter Three

Her office was on the fourteenth floor of a professional building that looked like most any other high-rise in upper Manhattan. From the street, a set of revolving doors opened onto a glass foyer with more greenery inside than Central Park.

The crowded lobby made Mike feel uneasy. Too open and public. Serious-faced businessmen and -women, dressed in designer suits, clattered across the gray marble floor to their offices and appointments. A stalker could easily blend into the crowd, pull out a 9 mm with a silencer, fire two quick shots at Brianna and get away before anyone would be the wiser.

Mike hurried her toward the bank of elevators. Thirty bronze nameplates, framed in glass, lined the wall. He gripped the attaché case and followed her into the first available car.

"Why don't I call you when my last patient leaves," she whispered when he moved beside her. "I'll be perfectly safe in my office."

"Let me be the judge of that."

She shrugged.

When they stopped at the fourteenth floor, the doors opened and a tall, bearded man in his mid-thirties, wearing a tweed blazer, corduroy slacks and loafers, waited. Mike instantly recognized him from the photo as Larry Cunningham. He dressed more like a college professor than a psychologist. He wore no wedding band.

Cunningham's face lit up when he saw Brianna. He smiled, his eyes crinkling. "Missed you at lunch, Brianna." His smile faded when he saw that Mike had stepped from the elevator with her.

"I took the morning off," she explained. "I had…an appointment." She gave Cunningham a weak smile as she strode beside Mike down the hall, rummaging in her bag.

Cunningham ambled on the other side of her, his attention back to Brianna. "I was hoping to have a moment with you."

She looked up, a key chain in her hand. "Can it wait, Larry? I'm running late." She paused in front of a frosted-glass door with her name stenciled across the window in gold letters. With an uneasy glance at Mike, she turned to Larry and introduced them.

Mike noticed that she didn't bother to mention that he was her ex-husband or that he was a surveillance specialist. No doubt Cunningham thought Mike was one of Brianna's clients, and he wondered if she'd meant to do so.

Cunningham gave Mike a sharp, assessing glance before leaving. "I'll see you tomorrow at dinner, Brianna."

So Cunningham and Brianna had a dinner date for Saturday night? Mike caught her look, and when Cunningham was out of earshot, she said, "It's a business dinner. A charity event. Hundreds of people will be there."

"I didn't say anything," he teased, but he didn't like the relief that knowing his ex-wife wasn't seriously involved with another man gave him. She could be dating a dozen guys and it was none of his business, he reminded himself.

Brianna pushed open the door and led Mike into a long, narrow waiting room. Warm, homey and welcoming. Two maple rockers flanked an oval coffee table. Two antique deacon's benches, covered in floral-print pillows, stood along each wall. Tiffany-glass shades adorned the lamps, and variegated ivy spilled from baskets on the side tables.

Installed into the ceiling were two inconspicuous air ducts, a perfect place for an unsuspecting video camera or recording device. So would the wall clock, the Tiffany lamps and the ivy arrangements.

"Do I detect a possessive streak in your friend Larry?" Mike asked after she motioned for him to have a chair.

"Heavens, no. I told you, we're only friends."

Mike wondered how happy Larry was about that arrangement, but he didn't say anything. Who could blame any guy for wanting to deepen a relationship with Brianna?

She frowned at the attaché case in his hand. "What will you be doing while I'm seeing clients?"

He hesitated. He didn't like being vague with her, but if the stalker had bugged her office, Mike didn't want to give out any information. "I'll be taking notes," he said finally. When she gave him a puzzled look, he put his finger to his lips, then pointed to the ceiling, in a gesture that meant whatever they said might be overheard. "Don't worry," he added. "I won't do anything we haven't already discussed."

She arched a brow and gave him a look that suggested he better be damn sure that he didn't. "Excuse me while I check my messages."

He strode back into the waiting room and leaned his briefcase against the bench. First, he'd sketch a preliminary layout of the office. After her clients left, he'd check the phones for listening devices. If someone wanted to overhear Brianna or her clients, the easiest place would be the telephone. All the stalker would need was a high-tech listening device, easily obtainable through the Internet.

He'd wait to check the office furniture and fixtures when Liam brought in the monitoring equipment and did a full sweep. He wished he'd been able to speak to Liam before he'd left for deep-sea fishing with his uncle. From what Liam's sister had said, Liam was expected back at the Cape by evening. Mike should hear from him as soon as he returned.

Damn, he couldn't ignore the sophistication of the timing-delay loop device that had been spliced into her apartment building's security system. He knew, firsthand, how mentally devastated Brianna would be if he found proof that the stalker had been listening to her every word. But she wasn't the kind of woman to fall to pieces when the going got rough.

He couldn't help thinking about his very first mission. For over two weeks, he'd played cat and mouse in the Colombian jungle, one-on-one with a sniper sent out by a drug lord. Living 24-7 with the knowledge that at any minute he might catch a bullet in the brain had taught Mike how to handle fear and turn it into an asset. When he'd finally caught the sniper at his own game, he became a different person than when he'd first parachuted into the jungle. It had taken him two more years to see the drug kingpin put behind bars, but Mike had become stronger for the ordeal.

Brianna would, too. But first, she'd have to live through that gut-wrenching terror. And when she did, he'd be there for her.

He sensed her, and when he looked up, she was leaning against the doorjamb, arms folded, studying him. She straightened when their eyes met. "My secretary's office adjoins my office and Larry's."

He nodded. "Under which doors were the photographs found?"

"The waiting-room door that opens into the hallway."

"Then the stalker wouldn't have needed a key." The idea gave him a feeling of relief.

In her office, she removed her suit jacket and draped it casually behind her desk chair, then glanced at the slim gold watch on her wrist. "My next client will be here any minute. I have one more after this appointment. Won't you reconsider and meet me back here at four o'clock?"

"Don't worry about me. I'll keep busy."

"Would you like some coffee while you wait?"

"No, thanks." He glanced at the stack of magazines on the coffee table. "This will give me a chance to get caught up on *Playboy*."

She feigned an indignant look. "I don't subscribe to *Playboy* magazine."

He frowned, trying not to grin. "Not even the swimsuit edition of *Sports Illustrated?*"

"'Fraid not."

"Okay. *Reader's Digest* it is." He winked as she smiled, then turned and went into her office, closing the door.

He was glad to see the tight lines of worry briefly fade from her eyes. He wished he'd tried harder to convince her to go straight home and rest. But Brianna could be stubborn. He didn't think she'd allow anyone, especially her ex-husband, to tell her what to do.

He scanned the address labels on the magazine covers sprawled across the coffee table. Brianna had the publications sent directly to the office instead of her personal address, he noticed with relief.

Just then, the hallway door opened and a young woman with large frightened eyes stepped inside. Her gaze widened when she saw him. She had black-rimmed eyes, spiked green hair and tattoos, and was probably in her late teens.

Mike grabbed a magazine and folded himself into a rocker. He crossed his leg and watched the girl out of the corner of his eye.

She stood, hesitating before finally taking a seat at the far end of the deacon's bench. After a few minutes, she

ignored him, intent on chipping away at her black nail pol-
ish, her hands and feet twitching to a tempo heard only in
her mind.

A minute later, Brianna's office door opened. "Come in,
Kristi," she said with a welcoming smile. The young
woman hung her head, jerked to her feet and silently followed Brianna inside the office.

Alone in the waiting room, Mike listened to see if he
could catch any of their conversation, but the interior walls
were adequately soundproofed.

He opened his briefcase and whipped out a camera. He
snapped various angles of the waiting room, the frosted-
glass doorway, the hall corridor and the office at the end
of the waiting area with the name Lawrence N. Cunningham, Ph.D., Clinical Psychologist stenciled on the frosted
window.

Did Cunningham and Brianna exchange keys to each
other's offices? If Brianna occasionally gave her secretary
her apartment key, how hard would it be for Cunningham
to get it?

Less than an hour later the door to Brianna's office
opened. "I'll see you again at the same time next week,
Kristi," Brianna said as she followed the teenager into the
waiting room. Shoulders bent, eyes downcast, Kristi left
without a word.

Brianna glanced at Mike, who was sitting in the corner,
jacket slung over the back of the rocker. Her gaze fixed to
the open black briefcase in his lap. He closed the case and
got to his feet when she came beside him.

"My next client left a message saying she needed to
cancel. There's a tearoom downstairs. I'm dying for a cup.
Care to join me?"

"Sure. But first, I need to go into your office for a few
minutes before we go."

He held up a countersurveillance device disguised as a

cigarette packet. If an eavesdropping bug or tap was connected anywhere in her phone lines, he'd find it immediately.

She glanced at the pack of cigarettes and frowned. ''I'd have thought you'd quit by now.''

He smiled. ''Come on, you might find this interesting.''

She arched an eyebrow and followed him into her office.

Mike began the electronic sweep at the desk-model telephone at her desk. He waved the cigarette pack alongside the phone and a tiny red bulb blinked.

Curious, Brianna took a chair and watched him extract a small wire from a leather packet and slip it around the mouthpiece cap. With a quick spin, the unit opened. He stared in concentration. Several seconds later, he withdrew a gray object, a little smaller than a dime.

Unsure what it meant, Brianna stared at the tiny object between his fingers, then at him. ''Is that a bug?'' she mouthed silently.

He nodded.

She leaned back into her chair, her knees weak as she stared at the evidence in front of her.

He held up a cautionary finger to his lips, his face grim. Reaching for a pad of paper from her desk, he picked up a pen and scribbled something, then pushed the paper toward her.

LET'S GET OUT OF HERE.

He crumpled the paper and put it into his briefcase. She watched numbly as he placed the listening device back inside the handset, replaced the cover, then hung up the receiver. As he returned his equipment into the briefcase, he motioned her to leave.

She grabbed her bag and glanced back at the desk telephone. Anger filled her with a fury she didn't know she possessed. *Her privileged telephone conversations with her clients had been overheard.* Whoever did this had to be stopped. She gazed at Mike, glad she'd found the courage to seek his help.

Mike grabbed her jacket from the back of her chair and came beside her. Gently, he draped it across her shoulders, and pulled her toward the door. Her hand shook as she opened her bag. When she found the key, she managed to steady it long enough to lock the office.

She felt his arm around her as she hurried beside him down the hall. Damn, she'd do everything in her power to find the bastard and make him pay for this.

Thank God Mike was here.

WHEN THEY WERE INSIDE the elevator, he warned her not to speak. She used the short wait to catch her breath. Besides, she needed to think through the pieces of the puzzle. One thing remained clear. The stalker had known her every move.

He might have followed her on foot from her office to the parking garage, or during lunch when she bought fruit at the farmer's market. He might have followed her by car to her apartment building. But he knew which apartment was hers. And in which bar she had met Larry for a drink after work. The stalker must have overheard her give out that information.

She'd made calls from her office only last week to have the locks changed on her apartment. She'd given her apartment number over the phone. Four days later she received the photograph that was slipped under her apartment door.

Dear God, what else had she said over the phone?

She'd called Mike's office. The stalker knew that Mike was on the case. By calling TALON-6, she'd put Mike in jeopardy, too, she realized as a frisson of fear shot through her.

She gazed up into his eyes. He gave her a crooked smile, fortifying and confident. "Still want to have that cup of tea? Maybe you need something stronger."

She closed her eyes for an instant. "I just want to get out of here."

"I know a place that's quiet and we can talk." He gave her an easy smile. "It's okay, sweetheart. Don't worry."

His comforting words tugged at something deep within her. Yes, she wanted to believe him, but her practical side knew better. Nothing would be okay again.

When the elevator reached the lobby, Mike took her arm and she gave in to the desire to be protected as he led her through the crowd and into the street. The blare of street noises mixed with the afternoon heat made her head pound. Mike hailed a cab, and she was still trembling when he opened the door for her. He gave the driver an address on Second Avenue, then settled back and put his arm along the back of the seat. Unable to help herself, she turned into him.

"Oh, Mike. I—I used the office phone when I called TALON-6 this morning." She dragged in a shaky breath. "I've put you at risk, too."

"Shh. Don't worry. This is what I do for a living."

"And my clients. Who knows how long their privacy has been compromised? I—I feel as though I should have done something to protect them."

He took her hand in his warm, firm grip. "You couldn't have known, Bria."

His special nickname for her and his comforting touch brought forth a flood of yearning. She had never liked nicknames when she was a child. She'd always refused to be called anything but Brianna. Yet when Mike had first called her Bria, they were making love for the first time, and the gentle way he spoke the name had sounded like poetry. No one had ever called her Bria since Mike had been a part of her life.

She should turn away from his strong, comforting embrace, but for this one brief moment she couldn't resist. Not just yet.

Yes, Mike made her feel safe, and dammit, that's what she needed right now.

No, cried a voice deep down in her soul. She was through leaning on any man. Hadn't she learned the hard way that the only person she could count on was herself? Whatever was going on, she would face the problem and triumph.

Bracing herself, she pulled her hand away and grabbed a tissue from her handbag. After blotting her mascara, she gave him a shaky smile. "I'm okay now."

His eyes narrowed. "I'm afraid it's worse than you think."

She glanced up at him. "What do you mean?"

"The device I found does more than just listen to your phone calls." His jaw clenched.

She could see his quiet anger toward whoever was behind this. Was he always this emotionally involved with his cases, or was she an exception?

"What do you mean by more than a listening device?"

"I won't know what the range of the transmitter is until I check it out in the lab." Mike whispered. "I know it picks up conversations while the phone is on the hook."

She shook her head in disbelief. "You mean the stalker has heard everything my clients have said while in session?"

He nodded. "Overheard and possibly recorded."

"But how?"

"It's a little more complicated than in the movies where someone sits in a van listening to tapes through a headset. Some P.I.s might still do that, but today's technology that allows visual enhancement of the rings of Jupiter can easily enhance a whisper on the street to symphony-hall clarity."

She was suddenly speechless.

"TALON-6 uses the cutting edge in surveillance equipment." His mouth firmed. "We'll find out who's doing this and put him away."

"But...he's already learned information that could be devastating." Her thoughts went immediately to Billie Ray Bennett. Could he possibly have the expertise to do something like this? From what she could remember, he was a high-school dropout. But if he wasn't behind the photographs, then who?

"Mike, are you absolutely sure that what's said in my office can be heard even though the phone is on the hook?"

"Yes, it's done every day. Any room sound can be heard and recorded up to as much as fifteen hundred feet, and more on some units. That means through two or more closed doors."

She shook her head. "I can hardly believe it."

"It's easy. The device is activated by sounds. All the stalker has to do to hear or record what's being said is to start an external stimulus that triggers the bug. It can be done simply by dialing your number. You think it's a wrong number, but it's enough to trigger the device."

"But why me? Who's doing this and what do they want?"

Mike clenched his jaw, determination darkening his blue eyes. "I promise you, Bria. I'm going to find out."

Nervously, she glanced out the taxi window at the pedestrians crowding the sidewalk. Hundreds, thousands, millions of people in New York City. The stalker could be any one of them.

"I'm not sure I feel better knowing all these things," she said finally.

"I'm not trying to scare you, but it's for your own protection. You've got to know what and who we're dealing with.''

''Of course. You're right,'' she said, realizing that she needed to protect her clients. ''I need to know.''

HE TAPPED HIS FINGERS along the computer pad, trying to control his fury.

Did they really think he wouldn't have known that they had found the bug? Stupid, arrogant bitch. She hires a wiretap man from TALON-6 and thinks he'll keep her safe. Well, she'd learn her lesson, and so would he.

He clicked off the monitor, then walked to the darkroom. The next photo will frighten the hell out of her. He could hardly wait.

A pity that he couldn't have seen the bitch's face when they found the bugging device inside the phone. It didn't matter. Soon he'd get what he wanted.

Very soon it will be over. And he knew exactly what it would take to bring her out into the open.

He laughed. Damn, she'd go willingly. She always did. Run right after one of her flock. He grinned, thinking of the way her eyes would bulge in shock, her mouth twist in terror while she begged him for her life.

Landis was an extra bonus, an added thrill. Once the incriminating evidence was planted, Landis would be the first person the police would think murdered her.

Thank you, bitch. He laughed. Yeah, now that he had a chance to think about it, he was ecstatic at the lucky turn of events.

He grabbed the telephone and punched in the numbers that were deeply burned into his memory.

Chapter Four

On the outside, Clancy's Pub, just off Second Avenue, looked like any other neighborhood bar. But Brianna sensed, soon after she and Mike entered the warmly lit, wood-paneled interior, that the pub was more than an accidental choice for a discreet place to talk. No one else was in the place. She sensed that this bar was yet another mysterious part of Mike's world. The idea was unsettling yet intriguing.

As soon as he ushered her into one of the half-moon leather booths, she slipped her oversize shoulder bag onto the seat between them. If he'd noticed the distancing tack, he gave no sign as he picked up the bag, slid in beside her, and leaned it and his attaché case against the back of the booth.

She looked up at the vaulted ceiling where brass containers of lush Boston ferns hung from exposed rafters. Soft indirect light spilled here and there, carefully planned to cast an intimate glow for patrons. Or for lovers.

She shuddered at that thought. They weren't a hand-holding couple on a date, in spite of the soft lighting and romantic ambience.

Looking around, she couldn't help wondering where the customers were. She eyed the bartender again. Mid-forties, with a touch of gray at the temples, he was a man whose deep tan contrasted sharply with a person who remained inside all day. Maybe he worked out in a health club, she decided, noticing his well-muscled forearms below his rolled-up sleeves. He had briefly looked up in response when they'd entered, yet somehow she sensed he and Mike knew each other.

For a moment, sheltered in this cozy booth, insulated from the blaring horns and hammering street noises outside, she felt protected, like a butterfly inside its cocoon. Or was it the man beside her who made her feel safe?

But she wasn't safe. The momentary absence of fear was her brain's natural reaction to overcoming stress. How often had she seen this in her patients? Mind games to fight off the panic gnawing within her; that is, if she'd admit to feeling afraid. But she wouldn't give in to her feelings. Or to Mike.

She turned to look at him. He was studying her. He was sitting so close. She could see the light and dark shards of blue in those extraordinary eyes. Her throat felt powder-dry, parched from nerves. She forced herself to meet his assessing gaze. "Interesting place," she said finally. "A private club?"

His grin hinted of dimples. "Very perceptive of you, Doctor."

It was the first time he'd called her doctor. Had he chosen that word for its impersonal feel? Was he feeling as unsettled by her presence as she was by his?

Of course he wasn't. And her nervousness had nothing to do with her ex-husband sitting so close to her. She forced a smile. "And you're a member of this…private club?"

He leaned back and stretched his long legs. "Clancy's is owned by a few ex-Special Forcers. Yes, I'm a partner. It's a safe place to come when we're in town."

So, her first hunch was correct. That minor victory made her feel more at ease. "This place has a calming ambience," she said, her gaze deliberately averted from him. God, she was making small talk as though he were a stranger standing beside her in line at the food mart.

She forced her brain to work. "Mike, what are you planning to do next?"

"Order something to help you relax." He turned around and raised his hand at the bartender. "Ben, the usual for me and—" He turned to her, waiting for her order.

"Chablis. Domestic," she said.

Ben nodded, unfolded himself from the stool and slipped behind the bar.

Mike leaned forward. "First, we'll go to your apartment so you can pack a few things for the next couple of days. While you're gone, I'll have a sweep done—"

"A sweep?"

"An electronic sweep. Check out any bugs or video cameras. That sort of thing."

A shudder crept up her spine. "Video cameras? How could someone install video…?" The words died in her throat. This morning she would never have believed someone could sneak into her office and plant a listening device, either.

"Just a precaution," he said gently. "Don't worry. We'll catch whoever's behind this." As though he noticed her tension, he added, "I'll see that you're safe, Brianna."

The bartender placed a frosted glass of white wine in front of her and a bottle of nonalcoholic ale by Mike.

"Thanks, Ben."

"You're welcome, Mike," Ben mumbled and hurried back to his stool at the end of the bar. The front door opened and two police officers came inside. Mike nodded to them when they waved and took seats near the bartender.

Mike's gaze met hers again. "Off-duty cops like to hang out here, too. The security is top-notch."

"Security?" She began to see the connection. "Is Ben really a bartender or does he…wear other hats?"

"He's what we call a freelancer." Mike used a fingernail to whisk a stray hair from her cheek. "Ben's ex-Special Forces, too, and a good buddy of one of my former teammates." He took a swig of his drink, swallowed, then put the bottle down on the marble-top table. "Freelancers hire on for assorted jobs. Law enforcement, police units, and TALON-6 hires their services when a particular situation comes up." He studied the ale left in the bottle.

"So Clancy's Bar is an employment office, of sorts."

He took another swig from the bottle. "Of sorts."

She waited for him to tell her more. When he didn't, she bit back the questions forming in her mind. Damn, she didn't want to give the impression that she was curious about him or the life he led. But as the silence lengthened between them, it was obvious he wasn't going to offer any more information.

It was none of her business, anyway. She took a sip of wine. Curiosity was a natural response to have toward an ex-husband, a man she hadn't seen in over seven years, who was now protecting her, she reminded herself. For a brief moment she had forgotten about the listening device planted in her office, forgotten about the photographs, the person or persons stalking her. She was relieved for that respite, however brief.

She was curious, but not interested in Mike. And what woman wouldn't be? He was fascinating, he lived an intriguing life. But he'd only be in her life long enough to catch whoever was stalking her, she reminded herself.

She closed her eyes and leaned her throbbing head against the leather-covered booth. "Oh, Michael. How am I going to tell my clients that their confidential information has all been compromised. It takes months to build trust between doctor and patient. With some clients, they'll never trust me again. Or any other therapist, for that matter."

"You've been through a lot, Brianna." Mike's voice was warm and gentle. "Try not to think about it right now."

"Remember that young woman who came in while you were in the waiting room?"

"Hmm. The one dressed up for Halloween?"

Brianna opened one eye and shot him a chastising look. "I'm terribly worried about her, Michael. I'm not sure if I helped her today. She just might..."

His blue eyes filled with sympathy. "Is she suicidal?"

Brianna nodded. She propped her elbows on the table. How she wished she could tell Mike that the teenager had admitted that she was pregnant and the father of her unborn baby—her slimeball boyfriend—was back in town. Not only had he introduced Kristi to drugs when she was thirteen, but he had the morals of an alley cat. Kristi thought he would marry her when he found out about the baby. When he had proved unfaithful before, less than three months ago, she had slashed her wrists. Who knew what the boyfriend would do when he found out about the baby?

"If you want to talk..."

"Thanks" was all she trusted herself to say. She'd forgotten what an easy listener he was. Whenever she'd had a problem, whether it was with her father, her indecision about a career or what kind of car to buy, Mike would patiently listen until she was all talked out. *How she'd missed that.*

She caught herself. Surprised to find her hand wrapped in his, she drew back. She couldn't tell Mike that Kristi was going to tell her boyfriend about the baby. She bit her lip. "I know it's not professional to get involved with one's clients, but there's something about this young woman. I really think I could help her."

"She's lucky to have you in her life." His voice warmed

again, flowed over her. Brianna glanced into Mike's caring expression. For a moment, she felt genuinely relieved that he had accepted her case. Nora had been right. Mike believed he could help her and his confidence was catching. Yes, she was beginning to believe he could keep her safe. And she wouldn't fight the secure feeling he gave her. But after all, this was his job.

More than likely, his charm was part of that service, too. The bond that was forming between them was merely the security in knowing she was in expert hands. Nothing more.

She never spoke of her clients to anyone outside the office, and she felt a bit embarrassed. Glancing at her watch to break the tension, she was surprised to see how late it was. "I should be going—"

"I've got a call to make. This will only take a minute." Mike reached for the black leather case beside him and clicked open the lid. "I'm going to check on one of my partners, Liam O'Shea. He'll be running the sweep on your apartment."

Surprised, she looked up. "You're not going to do it?"

"Liam is the team expert on eavesdropping detection." Mike reached for her hand. "Don't worry. He'll be discreet."

His hand cupped over hers felt warm, protective and strong. A sudden memory of how those hands had felt touching her skin, how those fingers felt teasing her, seducing her, brought with it a stab of incredible yearning.

She pulled her hand away and rubbed the stem of her wineglass. When their eyes met, she thought she saw a flash of remembrance in his face. But she must be imagining it, for in the next moment he removed a boxlike phone from its case and punched in a series of numbers. She sipped her wine again and forced herself to relax.

"Hello, Bailey?" Mike said. "Page Liam this time and

have him call me on the bubble machine in about an hour. I'll be at the Crib.''

His eyes leveled on her as he hung up the receiver and tucked the phone back inside the case.

Surprised, she asked, ''Bubble machine at the Crib?''

He flashed a smile. ''The bubble machine is our satellite phone. And the Crib is the name of our safe house in Brooklyn. TALON-6 owns it.''

''Why can't I stay in my apartment?''

''Until Liam runs a thorough check on your home, car and office, I want you safe with me.''

She clutched at his arm. ''I can't, Michael. I'll stay at a hotel.''

''Very well, but you won't have the same security. We'll get adjoining rooms.''

She glared at him. ''Let's get one thing straight. I'm extremely appreciative for what you're doing, but I'm perfectly capable of staying by myself.''

His features settled into an unemotional mask. ''When I said you'd stay with me, I didn't mean that literally. The Crib is a secure building where our clients, those in need of top-security protection, stay. Celebrities, politicians, people in the witness-protection program, that sort of thing. You'll be safe, comfortable, and you can relax and catch up on some needed sleep.''

''This is not where you live, right?''

He flashed a grin, a dimple deepening in his left cheek. ''True, I do keep a small apartment there, but there's plenty of room for both of us. You'll have your own suite and you won't know I'm there, if that's what you want.''

She arched an eyebrow as her gaze met his. ''I'll consider going on one condition. If I don't like it, I leave for a hotel. Okay?''

''Okay.'' He gave her another devastating grin that

melted her insides. "You're the boss in this business relationship," he added.

"I'm the boss," she repeated. But when she looked deeply into those familiar blue eyes, she felt as if she was sitting in the front seat of an out-of-control roller coaster, holding on for the ride of her life.

ON THE WAY to the Crib, they stopped at Brianna's apartment only long enough for her to pack an overnight bag, pick up the mail and replace the recording tape from her answering machine. Mike had suggested she not listen to her messages until she was safely ensconced in her new quarters at the Crib.

It was after four o'clock by the time their cab pulled up in front of an elegant Greek Revival building that blended right in with the picturesque Brooklyn neighborhood. The street looked deserted. From the back seat of the taxi, she craned her neck to see the three-story, brick and brownstone dwelling. A wrought-iron set of urns housed red geraniums and white petunias set on stone pedestals. "*This* is the Crib?" she asked, unable to hide the surprise from her voice.

"Uh-huh." Mike peeled several bills from his wallet, then handed the cash to the driver. After the cab drove away, she glanced up at Mike.

"I was expecting something more...I don't know, snarling pit bulls chained at the door, bars over the windows, concertina wire on the roof." She bit back a laugh.

He grinned. Clutching his briefcase in one hand, he grabbed her suitcase with the other. "Looks can be deceiving."

Her high heels clicked in step beside him as they strode over the cracked sidewalk toward the white door. Inside, an old-fashioned wrought-iron and brass elevator loomed a few feet from the entrance. With a trust she didn't feel, she followed Mike into the polished cage.

The metal gates clanged shut, and the car, instead of the clattering, bone-jarring climb that she'd expected, sped smoothly to the top floor.

Mike took her arm as they stepped out of the elevator into a room the size of Yankee Stadium. Bookcases stretched to the ceiling along one wall. Opposite, bare windows overlooked the Manhattan skyline and the rosy sunset beyond.

Natural-leather sofas adorned with oversize russet and teal pillows nestled in cozy groups. A modern painting leaned against an easel. A granite egret wading in a metal lily pond shone with unseen illumination. Glass tables with black urns filled with white moth orchids flanked each side of the sofas.

"I'm very impressed," she said, feeling a surge of admiration at his obvious success. Mike was self-made, receiving little help from his alcoholic father or the mother who had abandoned them.

He didn't look at her when he shrugged off his leather jacket and slung it over a chair. His black T-shirt showed off his well-developed chest and biceps to perfection. "You mean it's a far cry from those tar-paper shacks along Mill Street?"

He was reading her mind and she felt suddenly self-conscious. "I'm very pleased that you're successful, Mike." She walked to the windows and gazed at the Brooklyn Bridge. "I'd like the name of your decorator," she said, half teasing.

He grinned. "What's important is that the Crib is electronically secure. This is my apartment when I'm in the city, but I don't think of it as home."

She paused to study an impressionistic watercolor in the hallway. She recognized the signature of an up-and-coming artist who'd had her first showing in a leading gallery last winter. "Where do you call home?" she asked, then damned herself for the question. On the way over in the taxi, she'd vowed not to ask him any more personal questions. She'd just broken her promise in less than twenty minutes.

"I own a condo at Beaver Creek," he said, "if that's what you mean."

"Colorado?"

When he nodded, she asked, "So you still ski?" She remembered that he had been captain of his high-school ski team, thanks to an anonymous contributor who had recognized Mike's exceptional athletic talent, even as a teenager. She'd often wondered if Mike's benefactor had been her uncle, the Judge. But Nora would never confirm nor deny it, regardless of how many times Brianna had asked.

"I bought it because I knew the owner and he wanted to sell. It was a good investment," he said, "but my work takes up most of my time."

Some things never change.

They had only been married two weeks when Mike insisted he work full-time tending bar evenings after working a full shift at her father's paper mill. She'd pleaded with him to reconsider. She had wanted Mike to enroll in college with her that fall. They could have lived comfortably on the more than generous allowance her mother's inheritance provided them.

But Mike would have none of it. He'd rather work day and night, leaving her alone in their cramped apartment, night after night, than take a penny of her money.

She had begged him to talk with her, but when he was home he was too tired. He would always find time to listen to her, yet when she asked for his thoughts, he'd shut down. She could see that he was exhausted, but Mike believed that a man didn't ask for help. So what could she have done?

Now she realized that some personalities didn't suit a long-term relationship. Mike would always put actions before his feelings.

She was amazed at the bitterness the memory brought back, and she quickly pushed it aside. Nothing would come from raking up the past. They'd both made good lives for themselves after the divorce. That was the important thing.

She moved to the bookcase where he stood, clicking numbers into a numeric pad on the wall. "There," he said when he'd finished. "All doors and elevators are locked. If any movement is detected within twenty feet of the building, the action will activate the video cameras and an alarm will sound."

"What about a dog running along the sidewalk?"

"That, too." He picked up something that looked like a television remote control and pressed the device into her right palm. "Click the red button and watch that monitor," he said, pointing to the walnut cabinet in front of them.

She clicked the button. The cabinet doors opened and a computer monitor swiveled into view.

She pressed the arrow keys. Views of the Crib's street entrance, outside metal fire escape and various exterior shots of the brick building materialized with each click of her finger.

"Touch the white button," he said, leaning toward her. He was so close she could feel his warmth and smell the lingering scent of his aftershave. He took her hand inside his large grip, and she felt a tiny quiver when their skin touched.

Okay. She found him attractive. He still had the magnetic personality and sinful good looks. She *was* human, after all.

Brianna took a deep breath and focused on each view on

the monitor. With each click of the control button, a different angle of the interior and exterior of the apartment came into view.

"Who do you have for clients, the CIA?" she quipped, aware of the top-level security clearance he must have to maintain and operate such advanced equipment for the authorities.

"TALON-6 has worked for the CIA among other government agencies. This is only one of many security features I've installed here." His voice was low, and she knew he meant to make her feel at ease, but he was so close, and that ragged quality in his voice brought back an unbidden desire she'd vowed not to feel again with him.

He took her arm and led her to a group of chairs. "What's important is that you feel safe. Then maybe you'll relax and catch up on your sleep." He gave her a slow, lazy smile that made her all too aware of what she might dream about.

"Thank you," she managed to say, dropping the remote device into his palm and disengaging her fingers from his. Instead of taking a seat, she broke away and strode to the far wall to view a metal sculpture suspended from an overhead beam in the corner. The artwork reminded her of an eagle with a broken wing. "A local artist?" she asked.

His grin came with a flash of humor. "That's the bubble machine's telephone antennae," he said, coming to stand close beside her.

She angled her head, studying him. "As you said, looks can be deceiving." She struggled to think of something to say, anything that would lift the heavy weight of her memories of what they once had together. He was standing so close she could feel his warmth, smell his faint aftershave. Was he trying not to remember, too?

She turned her back to him and focused her gaze on the Manhattan skyline. *Someone was out there roaming the city, listening to her private conversations, following her, stalking her.*

"Don't be afraid, Bria."

She started to believe that he would keep her safe, and she was filled with a gratitude she hadn't felt in a very long time. She was safe with Mike. Safe from the unseen danger of the person out there, determined to wreck havoc on her life. She could trust Mike with her life, but not with her heart.

She felt his solid hands on her shoulders and she stiffened. His strong fingers began their magic as he kneaded her tense muscles. A shiver curled down her spine when his thumbs stirred the fine hair at the nape of her neck.

Closing her eyes, she fought back a moan of pleasure. If she turned around, what would she see in his eyes? Did touching her remind him of how his hands had played other parts of her body? Was his mind flooded with erotic memories, too?

Dear God, she should stop this. He was so sexy, so powerful, and too available for her own good. Attraction was only physical, she reminded herself. What female under eighty wouldn't be sexually excited by Mike Landis?

She hadn't been involved with a man since her ex-fiancé, Jordan, over two years ago. Since then, none of her casual dates had ended in bed, nor had she wished they had. Her work was now her passion, and much less complicated. Or so she thought before her uncontrollable rush of female hormones when Michael Landis returned to her life.

But she was a woman in control, a woman who understood the raw physical power of attraction. She wasn't a teenager anymore. She wasn't about to lose her head over a charming, sexy male. "Thanks, Mike," she said, her voice huskier than she'd like. "I'm quite relaxed. You don't have to—"

His strong hands swung her around to face him. Slowly

she gazed into those blue eyes and knew his thoughts were running parallel to hers. She felt a frisson of excitement. "Michael, I don't think—"

"Don't think," he growled, then he lowered his head and locked his mouth with hers.

Chapter Five

He slid his hands to the rounded curve of her bottom and drew her closer. She moaned a plaintive sigh as their kiss deepened.

He felt the unsteady rise and fall of her breasts crushed against his chest. He angled his body against her soft curves and felt her surrender flicker through her body as she melted into his embrace. She whispered something against his chest as he pulled her lower body against his legs. Her hands tightened against his neck and he lifted her as he'd done a thousand times, the motion as familiar and natural as breathing.

But instead of sliding her legs around his waist as he'd remembered, she drew back. Her fingers unlocked from the back of his neck and her arms folded behind her.

He released her, trying to ignore that his loins ached with need and built-up frustration. He had thought that maybe, just maybe, if he'd kiss her and got it over with, the curiosity or fascination, or whatever the hell fueled his building arousal, would stop. Because ever since she'd walked into his office this morning, looking better than he'd imagined possible, he'd wanted to take her into his arms and kiss her senseless.

"This isn't going to lead anywhere," she said.

"You think not?" He couldn't hide the challenge in his reply.

"I'm absolutely positive." Her green eyes glittered with determination, yet she couldn't quite hide her breathlessness. "I'm attracted to you. There. I've admitted it. Now you can stop trying to test me—"

"Is that what you think I was doing?"

"Well, what the hell would you call it?"

"Some things you can't label, Brianna."

"Well, I can." The stiffly polite tone was back in her voice. "You kissed me because you were curious to know how I'd respond. The primal action by the dominant male. But on a subconscious level, your desire to keep me safe transfers itself to what you believe is sexual attraction. You're feeling protective, but your male response is sexual. A textbook case. Nothing more."

He hooked his thumbs in the belt loops of his jeans and studied her. Despite her cool facade, her hands trembled and that breathy quality of her voice indicated a vulnerability she was trying desperately to hide. "A little presumptuous, aren't you, Dr. Kent? Telling me what I feel?"

"I usually try to guide my clients into discovering their own feelings, but in this case we don't have that much time. I thought we needed a more immediate approach."

"Save the psychobabble for your clients, okay? Me, I know what I feel and why. And I'm not afraid of the truth, which is more than I can say for you."

Her lips, still moist from their kiss, fell open. "Are you suggesting I'm denying my feelings?"

"Bingo."

She closed her eyes and took in a deep breath. "Michael," she said in an even tone he'd wager his last dime she used on her more difficult clients. Her eyes opened to meet his and her changeable eyes glittered. "Very well," she said. "I'll cut to the chase." She lifted her chin. "If we can't keep this professional, then I'll hire someone else.'' She whirled toward the door.

"You kissed me back like I remembered, honey. Don't try to deny it.''

She paused in midstep, then turned to face him. "I admitted that you're an attractive man and I'm human.'' She shrugged. "But I won't go to bed with you. Not now, not ever. Been there, done that, and I won't make *that* mistake ever again.'' Her eyes flashed with uncontrolled anger. "Now please show me to my room,'' she said, glancing at her watch. "That is, if you're willing to keep this relationship professional.'' She spoke through clenched teeth. "Or shall I hire someone else?''

He felt the chill in the air. It was as though she had dropped a force field around herself. Yes, this was a new tack for Brianna. The woman he knew could never hide her passion nor would she want to. He gave her a lingering look. She was correct about his feeling protective of her, but she was kidding herself if she believed the rest of that crap. She was right about this being a business relationship, though. He'd been a damn fool to think that kissing her would banish his ex-wife from his mind. Brianna Kent was temptation personified, a temptation that he'd resist, if it killed him. If she could make-believe she had ice water in her veins, then so would he.

HE REACHED DOWN and grabbed her suitcase. "Right this way,'' he said, his tone as flat and emotionless as hers.

Brianna stood where he'd left her. She still trembled with a mixture of surprise, anger and arousal as she watched him carry her Pullman case down the hall, his biceps bulging. The luggage was heavy, yet he carried it as effortlessly as if he were carrying a pillow.

Dear God, she should turn and run. Her heart was still clamoring wildly from his kiss. That kiss. All reason and logic shut down in her mind when he'd pulled at her lips, filling her mouth with the taste of him. For a moment, she'd gone limp within the heat of his powerful arms. For a moment. Then a spark of sanity brought her back to the present. *No, not again* warned in her fogged brain. It was insanity to think she could remain under the same roof with Mike.

But she had no choice. Until she found out who was disrupting her life, she needed him.

She needed him.

A shiver of primitive awareness shimmered down her spine. She ignored it as she followed him along the long corridor. Mike paused at the last door on the left. "Hope this suits you," he said as he swung open the door and stepped inside the spacious bedroom.

Her gaze dropped to the king-size bed flanked by bare, ceiling-to-floor windows. She forced her gaze to the broad expanse of glass. The Brooklyn Bridge spanned the horizon.

"All the windows in the apartment are one-way glass," he said, guessing her thoughts.

"The view is breathtaking," she said, her mind unable to think of anything except how his long-legged frame would look stretched out on that bed. *But she knew how he would look.* She forced away the memories with a determined mental shake. "It would be a shame to cover the windows."

"Especially at night."

Especially at night. Where they would be sleeping together in the same apartment for the first time since their divorce.

He motioned to the open door at the far wall. "The bath, dressing room and closets are through there."

"Where is your bedroom?" she asked, her throat dry.

"Across the hall. This way."

Her gaze followed him as he strode through the door and went directly across the hall. When he opened the door to his bedroom, her gaze was drawn to the corner of a black-and-white striped spread covering what she could see of a king-size bed.

What was the matter with her? She dragged her gaze away from his bed and ran her trembling fingers through her hair. She was extremely tired and not herself. After she finished her reports tonight in her room, alone, she'd turn in for a good night's sleep. Tomorrow, she'd be ready to face her predicament and plan what she was going to do about it.

But could she relax enough to sleep knowing that Mike Landis would be sleeping across the hall?

Of course she could. She was safe here. Whoever was playing games with her life had no idea where she was. Tomorrow, after she was rested, she and Mike would come up with a game plan to catch this person.

"The accommodations are lovely. Thank you," she said, attempting to sound relaxed.

"I'll send out for some coffee," Mike said from the doorway. "Why don't you take a hot bath. I'll be in the kitchen if you need anything."

"No coffee. I'll settle for a quick shower." She unfastened the lid of the suitcase and took out her jewelry bag. "Do you have a microrecorder?" she asked, retrieving the answering-machine tapes she'd taken from her apartment. "I'd like to listen to my phone messages while I unpack."

"Sure thing," he said, and left the room.

She pulled a tiny cassette tape from the jewelry case. In what seemed like less than a minute, he stuck his head in the door, carrying a palm-size gadget in his hand. "Keep it," he said, tossing it to her. "I've got plenty more."

She caught the object in midair. The device was the size and weight of a candy bar and made from a shiny canvas material that she'd never seen before. "Another one of your gizmos?"

His mouth lifted in a crooked grin. "Yeah. That model tells time, is waterproof and floats."

She grinned, then glanced at the watch face, the size of a quarter. "Five-thirty! Oh, I almost forgot."

He craned his head inside the bedroom doorway. "Forgot what?"

"I forgot to call Larry Cunningham. He's planning to pick me up tomorrow night on the way to the business dinner." She rummaged in her bag for her cell phone. "What's the address here, Mike? He'll show up at my apartment if I don't tell him—"

"You can't tell Cunningham where you're staying." Mike leaned his hip on the doorjamb and folded his arms across his chest. "You can't tell anyone. That's the point in staying here." His gaze was unreadable but there was a determined set to his jaw.

She sighed. "Mike, surely we can trust Larry. Simone, my secretary, must know where I'm at, and—"

"Until we know if Cunningham's phones are secure, we can't risk it. All they need to know is that you're in a safe place and they can page you or reach you on your cell phone."

She pushed back a lock of hair from her cheek. "I'm sorry. I wasn't thinking."

A grin laced with understanding lit his face. "Tell you what. Why not cancel the business dinner tomorrow. I'll take you to dinner."

She shook her head. "It's more than just business. It's the annual awards dinner for the city's shelter for abused women. The mayor will be there, along with celebrities and very important volunteers who've worked unselfishly to bring this dream to fruition. I work closely with these people and they're expecting me. The proceeds from the dinner alone fund the shelter for the year.'' She took a deep breath. ''Besides, I want to be there.''

''Okay,'' he said, barely missing a beat. ''I'll be your escort.''

She countered with a small sigh. ''Larry Cunningham is my escort, thank you.'' She tried not to smile when his mouth twitched. ''There's no reason for you to go with me, Mike. I'll be perfectly safe. Besides, you'll be bored to death. Long stuffy speeches.''

''You think you know me that well?''

The question unnerved her. She wished he wouldn't keep bringing the subject back to *them*, making everything seem so personal between them. But he was right. He wasn't the same man she knew seven years ago. How did she know what bored him? ''I'm sorry, Michael.'' She waved her hand in a dismissive gesture. ''What I'm trying to say is that you don't have to baby-sit me. I doubt that whoever is following me will fork out a thousand-dollars-a-plate dinner donation just to snap my picture.''

''A thousand—'' He whistled. ''I'm glad I'm on an expense account.'' His mouth curved. ''That's mighty steep, but you're not going without me. Besides, I'm charging you a hefty fee for my protection. You want your money's worth, don't you?''

She smiled. ''I'll call Larry and tell him.''

He returned her smile with a wry one of his own. ''Just remember, I'm not letting you out of my sight.'' What he didn't want to do was frighten her. But from what he'd seen so far, Brianna's secretary and Larry Cunningham had access to her client files. Brianna wouldn't agree with him, but both must be considered suspects until proven innocent.

Mike remembered the photograph of Brianna and Cunningham in the bar. If Cunningham had the hots for Brianna and she'd rebuffed him, even gently, then maybe he was paying somebody to take those pictures. He'd know that

Brianna would turn to him, especially if the action seemed like that of someone mentally unbalanced. If Cunningham was also in the shot, she'd never think that he was behind the scam.

And why wouldn't Cunningham fall for her? Any red-blooded male would, given half the chance. Cunningham had opportunity. He might have motive. Even though Brianna might never believe it, Cunningham was definitely a suspect.

"Call Cunningham," Mike said, "and tell him we'll pick *him* up tomorrow night in a cab." He smiled at what Cunningham's face would look like when Brianna and Mike arrived at his home.

Brianna raised an eyebrow. "Let's compromise. I'll call Larry and tell him to meet us there."

"Fine. Oh, by the way, where's the dinner being held?"

"The Plaza." Her gaze held his briefly, and he guessed that she was wondering if he had anything in his wardrobe besides the blue jeans and leather jackets he was wearing. "Black-tie," she said almost as an afterthought.

"Of course. I must have one stashed around here someplace." Mike turned before he saw her wince, a satisfied smile on his lips.

THE NEXT DAY, Brianna stepped into the living room and hesitated in front of the row of security monitors. She scanned each screen and the different scenes of the exterior of the building. Directly across the street, a man, dressed in a green jogging suit retrieved his newspaper from the front sidewalk. A white poodle yapped noisily at him from the front step. A young mother wheeling a baby carriage along the shady street crossed at the corner, while three young girls on in-line skates wheeled in a line along the street.

She smiled. A typical neighborhood on a Saturday afternoon. But was it typical? Really? How many, if any, of Mike's neighbors knew their actions were being video-taped? Did they know that the attractive Greek Revival dwelling was owned by an international surveillance agency? Of course not.

Mike was right. Nothing was as it seemed. The thought raised goose bumps on her arms. And the stalker who was taking pictures of her, was it someone she knew and trusted? Someone she thought of as a friend? Someone who smiled and said hello to her at the women's shelter? Her office building? Or the man who sold her fresh fruits and vegetables at the greengrocer's?

She rubbed her arms briskly, pushing away the paranoid thoughts. She glanced at her watch. Where was Mike? He should be back by now. She hadn't wanted to go with him when he went out to pick up lunch. He seemed to accept her excuse that it was too hot outside. She'd preferred to remain in the air-conditioning, but the truth was, she needed a few minutes alone. Away from her ex-husband.

She was still reeling from waking up and joining him for breakfast. Just as they'd done when they were first married. He'd come home after working all night at the paper mill, and she'd be waiting breathlessly for him in the bath. Candles, flower petals and soft music. One look and he'd crack that sexy grin, pull her from the water and show her that what they had together needed no special effects. The two of them were enough. And after enjoying the slow-building lovemaking that could drive her wild, they experienced that incredible wonder of climax that left them both breathless and sated. Their time together was precious, as she only saw him in that short span between her morning classes and when he returned from working all night.

She couldn't help the onslaught of memories as she sat across from him at the neighborhood breakfast bar a few hours ago. He ordered the same brand of cereal as he liked when they were married. She could barely swallow the dry toast she'd ordered, but he ate heartily, looking as sexy and heartbreakingly handsome as he had back then. It was as if time had stopped. She couldn't ignore the admiring glances from the feminine staff and other diners, yet he'd acted totally oblivious to them.

She paced in front of the windows. She hated to feel so vulnerable to her emotions. It wasn't like her. She was still reacting to that kiss, dammit. And to her own foolish response. She'd put a halt to the kiss, but it had taken almost all of her willpower. She had wanted him to kiss her, to keep kissing her until he dragged her back into his bedroom and did those magnificent things to her body that she knew he could do.

She wanted him, with a desperation she'd forgotten she possessed. Well, she couldn't have him. He was poison to her system, and she better well remember.

She glanced at her watch again. Forcing herself to be sensible, she turned and strode back to her bedroom. In one corner of the room, she'd assembled a small office for herself from a long, rectangular table. She'd work more on her reports, then it would be time to get ready for the award ceremony tonight. When Mike returned with lunch, he could eat alone. She wasn't hungry for food, anyway.

HE STARED at the vial of morphine while the telephone number rang. Soon, very soon, she would be his. In less than a few hours, she'd be walking into his trap. And if his luck held, she'd bring Landis with her. He'd have them both.

The phone answered and his heartbeat quickened.

"Dr. Brianna Kent's answering service. Please hold."

Damn. He hated to be left dangling like some flounder caught on a line. An uncontrollable anger began to claw at him. He almost hung up but thought better of it. The timing was too perfect. She was expecting that hopeless namby-pamby to try and kill herself. She wouldn't think twice before rushing to her side. He could be patient, for as long as it took.

"I'm sorry to keep you on hold," the woman's voice said. "I had a client on the other phone." After a moment's pause, she said, "How may I help you?"

Even though she didn't give her name, he knew by the voice that she wasn't Simone Twardzak, the bitch's secretary. His luck was holding. It was possible the secretary might recognize the real Dr. Raynard's voice.

"This is Dr. Raynard." He hesitated a moment, checking his hunch. When she didn't say anything, he continued. "I need to get in touch with Dr. Kent. Her client, Kristi McFarland, is in ICU at St. Luke's Hospital. She's cut herself and she's asking for Dr. Kent. Will you give her the message and tell her to hurry?"

"Yes, Doctor. If you'll hold on, I can connect you—"

"No, I've got to get back. Give her the message, STAT."

"Certainly, Dr. Raynard. Should I have her call you?"

"That's not necessary. I'll see her when she arrives."

He hung up before he had to listen to any more useless chitchat. God, how he hated incompetents.

A LITTLE AFTER FIVE O'CLOCK, Brianna had just finished dressing and was fastening her diamond earring at the mirror, when her private cell phone rang. Only her aunt and her secretary, Simone, had access to this number. Nora had called last night from her sister's home in Denver and left word that she'd arrived safely. Brianna had returned her call to reassure her aunt that she'd contacted Mike and was in a safe house. She hadn't explained that Mike was also with her. She didn't want to hear that it's-about-time-you-came-to-your-senses tone in Nora's voice. To an incurable romantic like her aunt, Nora would never believe Mike and Brianna could maintain a strictly business arrangement. But why shouldn't Nora be a romantic? She'd been happily married to the love of her life, the Judge, for almost thirty years before he'd died. That kind of love happened only to a special few.

The cell phone rang again. For an instant, she was afraid to answer it. *What if the stalker had found out her private number? After all, he knew everything else about her.*

She pushed the thought aside as she picked up the phone. "Hello," she said, praying that she'd hear her secretary's voice.

"Dr. Kent? This is Simone."

Brianna sagged with relief.

"I hope I'm not disturbing you," Simone continued. "But you didn't answer your pager or your other phones and I haven't heard from you since yesterday morning."

"It's okay, Simone. For the next day or so this number might be the quickest way to reach me. What's up?"

"The answering service just called. Dr. Raynard called from St. Luke's Hospital. Kristi McFarland was admitted a little while ago. She cut herself—"

"Oh no." Brianna let out an unsteady breath. Damn! Kristi must have told her boyfriend about the baby. He must have walked out on her again. "How badly is she hurt?"

"Dr. Raynard didn't say. The doctor said she's asking for you."

"I had a feeling something was going to happen. Did he say if the baby is all right?"

"I don't know. That's all the doctor said." Simone's voice warmed with a maternal tone. "No news is good news, my mother used to say."

"Right." She couldn't help but smile at her secretary's positive sayings, however cliché. Brianna glanced at her watch. If she left immediately, she'd have time to get to the hospital and see Kristi before she was due at the Plaza.

"I'm on my way."

"Okay, Dr. Kent. Good luck."

Brianna shut off the phone and slipped it into her beaded purse. She started toward Mike's bedroom, when she heard the shower running. His bedroom door was ajar.

"Mike?" she called. She glanced into the dimly lit bedroom and realized it was a replica of the guest room. A large bath connected behind the closet alcove and dressing room. If he was in the shower, she didn't have the extra time to wait until he finished dressing.

His words came back to her. *I'm not letting you out of my sight.* She glanced at her watch again. She didn't have time to wait for him to finish dressing. She didn't have a moment to lose. Besides, how long would it take to hail a cab in this neighborhood?

She would leave him a note, explaining the situation. Mike could meet her at the Plaza.

She'd be perfectly safe at the hospital. She knew the staff and Dr. Raynard. Wasn't her first consideration to her client? Kristi needed her.

"DAMMIT TO HELL." Mike crushed the note that Brianna had left on his bed with his fist and tore out of the bedroom. He was still swearing by the time the elevator doors opened to the street level and he hailed a cab.

Twenty minutes later, the Saturday late-afternoon traffic crawled to a stop along the expressway. Impatient, Mike rolled down his window and called to the police officer, who was standing along a row of honking vehicles, directing traffic.

"What's the matter, Officer?" Mike yelled over the noise.

"Fuel truck jackknifed up ahead. Traffic will be tied up, maybe several hours till we clean up the leakin' diesel."

The cabdriver waved his hands in frustration, swearing in a Cambodian dialect that Mike understood.

He clenched his jaw. Damn, he had no one to blame but himself. He should have known that Brianna wouldn't respect any rules he'd given her. He took out his wallet and pushed a large bill into the cabbie's fist.

Mike burst out of the door. His long strides carried him steadily past the bumper-to-bumper, honking cars and trucks.

His fingers trembled with excitement as he saw the blond woman cross the driveway in front of St. Luke's Hospital. Any minute now she would dash into the lobby and bound past the bank of elevators toward the E.R.

Yes, she was running. The troublesome bitch could hardly wait to give comfort to the weak and helpless.

He grinned. No doubt she'd be out of breath when she finally saw him, face-to-face, when he stepped into the elevator with her.

Then, before she even knew what happened, he'd stick her with the morphine syringe. By the time they reached the top floor, all the fight would be gone from her body. He'd load her on a gurney, cover her up and head down to the morgue in the basement.

His grin widened as he thought how weak and helpless she'd be. Never again would she tell lies that put young, innocent men behind bars.

Too bad he couldn't let the bitch live a little longer. How he'd love to see her eyes bulge with terror when she realized who he was and the revenge that awaited her.

He relished driving her crazy with the waiting.

But damn, he couldn't let her live any longer. Time was running out.

Chapter Six

Brianna hurried through the main lobby of St. Luke's Hospital, her high heels clicking on the polished tile. She glanced at her watch: 6:38 p.m. Forty minutes had passed since Dr. Raynard had called and left his message with her service. If Kristi's wounds were minor, by this time she might already be resting comfortably in a room in the Psych Unit on level 8. A nurse would have been assigned suicide watch for the first eight hours, at least. But if Kristi had arrived in critical condition, she might still be in E.R.

Wherever Kristi was, Brianna needed to speak first to Dr. Raynard. She would feel better knowing the attending physician's prognosis before seeing the teenager.

Making her way past a very pregnant woman waiting in front of the visitor elevator, Brianna headed toward the E.R. at the end of the corridor. She paused when a tall, broad-shouldered man dressed in green scrubs stepped forward from behind a potted palm and walked swiftly toward her.

"Dr. Kent?"

She turned toward him. His full dark beard and thick eyebrows matched the color of his brown eyes. Her gaze dropped to the large paunch that hung over the shirred waistband of his uniform. She hid a smile. He looked pregnant, she thought for a brief instant.

"Yes?" she said. "I'm Dr. Kent."

"Dr. Raynard asked me to tell you that Kristi McFarland has been taken to her room. If you'll follow me." He turned back toward the bank of elevators, then pressed the up button.

She felt a tug of relief. If Kristi was already in her room, then her injuries couldn't have been severe. "Where's Dr. Raynard now?"

The orderly shrugged. "He's helping E.R. get prepped. There was a five-car pileup on the expressway. He thought it would be better if you went directly to your patient's room. He'll join you there as soon as possible."

Brianna hesitated, glancing at the E.R. doors at the end of the hall. How much had Kristi told Dr. Raynard about what caused her to cut herself? Had Kristi's boyfriend brought her here? Was he still in the E.R. waiting room?

"I'll only be a minute," she called over her shoulder at the orderly. "I need to speak to Dr. Raynard."

"That's impossible. You can see him later."

The man's commanding voice caught her by surprise. She studied him closer. He was dressed in hospital green scrubs, but maybe he wasn't an orderly. Was he a specialist or a visiting doctor from another hospital? But before she could read his title on the ID tag clipped to his front pocket, he turned and strode toward the first open elevator.

Brianna followed him, her gaze on his shoes. As she hurried to keep pace with his long strides, she noticed that instead of the soft-soled footwear most hospital personnel wore, he wore hard-soled leather oxfords. Expensive leather.

Maybe he was a doctor. "I didn't get your name," she called out to him. "Are you a doctor?"

"No."

So, her first assumption had been correct. Besides, a doctor would have introduced himself, if only for professional courtesy. Well, whoever he was, this guy wasn't very talkative. "What room is my patient in?" she asked, matching his no-nonsense tone.

He stepped into the empty elevator, leaned over to press a button on the control wall, then held the doors open for her. When he turned around, she noticed a stethoscope dangling from his neck. Unusual for an orderly, she noted.

Something wasn't right, but she couldn't put her finger on it. "You don't have to go with me," she said as she stepped inside. "Tell me the room number and you can return to your duties."

"I'm going upstairs anyway." He released his left palm from the doors. Before they began to whoosh shut, she jabbed her right hand against the door to keep them open. "What floor is Kristi McFarland on?"

Before he could answer, a red-haired woman called to her from a room farther down the hall.

"Dr. Kent! Hold that elevator for a sec, okay?"

Brianna recognized Karen, the technician from X-ray. Karen often helped comfort Brianna's battered clients from the women's shelter with her gentle manner while she processed their tests. Brianna grabbed hold of the doors to keep them open while Karen disappeared into a cubicle room. In a flash, she reappeared in the hall, wheeling a white-haired woman in a wheelchair, an IV pole loaded with bags of fluids wobbling beside her.

Karen kept her gaze on the wheelchair wheels as she carefully pivoted the woman's chair into the car. "Thanks for waiting, Dr. Kent," she said brightly. "These elevators are so slow. I'd be waiting forever for another one and we're in a hurry, aren't we, Mrs. Cavanaugh?" She smiled at the old woman as Karen stabbed a finger at the third-floor button. "Want me to press eight for you?" she asked Brianna. "You're going to Psych, right?"

Brianna glanced at the wall panel. She distinctly remembered that the orderly had pressed the button for Kristi's floor. But instead of the eighth floor where the Acute Psych Unit was located, the sixth-floor button was lit.

Brianna stared at the orderly. "That's odd. Where did you say Kristi McFarland is?"

Instead of answering, he glared straight ahead, a muscle twitching above his left eyebrow.

Karen glanced up at the orderly, waiting.

"It's confidential information," the man said finally, scowling at Karen. "I'll tell you, Doctor, when we don't have nosy people listening."

Karen rolled her eyes, and dropped her gaze to stare at the back of her patient's head. But the gesture wasn't lost on the orderly. "I'm only following hospital procedure," he said coldly. "Something that wouldn't hurt you to do," he said to the technician.

Karen's head jerked up at him. "I beg your pardon?"

"Your ID tag is crooked," the man said. "And your client doesn't have her lab orders with her."

The elderly woman's head bobbed, her right hand jerked the plastic tube in her vein as her eyelids fluttered open.

Karen quickly checked the plastic IV lead around the woman's arm, then narrowed her eyes at the orderly and gave him a who-the-hell-do-you-think-you-are look. "I faxed my patient orders to the lab a few minutes ago," she said in a deceptively soft tone. "And my ID tag is just as straight as yours."

Brianna noted the orderly's name on his tag: Leonard Braewood. She would definitely report him when she finished here today. His rude attitude was not only inappropriate but offensive, especially in front of a patient.

The elevator crept its way up to the third floor. Most days she didn't mind the slow speed, but today she was impatient to know Kristi was all right.

The elevator doors slid open and Karen hurried the patient's wheelchair into the corridor. Impulsively, Brianna stepped off beside her. "I'll take the stairs and meet you up on Psych," she said over her shoulder to Leonard Braewood. It wasn't her place to say something about his rudeness, but she wasn't sure she'd be able to keep quiet if she remained with Braewood another minute.

"What a creep," Karen whispered under her breath, yet loud enough for Brianna to hear.

She smiled as Karen wheeled her charge along the west corridor. "Takes all kinds."

Brianna glanced back to see Braewood leaning out of the elevator, his face red.

"Dr. Kent," He stepped into the hall, one arm holding the door open. "I'm supposed to take you to your patient. What'll I tell Dr. Raynard?"

"You'll think of something." She opened the fire doors to the emergency stairway and raced up the stairs. Thank God the elevators were slow. She'd probably beat Braewood to the eighth floor with time to spare.

When she reached the nurses' station on the Psych Unit, Rita, the head nurse, looked up from her computer terminal. "Hi, Dr. Kent." She smiled. "Here to visit a patient?"

"What room is Kristi McFarland in, Rita?"

"Let me see…" Rita scrolled the computer screen.

Brianna glanced at her watch: 7:03 p.m. Mike would be on his way to the Plaza by now. With luck, she could leave here by 7:30 p.m. and be in time for the opening speech at 8:30 p.m.

"Sorry, Dr. Kent," Rita said, her gaze intent on the computer screen. "Is there another name she might be listed under?"

Puzzled, Brianna shook her head. "No. My patient was brought in within the past hour. Dr. Raynard was the admitting physician." A shimmer of regret coursed through her. No wonder Braewood was sent to take her to Kristi. More than likely, the hospital was overcrowded and Kristi *had* been taken to a different floor. Oh, why couldn't she learn to curb her impatience?

"Never mind, Rita. Hand me the phone, I'll call E.R. to see what room they assigned for her."

"Of course, Doctor."

Brianna took the phone and punched in the numbers for E.R.

When the reception clerk answered, Brianna quickly explained the situation.

"Sorry, Dr. Kent, but we have no listing for a patient named Kristi McFarland."

Damn. "Could I have a brief word with Dr. Raynard? I know he's busy, but—"

"Dr. Raynard isn't on duty today. Would you like to speak to Dr. Davis? He's been on call since noon."

Her mind was spinning with questions. "Y-yes, please."

"One moment, Dr. Kent."

In the lengthening silence, a thread of alarm edged up her spine. What the hell was going on? *Where was Kristi?*

"Hi, Brianna," Tom Davis said. "What's up?"

"Tom, a teenage patient of mine was brought in a little over an hour ago. Kristi McFarland. She's a cutter. I think her boyfriend might have brought her in. I was told that—"

"Are you sure she was taken to St. Luke's? We've had no cutter in here today. In fact, it's unusually quiet for a Saturday afternoon."

"Quiet? You're not expecting the victims from the five-car pileup on the Lincoln Expressway?"

"What pileup?"

A shiver rose through her as she realized something was terribly wrong. The strange Leonard Braewood who had been waiting for her. *Dear God, who the hell was he?*

"Apparently there's some mistake," she said into the phone. "Sorry to bother you, Tom." She forced the panic from her voice, not wanting to alert Tom or any of the hospital staff. First, she'd try to reach Kristi at her home. Once Brianna knew that her patient was safe, she'd deal with—

The elevator beep sounded, breaking into her thoughts. She turned to watch the doors open. She stared, telephone pressed against her ear as her eyes locked with Leonard Braewood's.

Recognition and something else sparked his expression. *He knew she'd found him out.*

She froze, her heart pounding. He glared at her with such hatred, she could feel it. Before she could move, he pressed a button and the elevator slammed shut. The arrow above the doors began its slow descent.

"Dr. Kent. Did you know that man?"

Brianna glanced at Rita staring back at her. She couldn't speak. Her hands shook as she rummaged in her bag for the card with Mike's cell phone number. She punched in the numbers.

In seconds she heard his voice. "Landis here."

"Mike!" Her knees felt as if they would collapse as she whispered his name.

"Brianna? Where are you?"

"I-I'm at St. Luke's. The Psych Unit on level 8. The north wing." She took a deep breath. "It's him. I—I think I just saw the man who…" She forced herself to say the words. "The stalker."

"Brianna. Are you all right?

"I-I'm fine," she said, knowing full well she wasn't. But damn if she'd let anyone know it. She forced away the panic. "His name is Leonard Braewood. He's a large man, over six foot. Dark thick hair. Full beard. He's dressed in green scrubs. He's in the elevator." Her gaze caught the arrow above the elevator. "He's stopped on the sixth floor." Her heartbeat raced.

"Brianna. Are people around you?"

"Yes. I'm at the nurses' station."

"Stay where you are. I'm downstairs. In the lobby."

An incredible feeling of relief flooded her. "You're at the hospital?" she asked.

"I'm in the downstairs lobby. I'll call hospital security and we'll get this guy, Brianna. Stay put till I get there."

MIKE RACED UP the steps three at a time. His gut instinct was never wrong, and the minute he'd read her note that said she was stopping off at St. Luke's Hospital on her way to the dinner, his inner radar had screamed an alarm inside him.

Level 8 appeared in bright-red letters on the wall alongside a corridor entrance. He pulled open the door and lunged through at breakneck speed. The corridor was empty. He dashed to the end of the hall and turned.

"Mike!" Brianna leaped from behind the nurses' station. "Oh, Mike, I've never been so glad to see anyone in my life." She flew into his arms.

He felt her tremble and he helped her to a group of chairs along the hall. "Tell me what happened." He brushed a hair from her pale face.

After she told him everything, Mike still couldn't believe it. How the hell could a stranger infiltrate hospital personnel so easily? "You said you never saw him before?"

"Never. I don't think Karen had, either."

Mike pulled his phone from his hip pocket. "I'll check his name from hospital personnel records, but my hunch is that it's a fake."

"At least we have his description," she offered.

Rita came around the corner of the nurses' station. "Are you Mr. Landis?" When he nodded, she continued, "There's a call for you."

Mike got to his feet and reached the phone in three strides.

"Landis here."

"Erickson at hospital security. No sign of him on six. All the patients have been vacated from this wing. They've been moved to the new section in the Jefferson Wing that's just opened last week. Your guy must have gotten off here then took the stairs down to the lobby."

"I just came up the stairs. I didn't see anyone."

"Then he must still be on the sixth floor. I'll go back up there myself and look around."

"You've put your men at all exits along the ground floor, right?" Mike asked.

"Yeah, and we've given this guy's description to the guards at the parking lot, too. If he's on the hospital campus, we've got him."

Another thought crossed Mike's mind. "Erickson, be sure to have your men check the ID of any hospital employees you meet on the sixth floor." The guy had obviously set this up for a long time. He's familiar with the hospital and with all the nooks and crannies of St. Luke's, especially the Psych Unit. He was or had been either an employee—or a patient.

"I'll check and call you right back."

Mike clicked off the phone. Brianna's eyes were wide as she watched him.

"They still haven't found him?" she asked.

"We will."

She ran a hand through her silvery-blond hair. "I've tried calling Kristi but she doesn't answer. No answering machine." Her lips pressed together.

"She'll call you if she needs you."

Brianna looked up. "Yes, I'm sure she will." She gave him a weak smile. "Thanks, I needed to hear that."

"Erickson of security is a good man. Nothing more we can do here."

"I'd like some air."

"Are you up to stopping off at the police station? I'd like you to give Braewood's description to a composite artist."

"Yes, I'm fine. Will it take long? Maybe I should call Larry and tell him I won't be able to make it to the awards dinner after all."

"Shouldn't take too long. Maybe you can reach Kristi later this evening."

She straightened her shoulders, then got to her feet. "Let's get going."

He walked beside her toward the elevator. He pressed the down button, and saw her flinch when the bell dinged just before the elevator doors opened. Damn, he'd catch this bastard and make him pay for what he'd put her through.

A maintenance orderly stood beside a two-tiered cart encased with a plastic cover. Mike grabbed the plastic and yanked it off, revealing a large cardboard box. The orderly's jaw dropped. "Hey, man, whatcha doin'?" His eyes widened as he stepped to the side.

"Just checking." Mike lifted the lid and looked inside to see that the carton contained a portable X-ray machine. "Sorry."

"Well, ya could ask, ya know." The orderly recovered the box, then wheeled the cart into the hall, giving Mike a strange look.

A few minutes later when Brianna and Mike were outside the front entrance, Mike hailed a taxi that had just pulled up with a fare.

It had taken them less than an hour for Brianna to give her statement to Police Detective Sanchez, then work with the composite artist until Brianna was satisfied that the sketch of Leonard Braewood was exact.

When Mike was finally settled in the back seat of the taxi with Brianna on their way to the Plaza, he turned to look at her. Sitting beside him, bathed in the flush of sunlight of early evening, she looked as he'd always remembered. He could smell her sexy perfume. For all that she'd been through, she looked incredible. "Is it professional for me to say how lovely you look?"

"No, but I'll match you." She grinned. "You look rather fetching in that tux."

"Fetching?" His mouth quirked. "Not sexy, or handsome, or—"

"Fetching." Her eyes sparkled with humor.

"I don't think I've ever been called fetching before. I can hardly wait to get home so I can look it up and find out if I've been insulted."

She smiled, but her eyes quickly filled with tears. "Thanks," she said. "I don't know when I've been more scared."

He covered her hand with his and forced himself to remember she was a client. All he could think of was to gather her up in his arms and never let her go. "From now on," he managed to say, "you don't leave my sight."

"So you think Leonard Braewood was—" she looked away "—the stalker?"

"We don't know. First, it may not be just one man. He might have other people, women." He squeezed her hand. "Liam called back. He's in New York and will do a full sweep of your office and apartment tomorrow. Good thing it will be Sunday. He won't attract much attention."

"He'll need a key. Should I drop one off—"

Mike smiled. "Liam won't need a key."

"But my apartment building has a security keypad on the front door."

"I know."

Her startled look faded and she shook her head. "I guess you know what you're doing." She leaned back and gave a deep sigh. "When will Liam have the results of the sweep?"

"Right away. He might have to send some samples to the lab. We'll know soon, Brianna."

"I'm very grateful for all you're doing, Mike." She turned to look at the cars and trucks whizzing by. "Do you realize how much the stalker already knows about me? My patients? My life?" She turned to stare back at him. "The way he looked at me. My God, Mike. He hates me. You could see it in his face."

"Try not to think about it anymore tonight. Tomorrow, I want you to rest."

"I can't. I work at the shelter on weekends. I'd be there tonight except for the awards dinner."

"Can someone else sub for you tomorrow? It wouldn't hurt to vary your schedule. Change the routes you travel."

"Because *he* knows my schedule, you mean."

He didn't have to answer her. She knew it as well as he did.

"Monday I have a full load of patients. Will Liam be finished with the sweep by then?"

"Depends on what he finds. Maybe you could set up a temporary office on the TALON-6 floor."

"I'd rather not. Some of my patients are very fragile. Not only have they built up a trust in me, but in my office, its location—" She stopped and he could see the growing irony in her expression. "That bastard took all that away, didn't he?" Her jaw clamped with determination. "Why can't I use my office after Liam does the sweep?"

He didn't want to frighten her any more than she already was. But if he told her that Liam had already checked out her car in the parking garage and found a tracking device, she'd be over the edge. Tomorrow, after she was rested, he'd tell her. But if the lab reports confirmed what Liam and he believed, then they were dealing with someone who was more than just a nutcase. The electronic tracking device found behind the left front bumper of Brianna's car was as sophisticated as anything the CIA uses today. That, combined with the sharp mind behind the electronic wizardry that Liam had found today, equaled someone who was a dangerous threat.

Mike struggled to bite back his anger. But every time he thought of the stalker so close to her, a storm of fury warred inside him. He needed to keep his professional distance with this case, but how the hell was that possible?

A car horn beeped and he glanced back at Brianna. "We'll talk more about this tomorrow. If you want to see your clients in your office, then TALON-6 will do everything possible to see that you do."

Her relieved smile was his reward. He looked out the window as the taxi climbed the viaduct ramp toward the expressway and St. Luke's Hospital slipped from view.

Wherever you are, I'll find you, Mike vowed silently. And when I do, so help me, you'll wish you'd never been born.

SEVERAL MEN in paint-splattered overalls and caps stood waiting for the elevator when it reached the sixth floor.

He stepped off, avoiding eye contact with the painters as he moved in front of them on his way down the hall to the supply room. Across the hall, the nurses' station stood deserted. The smell of fresh paint and cleaning supplies filled his nostrils. In this section of the wing, the patients and staff had moved to their new quarters a week ahead of schedule. That had been a bonus.

He gave a quick glance along both ends of the hall before opening the supply-room door. Once inside he flipped on the light then shut the door. Reaching for the cardboard case of hospital supplies on the back shelf, he opened it. Instead of boxes of catheters, he pulled out a black over-

night bag containing the getaway clothes that he'd stashed earlier.

With orderly precision, he yanked the stethoscope from his neck, unclipped the photo ID from his pocket and whipped off the dark wig from his head. Next he removed the brown contact lenses from his eyes and dropped them into the lens case. He slipped the green shirt over his head, then rolled everything into a tight ball. In one deft move he unsnapped the belly pouch from around his chest, then the padded shoulders and vest he'd worn. Untying the drawstring around his waist, he slipped out of his trousers.

In less than five minutes, he'd sailor-rolled all trace of Leonard Braewood and packed the gear into the black bag. He snapped off the light then peered into the deserted corridor before making his way toward the elevators.

The black ankle-length cassock brushed his calves as he limped along the corridor. An old man's limp was enough contrast to that of the lumbering Leonard Braewood. When he turned the corner, he saw a bald man wearing a furniture mover's uniform leaning against a file cabinet loaded onto a dolly.

The man turned. "Hello, Father."

"Good day to you," he said pleasantly, a slight Irish brogue to his words. He gave the worker a welcoming smile, one that would be expected of a man of the cloth. Within a few minutes, the elevator dinged, then the doors opened and two uniformed hospital-security men bolted onto the floor.

The ruddy-faced man, Rafe Erickson, by his name tag, blocked his way into the elevator. "Excuse me, Father. Did you happen to see a large, heavyset man dressed in scrubs come by just now?"

"Why, no, sir." He shook his white head for effect. "I was here to visit a friend, but he's been moved to another wing, I'm told."

Erickson looked at the bald-headed mover.

"Me neither, but I wasn't payin' much attention. Folks have been parading up and down all day. We're supposed to have everything moved out of here by third shift."

"Thanks," said Erickson with a scowl. "Sorry to detain you." He took off down the hall, the younger man after him.

Idiots, he thought as he stepped inside the elevator. The rage he'd felt when that dumb bitch had gotten away from him had faded. Now he was almost glad that this attempt had failed. For, in that one brief moment when their eyes had locked, he knew by the terror he'd seen in her face, that the bitch realized he was the one hunting her.

He'd felt a thrill akin to sexual pleasure in that one brief moment. Just think how pleasurable it will be to finally get his hands on the bitch.

He'd made one miscalculation, however. Even though he'd staked out the hospital and knew its inner workings, it was still her turf.

Next time, he'd get her on his own turf, by his own rules. She'd be so caught up that she wouldn't know what hit her until it was too late.

Chapter Seven

The dessert course was being served by the time Brianna and Mike finally arrived at the guest table and took their places. "What happened?" Larry Cunningham asked Brianna as soon as she took her seat beside him. He scowled at Mike when he sat down at the reserved chair across from Brianna.

"Nothing to be concerned about," she whispered, nodding and smiling to several colleagues seated farther down, at the end of the table. She turned her attention back to Larry. "I'll be away from my apartment for a few days. But if you need to reach me, call my answering service. And I hope to be in the office on Monday."

"You hope?" His thick eyebrows furrowed in surprise. He shot a look across the table at Mike. "And where does he fit into this?"

Brianna felt the first stirring of irritation. She and Larry had no personal relationship. However, if she hadn't initially stated in their partnership agreement that there would be no personal fraternization between colleagues, Larry might have come on to her. She knew he wanted more than what she was willing to give. The few times they'd had drinks after work or attended a black-tie affair, he'd often held her hand a little longer than necessary, been a little too attentive or lingered a little too long after they'd said goodbye outside her door. But she respected him for never crossing the line at what she'd considered inappropriate behavior. Until now.

"Not now, Larry. This isn't the time or the place to discuss it."

He grabbed the goblet of water by his plate and took a few gulps. Then he settled back in his chair, crossed his arms and gave the appearance of listening to the president of the Cityside Women's Shelter deliver the opening speech.

Brianna gave an embarrassed glance to Mike across the table.

Although his expression was neutral, she knew he'd heard Larry's questions and her reply. Feminine instinct told her that Mike didn't approve of Larry, although Mike would never say so. She wondered if Mike had really believed her when she'd told him that Larry was just a colleague and that they didn't have a personal relationship.

If Mike were to probe into her personal life, it wouldn't take him long to learn that she hadn't been involved with anyone since her last relationship. Something Mike might offer to remedy, she thought, the idea causing her insides to tremble. Good thing she wasn't interested.

Was Mike dating someone special? More than likely, yet he'd been too professional to mention it.

Dear God, whom he slept with was none of her business. She glanced back at the speaker, forcing her mind to focus, but try as she might, her mind wouldn't concentrate on Helen Warren's speech.

She glanced at her watch: 9:05 p.m. Had hospital security found Leonard Braewood yet? How could he have slipped past all the guards and disappeared from the sealed building?

A mixture of fear and frustration spiked through her. She jumped when a waiter approached her side to remove the untouched chocolate-filled whipped-cream concoction in front of her. Her throat felt so tight that she couldn't swallow.

Applause rippled through the ballroom and she glanced up to see that Helen Warren had introduced the mayor to the speaker's podium. Brianna scanned the ballroom and the hundreds of smiling faces seated at the round white linen-covered tables. Several prominent sports figures and Hollywood celebrities were here for special awards. Their charitable work with the women's shelter was deeply appreciated.

Her gaze continued to roam the faces in the ballroom. *Was Leonard Braewood here?*

She blinked away the question. Of course not. The charity dinner for the Cityside Women's Shelter attracted a great deal of attention. Not only was the event covered by tight security, it was a media circus. Even the bold Leonard Braewood wouldn't run the risk of a cable-news camera catching him on film.

She risked a glance at Mike, who was engaged in small talk with Lisa Caleb, a vivacious, brown-eyed woman seated to his right. She was a child psychiatrist, one of the finest in the city. And she was also an incurable romantic. Brianna knew by the gleam in Lisa's eyes when Mike had escorted Brianna to their table that Lisa would want to know everything about Brianna's handsome escort.

Mike Landis in a tuxedo was something to notice. She'd never seen him wearing a tux before. Those broad shoulders and lean hard body were outlined to advantage by the expensive tailoring of his suit. Custom-made, no doubt. She smiled when she remembered how she'd told him the affair would be black-tie, and his offhand remark about finding something suitable.

Mike said something amusing and Lisa laughed. God, how could he sit and banter back and forth, pretending he didn't have a care in the world? Yet she also knew that Mike was spring-loaded, ready for anything.

Never had she seen a man take control of a situation with such authority and control as Mike had. Once she had seen Mike bolt onto the Psych Unit floor, she knew he'd risk his life to keep her safe.

His blue eyes met hers for an instant while he conversed with Lisa, and she felt a shot of desire. God help her, but on a primitive level, she still wanted him. And in a few hours she'd be spending another night with him under the same roof.

Oh, Mike, why couldn't we have been more suited to each other? But some personalities could never be compatible. She and Mike were complete opposites who, unfortunately, had been drawn to each other physically. From that first flush of hormonal attraction, their relationship was doomed.

She knew the dynamic of a relationship. Sex wasn't a relationship. And sex wasn't something she wanted with a man who was so unsuited to her personality. If only she would remember that, she'd survive this ordeal, and when the stalker was caught, she'd return to her well-ordered life and never have to think about Michael Landis again.

A waiter appeared to fill her coffee cup, but she refused with a shake of her head. She forced her attention back to the podium, but her thoughts kept straying back to the man seated across from her.

Had their divorce hurt him more than she realized? Funny, after all these years, this was the first time she'd ever considered the question. Before, she'd always remembered what he had done to her. He'd never tried to stop her when she threatened to leave him. Although the deep pain of that rejection had faded, she had been wrong to think that he didn't love her enough to want to work on their marriage. Her training and work as a psychologist had proven, over and over, that some people simply weren't meant to be together for the long haul.

She thought with her heart; Mike thought with his head. *Because he's afraid of his feelings.* That didn't mean he didn't care for her. But she wanted more from the man who would share her life. She wanted someone who needed her, who wanted children as much as she did, and who would be true to their marriage vows. And until she found such a man, she wouldn't settle for second best.

The room filled with thunderous applause. Glancing at the podium, she was surprised that she hadn't heard a word of the mayor's speech.

"And now, I'm pleased to present this year's Award for Outstanding Achievement. This year's winner is an exceptional woman who has given unselfishly of herself by initiating the dream of helping unfortunate women and their children, and culminating that desire into the founding of the Cityside Women's Shelter. I'm pleased and honored to present the Crystal Award to Dr. Brianna Kent."

The ballroom burst into applause. As Brianna rose to her feet, she didn't fail to catch Mike's surprised look, then exhilaration crossed his face as she smiled at him. He was the first at their table to stand when the crowd gave her a standing ovation. Hundreds of cameras flashed as she shook hands with well-wishers along the route toward the dais.

Mike's gaze followed her past the tables of admirers as she climbed the steps and took her place at the microphone. He'd been surprised when her name was called, but admiration and pride quickly won over his surprise. Now he realized why she'd said she couldn't miss the awards ceremony. A business dinner, she'd called it. She'd known the award was for her, yet she hadn't said anything. What the mayor had said about her service and devotion to the battered women and children of Cityside Shelter wasn't a surprise, but Mike didn't know that she'd been its founder.

He could imagine her clients admired her, as well. Brianna had the knack to delve right to the heart of a problem, forgoing hand-wringing and fretting. It took a lot to ruffle her feathers. And she'd proved it again, today.

Standing there in that sexy short black dress, which showed off her long shapely legs, diamonds gleaming at her ears, her hair twisted in a shiny blond coil at the nape of her neck, and a soft smile on her lips, he found it hard to believe that less than two hours ago she'd been face-to-face with a stalker.

She'd always been cool under pressure, and he'd always admired that. Most women he knew would have fainted or been in hysterics if they'd faced what she had today.

Yet, standing on the stage of a ballroom the size of Rhode Island, she appeared as cool and elegant as a goblet made of Waterford crystal.

He thought of the other wealthy women he'd dated since his divorce. Most of them cared very little except for themselves. Brianna gave of herself because she believed in being generous. It was as ingrained in her nature as breathing.

But someone out there didn't appreciate her. Someone was in the city, lurking, watching, waiting to strike. And Mike's hunch was that the stalker was connected to her clients. A psychologist as nurturing and giving as Brianna might not see the danger signs, especially if the nutcase disguised it well.

He made a mental note to ask Cindi Nichols, the FBI profiler whom TALON-6 had used successfully in the past, to give him a call. If Brianna would talk to Cindi, maybe she could help her pinpoint which of Brianna's clients might be the stalker. It was worth a try.

"Known Brianna long?" Larry Cunningham asked from across the table.

Obviously Brianna hadn't told Larry that Mike was her

ex-husband. "Yeah," Mike said, amused at Larry's obvious curiosity.

"From college?"

"Before."

Larry scowled. "Before college?" He paused, and Mike could see his gears whirling, wondering how she could have met Mike when she was a student during her sheltered boarding-school years. "Then you're not a patient?" Larry asked finally.

Mike grinned at his attempt at humor. "Not yet."

Larry's eyes narrowed, not sure whether Mike was leading him on or not. Mike's first hunch had been correct. Larry was definitely attracted to Brianna, might even believe himself in love with her. But she obviously didn't return the feeling. She'd admitted as much, and Mike knew that when Brianna cared deeply for someone, she'd never deny it.

Did Larry think that if a stalker was after her, she might turn to him?

"Did you return to the office yesterday afternoon, Larry?" Mike asked innocently.

"No. On Fridays I teach at Princeton."

Mike remembered seeing him about midafternoon when Brianna and Mike had stopped at her office. "You didn't teach yesterday?"

"Yesterday was unusual," Larry snapped back. "I'd taken the day off. I had a matter to discuss with Brianna and I'd been waiting to see her. That is, if it's any of your business." His scowl deepened. "Why the questions? You sound like a cop."

Mike grinned. "I'll take that as a compliment." He reached for his wine and took a sip, ending the conversation as he turned back to watch the proceedings onstage.

The microphone filled the ballroom with Brianna's smoky contralto, the words of her speech outlining her vision of the future for the Cityside Women's Center. Mike listened, transfixed as she wove a spell around the audience, calling upon them to work even harder for the cause. Mike felt transported as he took in her every word, his lips slightly parted.

WHEN BRIANNA FINISHED her acceptance speech, the applause was deafening. She smiled at Mike, who was clapping wildly. Her heart lunged as she realized that all the applause in the world wasn't as important as Mike's approval.

The thought brought a sharp intake of breath. She turned, forcing herself to feel composed as she greeted the mayor, shaking his hand again as a swell of well-wishers swarmed around her. Simone, her secretary, clasped her hand and gave her a hug. ''Well done,'' she said, wiping a tear from her cheek.

''Thank you, Simone.'' Briefly, she introduced Mike to her secretary. Several doctors who had donated their time to the women's center offered their congratulations.

She felt claustrophobic for the first time in her life. She tried to break through the wall of people, but the long procession of admirers and greeters seemed endless. She looked up to see Mike come up beside her, his eyes gleaming. A flood of relief made her realize how nervous she'd been. How had he managed to wade through the crowd and appear at her side so quickly? All she knew was that she was so grateful. If only they could escape and go someplace where they could hear themselves breathe.

''Let's get out of here,'' she whispered in Mike's ear. Lisa Caleb, a huge smile on her face, stuck her hand out. ''I couldn't be more delighted, Brianna.'' She winked, then cocked her head, motioning at Mike. Brianna caught Mike watching and could tell by the grin on his face he'd been aware of Lisa's double entendre.

"Thank you, Lisa," Brianna said, then laughed as she gave her friend an it's-none-of-your-business look.

"Call me if you have the chance," Lisa said as Mike drew Brianna from the ballroom.

Outside the crowded entrance of the hotel, Brianna tucked her beaded bag under her arm and cradled the tall crystal statue in her other arm. She saw a uniformed driver standing beside a white stretch limo waiting for them at the curb. Surprised, she looked up at Mike for an explanation.

"I thought we should celebrate," he said, taking her arm as they strolled under the canopy-covered walk to the curb. "Besides, what could be more fitting for the first lady of Cityside Women's Shelter."

She frowned. "Mike, do you have any idea how much food the shelter could buy with the money a limo costs for one night?"

He laughed. "Don't worry. I wasn't planning on adding it to your bill. Let's say this is my treat." He smiled that crooked smile that caused her insides to flutter.

She was surprised that with everything else on Mike's mind, he had found the time to order the limo. Then she remembered when they were first married, he had always surprised her with little gifts and unexpected tokens that let her know she was never far from his thoughts.

"Thank you," she said, forcing her mind back to the present. "I appreciate your thoughtfulness." When she saw him smile, she narrowed her eyes in feigned disapproval. "Just be sure you don't do it again."

"Point taken."

She grinned. It felt good to kid with him again, especially after such a nerve-racking day.

The limousine driver reached over and opened the door for them. When they were comfortably reclined against the supple leather of the back seat, Mike gave the driver the address of the Crib, then closed the panel of the door that separated them from the front seat.

When he leaned back in his seat, she looked over at him. "I'm glad you were at the dinner tonight."

He rolled his head to look at her. "Because the stalker might be there?"

The car drifted quietly into the stream of heavy Saturday-night theater traffic. In the insulated luxury of the back seat, they heard nothing of the blaring horns and screeching tires of the outside world. "No," she said finally, her gaze on the clear crystal in her lap. "Receiving this award means a lot. It's nice to have someone there who…" Someone who means a lot to me, she realized, but instead said, "Who knows how much my work means to me."

His eyes, darker than midnight blue in the passing car headlights, told her that he understood perfectly. She put her hand on his and squeezed it. "Thanks," she said, her throat tight with a mixture of emotions she didn't want to analyze.

As the limo turned down a wide avenue, a familiar tune began playing on the stereo.

Their song.

She glanced at the built-in shelf along the side of the limo. A bottle of Dom Perignon sat surrounded with ice in a bucket. Two gleaming champagne flutes stood waiting in the rack.

"What's going on, Michael?"

"What?"

"If this is some kind of prelude to seduction, you can stop right now."

"What are you talking about?"

"The champagne? The music?"

He chuckled deep in his throat, which only irritated her further.

"The champagne comes with the limo. As far as what

music the driver picks, hey, I had nothing to do with it.''
He couldn't quite hide the grin from his face. "Now, relax
and let me take care of you." He took her hand. "After
the day you've had, you deserve some pampering."

She pulled her hand away. "There's a vast difference
between pampering and seducing."

"Dammit, Bria. I'm not trying to seduce you."

She looked at him and realized he had no idea how se-
ductive he was. She felt a little disappointed and deeply
chagrined. He was right. After all, he hadn't even offered
her a drink or opened the champagne. Ordering the limo
was a thoughtful thing to do, and she was reading suspi-
cions into everything he did because…because she wanted
him to seduce her.

She took a deep breath and forced herself to face him.
"I'm sorry, Mike. I'm not myself tonight."

His eyes gleamed in the shadows. "Don't apologize.
Anyone would feel vulnerable. You've been through hell.
Sit back, close your eyes and try to enjoy the evening.
You're safe now." His voice was low, as soft as a lover's
sigh in the moonlight. Damn, she had to stop thinking this
way about him.

She laid her head against the supple leather and drew a
long breath. The words to their song swept through her
mind, making her deeply aware of the man beside her.

How could he sit back and enjoy the music? she wondered. She wanted to order the driver to play something
else, but if Mike could sit here and listen to those plaintive
words, then so could she.

He crossed his legs, and she was aware of the sharp
crease at his knee so close to hers. She was aware how the
side seam of his tuxedo shone in the passing headlights.
How his thigh touched her leg whenever the limo turned a
sharp corner. How his hands rested in his lap, his index
finger keeping time with the beat of their song.

Thank God he wasn't singing along, as he used to do. How she loved his rich, resonant voice. "You should form a rock band," she'd teased, and they'd laugh as he broke into a perfect imitation of their favorite singer.

"What are you thinking about?" he asked.

"Nothing in particular. And you?"

"I was wandering down memory lane." He shot her a long, thoughtful look. "Must be the music."

"Yes, next to the sense of smell, music is the best trigger for inducing memory." She laughed nervously. "I sound rather clinical, don't I?"

"Hmm. I notice you become quite clinical whenever I touch a nerve."

She gave him an indignant huff. "What do you expect? I'm a psychologist."

"You're also a woman."

"Meaning?" She waved a hand. "Oh, never mind. I have no wish to pursue this."

He began humming along with the melody.

She couldn't believe it. She tried to keep a neutral expression, but he must have sensed that she was uncomfortable because he asked, "What's the matter? You used to love that song."

She forced a grin. "Some things change."

"And some things stay the same, Bria. What we had together was good. Most of it, anyway. Don't toss away all the good memories with the bad. I sure as hell don't."

She felt he'd turned the tables on her. *She* was the one who gave advice, not the other way around. She tried to make light of the matter, think of something glib to say, anything to lighten the mood. But all she could think of were those damn lyrics she knew so well.

"Stop humming," she said finally. "I want to hear this part. I've always loved this riff of baritone sax."

He quieted, and in the darkness, she could almost see his grin. "Still like to dance?" he asked.

"None of your business."

"We were quite the couple on the dance floor. I still have that trophy we won in that little club in that Bangor hotel. Remember?"

"No."

"I'd made a deal with the hotel manager to tend bar on New Year's Eve in exchange for a room for the holiday weekend."

She would never forget. It had been his Christmas present to her. Two nights and one day at one of the nicest hotels in the city. They'd arrived on Friday night, as excited as two teenagers. They'd only been married a few months and were living on Mike's salary as a bartender. He also was the custodian at the apartment building where they lived, rent free. A wistfulness filled her as she remembered how completely ill equipped she'd been for that lifestyle. But she'd loved being a wife. Mike's wife. For the little time it lasted.

"I'm not really interested in a ride down memory lane, Mike."

"You were so beautiful. Almost as beautiful as you are now."

She turned away from him. What was he trying to do? Her throat tightened with…dear God, she was going to cry. She cleared her throat. "Why don't you call and see if they've caught the stalker?"

"Erickson will call me if they have any news."

She whirled her head to look at him. "Do you think Leonard Braewood is still at the hospital?"

Mike leaned his head back against the seat, his eyes closed.

"He got away."

"How is that possible?"

"How did he plant that bug in your office phone? How does he know so much about your routine?" He opened his eyes and looked at her. "Try not to think about Braewood tonight. Tomorrow morning, we'll meet with Liam and go over our new strategy. For now, just put everything out of your mind and let me worry about it."

She rubbed her temples. "Easier said than done."

His warm hand came up behind her neck and gently massaged her tight muscles. *Just as he used to do.* Stop it, Brianna, she told herself. She closed her eyes and forced herself to enjoy the delicious feeling that his experienced hands played on her shoulders.

"Larry didn't seem to be enjoying himself," he said a few minutes later.

"Why do you say that?"

"Oh, kind of the way he looked. It was obvious he wanted to know where I fit into the picture."

"Larry is the model of decorum. If he was curious, he'd never give in to it."

She heard him chuckle and she opened her eyes and looked at him. "What does that dirty little chuckle mean?" she asked, brushing away his hand from her neck. But when she touched his fingers, he caught and held on to hers, and for the moment all she could think of was how very close he was, so very close. She could feel the warmth of him, the brush of his knee against hers. She could feel his strong, steady hands curl her fingers within his palm as their gazes fixed with one another in the shadowed darkness.

Without a word, he lifted her face to his and captured her lips. Her eyelids fluttered shut, and something twisted inside her. Her mouth opened, so willing. Too willing. No hesitation, no little start of surprise. As their kiss deepened, she knew she should stop this, but the lyrics of their love song from another time filled her mind, their promise and meaning as heartfelt now as then.

When his tongue came inside, she knew this was what she'd wanted. Just this once, she thought, drawing him closer. What harm could one kiss do? She leaned into him, so familiar, so comfortable. Her eyes stung from wanting this for so long.

His breath quickened against her cheek. She moaned, feeling herself soften against him. So safe, so glorious, so familiar.

His mouth took hers sweetly, persuasively. She craved more, suddenly impatient with what was building between them. This moment had been inevitable and irreversible, gaining speed the moment she'd walked into his office.

She had wanted this. From the moment she'd first seen him in his office, she'd wanted him to hold her, to kiss her, to comfort her.

A deep growl rumbled in his chest and he whispered her name against her ear. He moved slightly, revealing that he was fully aroused. Her heart hammered when his hand slid over the swell of her left breast, his thumb rotating the nub in exquisite pleasure. Suddenly she felt as if she were stepping out on some high, thin wire like a tightrope walker working without a net. A shock of understanding pulled her away, away, away, back to firmer, safer ground.

Merciful heaven, what was she doing? She forced her mind to work. How long had it been since she'd felt the comfort of a man's embrace, or sensed a man's genuine desire? No wonder she was temporarily insane with passion.

"Mike, we have to stop," she whispered in a shuddered breath. Gently, she withdrew her arms from around his neck. His chin rested against the top of her head while they caught their breath, their hearts thudding side by side.

"I hadn't planned to do that," he said finally, his arm still around her shoulder. When she didn't answer, he drew back and looked at her. His gaze flicked down to her lips. "I don't think I ever got you out of my system."

She needed control, and the only way she knew was to take it. "You're feeling lust. Plain and simple. Understandable, after what we've been through today."

In the shadowed darkness, she saw his dark eyebrow arch. "Hormones?"

She straightened the black strap of her dress then checked each diamond earring. "Grownups have hormones as well as teenagers," she said lightly.

"You still like to pigeonhole feelings, don't you?" His voice was hard, accusing.

She didn't want to have this conversation. Why couldn't he just drop it? "It was just a kiss." She brushed at her skirt. "It won't happen again."

"The hell it won't."

She turned to look at him. In the headlights from the car behind them, she could see his jaw clench. "Bet on it."

His eyes flashed and a ghost of a smile lit his mouth.

She glanced away, afraid he might see the crack in her confidence.

"MIND IF I TRY SOME of your vegetable moo shu?" Mike asked while he opened the last of the white food cartons they'd bought at the Szechuan and Peking take-out place around the corner. No sooner had the limousine dropped them off at the Crib, a little more than an hour ago, than they realized they were starving.

"Go ahead," Brianna called from the hallway. She stepped into the kitchen, towel-drying her damp hair. He looked up to see that she'd changed into a pair of faded denim shorts, a yellow T-shirt, and she was barefoot. With her face free of makeup, he was reminded of how she'd looked when they were first married.

"Smells delicious," she said, gazing at the cartons he'd

lined up along the marble counter. She bent over the one nearest her. "Mmm, what's this?"

He took a breath before daring to speak. "Char su ding." He watched as she peeled the paper away from a set of wooden chopsticks. "Roast pork sautéed with vegetables and almonds."

"I don't remember when I've been so hungry," she said, spearing a mushroom and plopping it into her mouth. She looked around the gleaming rectangle of stainless-steel cabinets. "Where do you keep your plates?"

He shook his head. "Sorry. Don't have any."

Her eyebrow lifted. "You don't have plates?"

He grinned. "I'm very seldom here." He picked up a mouthful of diced vegetables between his chopsticks. "And when I am, I order takeout."

She glanced at the large refrigerator beside the dishwasher. "Don't tell me. You use the fridge for storing bacterial cultures?"

He feigned a scowl. "Don't be silly." Trying not to laugh, he added, "Go ahead, nosy. Take a look."

She shot him a wary glance before she opened the door. Her jaw dropped. The shelves were filled with camera film. Cases upon cases of various brands and speeds. "Film?"

"There are chemicals in the back for developing, too."

"No one can say you're not full of surprises." She closed the door, unable to keep the amusement from her voice.

"Eat your moo shu before it gets cold." He watched her pick up the carton, her eyes fixed on its contents. He was relieved that she'd agreed not to talk about the stalker until the following morning. But small talk between them was like walking through a minefield. Any subject, no matter how trivial, could remind them of who they were and what they'd meant to each other. He could sense she was thinking the same thing.

"Do you cook?" he asked finally, hoping to fill the awkward silence.

She swallowed a mouthful then met his gaze. "Does nuking frozen meals from the health-food store count?"

He grinned. "Remember that fancy cooking class you took?" By her uncomfortable pause, he was sorry he'd mentioned it. She had enrolled in a weekend class in culinary arts the summer he'd first met her. She'd surprised him with her first home-cooked meal, a huge strawberry molded from cream cheese. He'd come home from working a double shift at her dad's paper mill, starving to death. One look at that tinted-red strawberry, well… He'd tried not to laugh, but he'd hurt her feelings just the same. Then she laughed and they ended their spat as they always had, by making love like crazy fools.

"I've picked up a few culinary pointers since then," she said finally, placing the carton on the counter. "Guess I'm not as hungry as I thought."

"Brianna, we need to talk about this."

"About what?"

"About the past. It's not going to go away."

"Look, Mike. We agreed we could work together if we kept the past where it belongs."

"That kiss we shared in the limo wasn't part of our past. Denying it didn't happen isn't going to make what's between us go away."

"I'm not denying anything. And there's nothing between us." She stared at him, her eyes wide and shadowed. "I care for you, Mike. I always will. But we have no future. That's not good or bad, it's just the way things are."

"How can you be so damn sure? You don't know who I am, yet you're ready to judge me."

"I know the signs."

"What does that mean?"

"Your lifestyle, for one." She waved her hands. "This.

This opulent apartment, with as much warmth as a Stealth fighter jet. Why, you can't settle down long enough to buy a loaf of bread." She closed her eyes and took a deep breath. When she spoke, her voice was soft. "You're right, Mike. I was judging you, and I have no right." She opened her eyes and met his gaze. "I'm sorry. Who you are and how you live is just fine."

"Tell me you don't want to go to bed with me and I won't ask you again."

She cringed. "You're not playing fair."

"Tell me."

"Okay, damn you. If that's what you want. I don't want to—"

He stepped toward her, closing the distance between them to mere inches. "Look me in the eye when you say that."

Her eyes glistened with vulnerability. "I'm going to bed. Alone." When she dashed from the room, he made no attempt to stop her.

Chapter Eight

The next morning, Brianna knew she needed to set up a regimen. Although she was an organized woman and enjoyed structure, a schedule would also keep her emotions concerning her ex-husband at bay. After last night and the way she'd eagerly returned his kiss—God, she had practically been all over him—she definitely needed an agenda. Or so she thought.

At 5:00 a.m. that morning, she had no sooner started out the door for her morning run, when Mike appeared from his bedroom. Freshly shaved and showered, he looked incredibly sexy in a white T-shirt that stretched across his powerful chest and broad, muscled shoulders. The casual beige running shorts he wore contrasted handsomely with his deep tan. It was enough to take her breath away.

"Mind if I tag along?" he said, humor twinkling in his blue eyes. He clipped a water jug to his belt and followed her down the hall.

"Do I have a choice?" She whipped her hair back into a ponytail, securing it with an elasticized band.

His smile was his only answer.

"How did you know I was going for a run?" she asked.

"At breakfast yesterday, you mentioned that you'd missed your run. You weren't going to leave without me, were you?"

She didn't answer directly. Instead, she said with a chuckle, "I hope you can keep up with me."

They didn't speak again until they were out on the street. "After our run, I know a little place around the corner that opens early for breakfast. Do you still love waffles?" he asked, the wind whipping his hair.

"Waffles sound great," she offered, not answering his question. Did he have any idea how painful it was that he kept bringing up the past? Even the little things he remembered.

"Have you heard from hospital security?" she asked, hoping to steer the conversation back on track.

"By the time we get back to the Crib, Erickson should be awake," Mike answered. "I'll call him to see if there's anything new on the case."

To see if Leonard Braewood was caught, Mike meant, but she didn't correct him. She had taken his suggestion not to think about the stalker and it had worked. Although she'd felt more relaxed concerning Braewood, her nervousness was replaced with increasing sexual tension. She caught a trace of his aftershave. The scent jolted her senses.

Dammit, what was the matter with her? She was long over her ex-husband, so why was she reacting to him like a teenager on her first date?

She couldn't even take comfort that Mike had been as aroused as she last night. He'd made it perfectly clear that their arrangement could include sleeping together as an added benefit for them both. But she'd seen from her practice, over and over again, how rejected spouses wanted their mates back, not for love but because they mistakenly believed if they regained their ex-partners, they would feel whole again. Mike didn't love her, although he might think he did. She was just another challenge.

She shoved her sweatband in place and forced her attention on the stately brownstones nestled between neatly clipped lawns. Petunias, begonias and impatiens splashed color from planters and window boxes. A dog barked from behind a fence. Church bells chimed for six o'clock mass. Baskets of cascading flowers hung from wrought-iron yard posts.

Block after block, the steady rhythm of their shoes striking pavement lulled her into an edgy peace. Acutely aware of Mike beside her, she could almost forget, for the moment, that Leonard Braewood was obsessed with her.

Several blocks later, Mike wasn't even breathing hard when she paused to catch her breath. Running in place, she took a swig from her water bottle. "You're in great shape," he said, his gaze assessing her. "Work out every day?"

"Never miss. There's a gym near my apartment building."

His face grew serious. "Keeping to a strict schedule makes it easy for someone to track your whereabouts."

She screwed the cap back on the bottle. "I've already thought of that. Guess I've been an easy mark for the stalker."

"I thought later today, if you're feeling up to it, I'd ask you some more questions. I'll need to know the names of the people you come into contact with during your everyday activities."

"I gave you my appointment book from the office."

"That's a start, but I need the nonbusiness things, too."

My personal life, she thought. He'd soon know there was no man in her life. Not since Jordan. "Okay," she said, knowing that having to confess to her ex-husband that she hadn't had sex in two years was anything but okay.

He glanced at his watch. "It's almost eight o'clock. Worked up an appetite? The Waffle House will be opening soon. If we head back now, we'll be just in time to beat the morning crowd."

SEVERAL HOURS LATER, Brianna stood on the Crib's sunroof terrace and helo pad, and gazed along the shores of the East River. The morning sun sparkled on the waters and shimmered off the streaming traffic on the Brooklyn Bridge that spanned Manhattan and Brooklyn. She hugged herself contentedly as she studied the rooftops and chimneys and church spires and belfries. If only the city were as safe and beautiful as it looked from this vantage point, she thought.

Behind her, Mike's cell phone rang. She glanced at him over her shoulder. Seated at the patio lounge chair, his sunbrowned, powerful legs stretched out in front of him, Mike reached for the phone, never taking his gaze from the laptop balanced on his knee.

His thick dark eyebrows furrowed in concentration as he listened. She held her breath, wondering if it was news from Erickson. Mike had called him earlier when they'd returned from their run. Erickson hadn't answered, but Mike had left word on his answering machine. Maybe Leonard Braewood had been caught.

Mike glanced up at her, and as though guessing her thoughts, shook his head. "It's Liam calling from your apartment," he said. "He's almost finished with the sweep. So far, he hasn't found any bugs." Although his smile was meant to reassure her, she took little comfort in it.

"Why would the stalker need to bug my apartment? You already said that Liam found a tracking device installed in my car. Who knows how long it's been there." The anger and cynicism she felt surprised her. Maybe one of her clients was the stalker's interest, and not her? Dear God, who knows?

Mike laughed, the sound distracting her from her thoughts. She watched him tap on the computer, his deeply tanned hand cradling the phone to his ear. After their run, he'd showered and changed into jeans and a black T-shirt, similar to the one he'd worn Thursday, when she'd walked into his office after seven years. Had it been only three days ago? God, it seemed as if those seven years they'd been apart had never happened.

She shook her head at her foolishness. *I've been out in the sun too long,* she decided. Taking a seat beside him at the umbrella table, she picked up her microrecorder. Sliding one foot out of her leather sandal, she crossed her bare leg as she sifted through the client folders she had stacked neatly in front of her.

Just then, Mike hung up and looked down at her pink toenails. "I've got another call to make," he said, his gaze on her foot. "If you want to dictate, I can make the call from downstairs and not bother you."

"No need," she said, sitting up straight and sliding her foot back into the sandal. "I have to catch up on notes for a court appearance tomorrow. I'm testifying for a mother whose spouse was trying to gain custody of their son." She opened a client folder. "If Liam is through with the sweep, I'd like to pick up a few more things from my apartment later," she added.

"How about now?" Mike tapped a few keys on the computer keyboard then closed the lid. "We'll take the car."

She put down her microrecorder and leaned back in the chair. "Car?" she couldn't hold back the surprise from her voice. "I didn't know you owned a car." Few people who lived in Manhattan owned cars, with the available city transportation. Besides, he'd never mentioned owning a car.

"Sure. Thought we'd take a drive after lunch."

"Where to?" A thread of worry coursed over her. "Did Liam say something to spur this trip?"

"No, this is something I'd already planned. Thought we'd drive out to New Jersey and pay a visit to your colleague, Dr. Cunningham."

She sat up. "Larry?" She leaned forward with her elbows on the table. "What's so important that you want to bother Larry on a Sunday afternoon?"

"Want to ask him some questions. Thought it would seem friendlier to visit him on his own turf."

She gave him a thin smile. "You mean if Larry's relaxed, he might let something slip?"

His mouth quirked. "Are you always so suspicious?"

She grinned. "I'm beginning to think that you do very little on the spur of the moment. What do you really want from Larry?"

"If it makes you feel any better, I don't think your friend Larry is the stalker."

"Quit calling him *my friend*." She slid the microrecorder back into its case and snapped the lid shut. "I told you there's nothing between Larry and me."

"I believe you."

You do? She felt a sting of disappointment, then immediately mentally chastised herself for her foolishness. "I'm glad," she said, hoping he believed her.

His slight grin revealed nothing as he jotted a few notes on the pad in his lap.

"I wanted to call Larry," she said. "It's time I told him about the photographs and the stalker."

"Good idea." Mike picked up his cell phone. "I'll call Erickson again. His phone didn't ring when I tried him earlier."

A wave of restlessness caused her to push away from the table and get to her feet. If Erickson had found any information, he would have called by now.

While Mike waited for Erickson's phone to answer, she stood beside him, bracing herself for further disappointment.

"MIKE. I was just about to call you," Erickson said, his tone no-nonsense.

"Any word on Leonard Braewood?" Mike asked.

"Not yet, I'm afraid. But something came up that puzzles me."

"Go ahead."

"Yesterday, when I arrived on the sixth floor, a priest and a moving man were waiting at the elevators. The moving man, Gary Hershall, said that the priest had just arrived before I got there."

"So?"

"Hershall said that he thought it was weird to see a priest. The patients had been relocated from the floor last week."

"So? Maybe he was lost."

"Yeah, that's what he said."

"What was the priest like?" Mike asked.

"Friendly. Spoke with a slight Irish brogue. Said he was visiting a patient, but that he'd gotten off on the wrong floor."

"It's possible. Did you get his name?"

"Father Patrick Halloran from St. Michael's. And Mike, I just got the police report this morning. There's no priest by that name at St. Michael's."

"SO WHY WOULD the priest give a false name?" Brianna asked a short while later after Mike had filled her in on Erickson's phone call. They were on their way to her apartment to pick up some more of her things, then head for Larry Cunningham's home in New Jersey.

Mike watched her adjust her seat belt, and lean her head against the passenger headrest. He turned the Escalade SUV left onto Brooklyn Bridge Boulevard, then glanced back at her. She'd changed from denim shorts and T-shirt into a yellow sundress that turned her eyes into pools of greenish gold. The simple cut of the dress exposed her back, showing off her smooth tanned skin, recalling erotic memories that he'd spent years trying to forget.

Damn, he'd never find the stalker if he kept thinking about what it would be like to get his ex-wife into bed. He forced his attention back on her question.

"Before I decide that the priest was using a false name, I want to rerun the name through the databanks myself. Maybe Erickson spelled the name wrong."

Her eyes rounded as she studied him. "You don't believe that," she said, her hands clenched in her lap. "Please, Mike, don't try to placate me. If you know something, I want to know it, too."

"I'm not holding anything back," he said, relaxing his hands on the wheel. "I've always admired the way you forgo hand-wringing and just handle the problem. But in this case, we need facts. And getting facts takes time." He looked at her and smiled. "Patience has never been one of your strong points."

Her look of surprise, then hurt, took him off guard. Then he realized that she might have thought he was referring to their marriage. She had not waited very long before filing for divorce.

"Maybe that's the difference between us," she said finally. "I don't believe in waiting around for a lost cause."

He felt the jab, but realized that her irritation was an attempt to hide the vulnerability he knew she must feel, and it hitched up his protective instincts a notch.

She closed her eyes then opened them. "I'm sorry, Mike. I—I didn't mean to say that." She leaned over and brushed the back of his hand with her fingertips. She'd barely touched him and the jolt to his system felt like a thunderbolt.

"No apology needed. And you're right. Let's talk about all of this tomorrow." The color that her temper had brought to her cheeks was fading.

"By then, we'll have the copies of the forensic artist's sketches from the description Erickson gave of the priest," he said, his gaze straight ahead. "For now, try to put this out of your mind."

"I'll try, but I'm not like you. I can't just put unpleasantness out of my mind. I saw him, Mike. Those eyes, so full of hate."

His hands clenched the wheel. Damn, he didn't know when he'd felt so helpless. Ever since Erickson had told him about the priest, Mike couldn't get a crazy thought out of his mind. *What if the stalker and the priest were the same man?*

What if the stalker had checked out the hospital beforehand and known the sixth-floor patients and staff had been evacuated? He could have easily stashed a disguise earlier, planning to make his getaway. If so, then the stalker was a lot more dangerous than he'd first thought. Lots of ex-military men could get their hands on black-market, cutting-edge security equipment. But the kind of mind who had schemed to lure Brianna to the hospital by impersonating an E.R. doctor, then eluding hospital security and him...

She looked out the window as he turned off the ramp and merged onto Center Street. "This isn't going to be easy, is it?" she said softly. She turned and looked at him, her eyes troubled.

"Nothing we can't handle," he said, hoping to God that this was a promise he could keep.

"THAT ABOUT DOES IT," Brianna said as she rummaged through the garments hanging in the walk-in closet of her bedroom.

"Want me to close the lid?" Mike asked, noticing how neat and organized she had packed her suitcase.

"Thanks, Mike, but I can do it myself." She stepped

back and pointed to a Pullman case on the top closet shelf. "I'd appreciate it if you could reach that bag for me."

He moved beside her and lifted the luggage with no effort. His gaze fell to several bathing suits hanging on the closet rod. "TALON-6 has a pool and an exercise room. You might want to bring along a suit."

Her eyes widened in surprise. "I'd like that. I'll miss my workouts, unless you want to accompany me to the gym each morning." She couldn't quite hide a smile.

"I won't rule it out. I'd like to ask the staff at the gym a few questions."

She rolled her eyes. "Mike, you can't be serious." Despite her casual tone, he saw her mouth tighten.

She took a black-and-white striped swimsuit and put it in her suitcase. Mike noticed a black lacy nightgown hanging on a padded hanger. He picked it from the rod. "Hmm. This might be something you'll need," he said, teasing.

A grin replaced her worried frown. "Oh, you think so, huh?"

"Definitely."

She moved to the closet and pulled a white, fuzzy terry-cloth bathrobe from a hook. "This is my favorite," she said with a grin. "Glad you reminded me. I almost forgot to pack it."

HE GRIPPED THE TONGS and carefully removed the photograph from the developing solution. In the darkroom's soft red light, he sneered at the image of the smiling teenager, caught with his telescopic lens, so unaware.

Freaky thing, with her nose rings, black lipstick and bands of color in her spiked hair. Just the sort of subcreature the bitch would take under her wing.

A quiver of excitement shot through him when he thought of how the bitch would react when she saw the photo. Her eyes would round in fear. Her face would drain of blood. She might even cry out.

But she had no idea of real terror. Soon, very soon, she would know what real horror felt like.

He slipped the proof into the stop bath, agitating it a few seconds. She thinks she's safe. Good. But she can't protect all of her flock. She'll drop her guard, then she'll come running, right into my trap.

Chapter Nine

"If you don't believe Larry is a suspect, why do you want to interrogate him?" Brianna asked once they were settled inside Mike's SUV, heading north along the New Jersey Turnpike.

Mike glanced at her. She was wearing designer sunglasses, and the amber lenses couldn't quite hide the distrust in her eyes. He could see that she didn't entirely believe that he didn't consider Larry a suspect. "Let's just say I want to be sure Larry doesn't know something that might help us. For instance, he might have seen something or someone and not thought it out of the ordinary at the time. I also want to watch his reactions."

"Reactions to what?" A ring of doubt still hung on her words.

His reactions to you, Brianna, but Mike kept the thought to himself. Whatever the relationship between Brianna and Cunningham, Mike sensed that she trusted Cunningham, and that was reason enough for her to be protective of him. For a fleeting moment he envied Cunningham that. She was a tigress when defending her friends and those close to her.

You're letting your feelings get in the way, Landis, he warned himself. Keep this professional, remember?

"Are you going to tell me what you meant, or are we playing Twenty Questions?"

"Sorry." He kept his eyes on the road as he pulled the Escalade into the far lane to pass an oil truck. "You can tell a lot about people by the way they react. That's all I meant." He gave her a quick glance. She was studying him and he knew she wasn't completely convinced. "I don't think Cunningham is the stalker. But I want to be sure that the stalker isn't using him to gain information about you."

After a long moment, she nodded. "I see."

He glanced into the rearview mirror then at her before bringing his eyes back to the road. She had leaned back and folded her hands on top of the client files she'd brought to work on while they drove to Cunningham's house. Mike figured she'd brought the work as an excuse to insulate herself from any further intimate exchange with him. Especially after their limousine ride from the Plaza last night.

A heat rose in him at the memory of that kiss, but he pushed it back. He'd made a hell of a lot of mistakes in his life and kissing her was about as foolish as they came. He remembered a definition of insanity that he'd heard somewhere. Doing the same thing over and over and expecting different results. Yeah, he was certainly insane when it came to his ex-wife. What the hell did he expect would happen if he kept kissing her? He was one crazy fool.

He stole another glance at her. She was staring out the side window, deep in thought. He marveled again at her natural look. With her face free of makeup and her hair swept back in a banana clip, she looked no older than a teenager, especially when she lowered her lids in that guileless way. A few silvery-blond tendrils escaped her hair clip; the draft from the air conditioner bounced the errant tendrils around her slightly flushed cheeks.

Her soft mouth opened slightly. "I don't know why I never thought of it before, but just because I don't know Leonard Braewood doesn't mean some of my friends aren't acquainted with him." She whipped off her sunglasses and turned toward him, her green eyes wide with alarm. "Dear God, do you think the stalker would harm them?"

He took a deep breath, choosing his words carefully. He wanted to be honest but he didn't want to worry her, either. His guess would be that the stalker was fixated on only one person—Brianna.

"I'll let you know," he said finally, "once we hear Liam's report on the sweep he did of your office and apartment. I've arranged a meeting for us with him at TALON-6 first thing tomorrow."

Her mouth twisted into a moue. "I'm in court all morning. Didn't I tell you?"

He shook his head. "No problem. While I'm waiting for you in the courthouse, Liam can call me on the Harpo with his reports."

She grinned. "The Harpo?"

"The Harpo is the secure ground phone line."

She frowned. "I thought that was the bubble machine."

His lips curved into a smile. "The bubble machine is the satellite phone. It's portable, its location can't be detected, and it can be used on ground or air. The Harpo is stationary, and is used from one secure ground unit to another." He gave her a quick glance. "All TALON-6 lines are secure."

"Figured." She slumped back in the seat and looked out the windshield. "You don't have to come with me to court. I'll be surrounded by security guards and people I know."

"You mean like when you were at the hospital?"

The flash of fear that widened her eyes made him wish he could take back his words. "I'm going with you to court tomorrow." Then, as if to lighten the mood, he added, "After all, I'm charging you big bucks for my protection." He grinned at her and it pleased him to see the worry fade as she smiled.

"Seriously," she said, her gaze on the folders in her lap, "I'm very appreciative for all you're doing, Mike."

"It's my job." He purposely didn't look at her when he said that, for sure as hell, she'd see through him. He'd give his life to keep her safe, and protecting his ex-wife had nothing to do with money or his job as a security specialist.

Mike signaled a lane change, then worked his way through the heavy Sunday-afternoon traffic. The soft brrr of her cell phone caused her to jump. While she answered it, he was grateful for the diversion from thinking about her. He'd been doing too much of that lately.

"Thanks, Jayne," Brianna said a few minutes later. "I hope everything turns out okay. Bye." She clicked off the phone. "That was my client's attorney," she said, slipping the phone into the beige straw bag at her feet. "The attorneys have agreed to a postponement, so I won't be needed in court tomorrow, after all."

She smiled brightly at him.

"Great. That means as soon as you give me the okay on the surveillance equipment I've suggested, the sooner we can install it."

"How long will it take to hook up?"

"We should have the latest bells and whistles installed by Tuesday."

"Perfect." Her eyes brightened. "Since I'd planned to be in court tomorrow, I'm not scheduled to see clients at my office until then." She sighed. "How can we be sure the stalker won't find a way to rebug my office?"

"I've got a little black box that can easily sweep a room. You can activate the device every morning."

She relaxed against the leather seat. "You make everything sound so simple."

"That's my job."

She chuckled as she rummaged in her straw bag. When she pulled out her cell phone, he looked up.

"Who are you calling?"

"I thought I'd give Larry a ring. Let him know he's about to have company." She shot him a look as she punched in the numbers. "We'll be getting off at the next exit."

By the time Mike keyed Larry's home address into the SUV's computer and followed the map that appeared on the small monitor installed into the dashboard, it was nearly four o'clock.

Mike pulled the SUV into the driveway and approached the modern trilevel house framed in carefully manicured shrubbery. He parked alongside a yellow BMW sports convertible in front of a three-car garage.

Brianna bounced out of the car as soon as he turned off the ignition, and hurried along the terraced walk that led around the back of the house.

Mike put his hands in his pockets and leisurely strolled after her. A swimming pool was behind the high fence, he would guess. The tennis court that he'd caught a glimpse of through the thick hedge along the east wall must be Dr. Larry Cunningham's property, too.

Business must be very good, indeed. Especially if that little sports car was registered in the good doctor's name. Mike decided it wouldn't be a bad idea to run Dr. Larry's name through ACS, the Access Control System that TALON-6 used for high-clearance operations. Mike had a hunch it wouldn't turn up anything, but where Brianna was concerned, he couldn't be too careful.

"Join us for a game," Cunningham called out to Brianna as he emerged from the shady path to greet her. The rim of his dark baseball cap with the red-cardinal logo above the visor shaded his eyes. He was dressed in whites, from his tennis shirt down to his shoes. He looked like a recruiting poster for the local country club. A long-ago memory of when Mike had first known Brianna flashed through his mind. Cunningham was a fast-forward version of the same kind of college studs who'd swarmed around her at the country club. Mike pushed back the uncomfortable feeling before he had a chance to analyze it. Some things were better left alone.

"Mike, you remember Larry," Brianna said when she came within earshot of them.

Cunningham's jaw clenched and his eyes narrowed, looking none too happy to see him. "Afternoon, Landis." He grabbed his hat's visor and adjusted his cap.

Mike's acknowledgment was a lift of his head. It was obvious that Cunningham knew this wasn't a social call. His inability to hide his emotions was hardly the mark of a criminal. To put it simply, Cunningham might be smart, but he didn't have the stalker's cunning.

"Have you met Lorna?" Larry asked as a petite, red-haired woman in her early thirties came up behind Larry. A tennis racket and ball were clutched in her left hand. Lorna's cool gray eyes swept past Brianna to fix on Mike. Her white teeth glistened from between red, collagen-filled lips.

"Lorna, how are you?" Brianna said after Lorna buzzed her cheek. Brianna turned toward Mike and quickly introduced them.

"We met last night," Lorna said, holding on to Mike's hand longer than necessary as she stared up at him.

Brianna gave Mike a surprised look before she turned to Larry. "We didn't mean to interrupt your game. I'm sorry we didn't call sooner."

"Nonsense," Lorna said, her gray eyes studying Mike. "One of the perks of living next door to Larry is that I can drop in anytime for a game of tennis." She drew her attention to Brianna. "My dear, why don't you have your talk with Larry. I'll show Mike the pool. I'll mix a pitcher of martinis.'' Although she was talking to Brianna, her Julia Roberts smile was directed squarely at Mike.

"Actually, I was the one who wanted to talk to Larry." Mike pulled his hand from her grip. "Nothing for me to drink. I'm fine, thanks."

Lorna blinked, her smile fading as she turned to Brianna. Brianna shook her head. "Nothing, thanks."

"I'll have a scotch," Larry said before Lorna sauntered toward the back of the house.

Larry strode purposely toward the arched gate within a thick evergreen hedge. The area behind the house reminded Mike of an English-garden maze. A few minutes later, the roof of a screened-in gazebo came into view. Beside it was an Olympic-size swimming pool. When they were inside the gazebo, Mike took the chair beside Brianna after she made herself comfortable on the floral-cushioned chaise sofa.

Larry stood a few feet in front of them, his arms folded. He turned his attention to Mike. "What's this about, Landis?"

Brianna leaned forward. "Mike, maybe it would be easier if I went first." He nodded, then watched Larry as she told him about the anonymous photographs she'd received, the listening device that was found in her office telephone on Friday, and finally the incident at the hospital yesterday with Leonard Braewood.

"Who is this Braewood?" he asked Mike.

"We're not sure," Mike answered carefully. "We're still gathering evidence."

Larry dragged a chair beside Brianna and sat down. "You must go to the police." He shot a glance at Mike. "No offense, Landis. I'm sure you're well meaning, but this calls for police work. The FBI." He looked back at her. "Why didn't you tell me about this sooner?"

"I didn't know anything to tell. I'd hoped it was some

joke. Someone trying to frighten me. I'd hoped once he'd managed to scare me, that would be the end of it.'' She took a deep breath, then her gaze met Mike's. ''Mike heads TALON-6, a specialized security agency. I couldn't be in better hands.''

''Doesn't sound like it from what you told me happened yesterday at the hospital.'' Cunningham's gaze on her never faltered.

''That's not fair, Larry,'' she said. ''I don't know what I would have done without Mike.''

Larry sat back, quiet for the moment. ''Great Scott. You acted as though nothing was wrong last night at the awards dinner.'' He let out a gasp. ''Christ, the stalker might have been in the audience, for all we know!''

''Larry, please.'' She took in a deep breath. ''Mike thought you should know what's going on. I realized last night that I should have told you before now. That's why we're here.''

Larry put his hand on her clenched hand. ''You know you can count on me, Brianna. I'll do anything I can.''

She moved her hand, then glanced at Mike before returning her attention to Larry. ''If you want to help me, you'll answer Mike's questions.''

''What questions?'' Larry frowned at Mike. ''You can't believe I know anything about this?''

''No, no, of course not,'' Brianna said quickly. ''But there's a chance you might know something that will prove useful. Maybe you saw something that at the time might have seemed meaningless.''

''Like what?'' Larry asked defensively.

Mike cleared his throat. ''Larry, you're not under suspicion. My questions are just routine.''

''That sounds like a line from a cop-TV show.'' He leaned back to face her, his face tense. ''Let me go with you to the police, Brianna. I'd feel better if—''

"I've been to the police. But so far, we have little to go on. Slipping photos under the door isn't illegal. We can't prove who placed the listening device in my phone. Besides, the police are understaffed and overworked. Using TALON-6, I'll get more immediate results. And I'm being protected, day and night."

Larry looked surprised. "Where are you staying?"

"I can't tell you," she said.

"Don't you trust me, Brianna?" Larry asked.

"It's not that." She abruptly got to her feet. "Mike, can you explain it to him?"

Mike noted the scowl of disbelief on Cunningham's face. "It's for her protection that you don't know. What you don't know you can't tell. That's standard operating procedure."

Larry shot to his feet. "This is ridiculous."

"Oh, there you are," Lorna trilled. She appeared from the open gate, carrying a tray of drinks in her hands.

"Mike, why don't you stay and explain things to Larry," Brianna said, moving to the door, "while Lorna shows me the gardens." Without waiting for a response, she stepped through the gazebo door and strode toward the red-haired woman. "Lorna, why don't you show me the roses. Larry had mentioned he's entering Golden Masterpiece in the rose show next week."

When the women were out of sight, Mike got to his feet and leaned to within an inch of Larry's face. "Look, Cunningham," he said, his low voice edged in steel. "If you want to help her, you'll answer my questions. But if you want to play hardball with me, just say so. Because if the lab reports from the tests my partner took from the evidence he found in Brianna's office come back tomorrow and reveal what I think they will, then I'll have the power to have the police haul your ass in for questioning. Then this little chat will be on the record. Now, whose rules do you want to play by? Yours or mine?''

Cunningham's eyes narrowed to angry slits. ''You're a regular caveman, aren't you?''

''Ah, now you went and hurt my feelings.'' Mike took a deep breath, aware of the anger churning inside him. ''Are you ready to answer my questions?''

Larry sat down. ''Depends on the questions. Should I call my lawyer or something?''

''No, this is just a friendly little chat between buddies.'' Mike pulled a microcassette recorder from his hip pocket. ''I'd like to record this, if you don't mind.'' He clicked on the machine. ''Now, tell me, Larry. Are you in love with my ex-wife?''

''THAT DROP-DEAD, gorgeous hunk is your ex?'' Lorna asked a few minutes later. Her face openly revealed her delight that Mike wasn't Brianna's new lover as Lorna had first thought. She took a sip from her martini glass. ''Is he…engaged or anything?''

Brianna bit back the stab of unadulterated jealousy and the anger with herself for feeling it. ''I—I don't…know,'' she said, justifying her answer with the knowledge that she really hadn't asked Mike if there was a woman, someone he was serious about, in his life.

She wanted to slap that silly smile from Lorna's face. Instead, she glanced at the thin gold wristwatch on her wrist. ''My, it's almost six. I think I'll see if the men have finished.''

Lorna slid her hand over her short bob. ''What's so important that Mike couldn't wait until tomorrow?'' She stood on tiptoe and peered around the weeping juniper to catch a glimpse of the gazebo.

''Mike won't be available this week,'' Brianna said, her cheeks warming at the white lie. Damn, she wished Mike would hurry. Lorna was getting on her nerves. She glanced back at the gazebo. The wind, or what there was of it, was blowing the other way or else she might hear what they were saying.

"Men like that can have any woman they want," Lorna said, pouring herself another drink from the pitcher. She speared a green olive onto a toothpick. "Sure you don't want something?"

Yes, I want to get out of here, Brianna thought. "Why don't you wait here while I see what's keeping them?" She rose from the bench along the poolside table and without waiting for Lorna to answer, hurried along the path toward the gazebo.

She noticed Mike before she saw Larry. Both men turned when her footsteps creaked upon the wooden steps leading to the gazebo screen door. "About ready?" she asked, trying to sense their mood.

Mike's mouth crooked slightly, his body language giving no hint to his emotions. Despite Larry's tan, his cheeks looked pale. His cap's visor slanted across his forehead, shielding his eyes. From the guarded way he'd folded his arms across his chest, Larry's posture appeared very defensive.

She gave Mike a tight smile before she spoke to Larry. "Why don't we finish your talk on Tuesday."

Mike looked at him in surprise. "I'd forgotten you're not in the office every day, are you?"

Larry stood and moved to the door, dismissing them. "No, I lecture at Princeton on Mondays and Fridays."

Brianna caught the puzzled look on Mike's face, but she would wait until they were on their way back to the city to ask him what was wrong.

"Give Lorna our goodbyes, Larry," she said, hoping to make a speedy exit. She was bursting with curiosity to find out what, if anything, Larry had told him.

Mike offered his hand to Larry. "Nice seeing you again, sport."

Larry mumbled something, then glowered at Mike, his right hand gripping the doorknob before he strode from the gazebo to join Lorna by the gate.

Brianna did a double take when she realized Larry had refused to shake Mike's hand. She turned and raised a questioning eyebrow at her ex-husband.

"Come on, honey," Mike said, taking her arm. "Goodbye, Lorna," he called out to where she and Larry stood.

Lorna lifted her martini glass, then took a sip. "'Nighty."

"CUNNINGHAM HAS ACCESS to your office key and to your apartment—"

"No, Mike. I told you that Simone and my aunt Nora are the only people who have access to my apartment—"

"You and Cunningham share Simone for secretarial duties," Mike interrupted. "If Simone kept your keys in her desk, it's not impossible for Larry to have made an impression of them—"

"Larry isn't the type to even think like that—"

"How do you know?"

"Will you stop interrupting me?"

"I will if you will." He grinned and she found it hard to stay angry with him. Oh, how she'd like to let go and pick a fight with him. Anything to keep her mind off how incredibly sexy he'd looked in contrast to poor Larry. Oh for Pete's sake, what was the matter with her?

Maybe if she could scream and yell, she'd release the bottleneck of tension that she'd felt since this nightmare began. How she'd love to hurl insults at Mike like the childish, dysfunctional brat she wished she were. But she wasn't, dammit.

She was a gracious, kind, practical woman. A Rock of

Gibraltar who kept her head in a crisis. She was a leading expert in the art of couple relationships. Damn, she'd even toyed with the idea of writing a book about the subject.

Well, Gibraltar was crumbling and all common sense flittered away with one of Mike's crooked grins that turned her heart to mush. Her emotions were riding Coney Island's tallest roller coaster and she didn't know what to do about it.

Dear God, she'd felt like a woman scorned when Lorna had flirted with Mike. Brianna had wanted to throw that iced pitcher of martinis over Lorna's head, and she might have if she'd stayed a minute longer.

Yet, whenever she was with Mike, she'd always been emotional. Passionate, he'd once called her. For the first time, she really understood. Because when she was with Mike, she could be herself. She could let down her guard and be however she felt, because she knew he'd understand.

When she was with Mike, the world seemed so much more. Rain was wetter, sunshine was brighter, laughter was sweeter...

Her eyes smarted with the threat of tears. Hell, she had only thought she'd gotten over him.

She blinked them back and stared out the side window at the slower lanes of traffic. She would get over him, dammit!

His warm hand pressed upon her knee, and she forced herself not to flinch. No need to alert him to how much his touch really affected her.

"I'm trying very hard not to let any loopholes get past us, Bria." His deep voice was a husky whisper. "If you were just another client..." He let the words drift in the silence between them.

She blinked back another threat of tears. *If I were just another client, what, Mike?* She dare not speak, the question lay buried inside her tightened throat.

"Bria? Look at me."

She swallowed, her head turned away from him. "Keep your eyes on the road."

She heard his soft huff of laughter; the sound made her want to throttle him.

"There's a seafood restaurant at the next exit." When she didn't answer, he continued, "On the drive down here this afternoon, I noticed their sign. I thought we might be hungry on the way home and you'd like to stop."

She took a deep breath. Maybe she needed food. Maybe she was having a low blood sugar reaction from not eating. The idea gave her hope. Maybe there was a practical reason for her foolishness instead of the impossible idea that she was still in love with him.

Maybe she didn't love him. Lust was what she felt. She sagged with relief. Yes, that was it. She was feeling lust, nothing more serious than intense physical attraction.

No, a tiny voice said in her mind. *Practical women don't lie to themselves.*

Blurred halos ringed the headlights outside the window, and she realized her eyes welled with tears.

She took a long deep breath. Regardless of what she felt for Mike, she was a practical woman. She would act like one. "Seafood would be great," she managed to say, relieved that her voice sounded almost normal. With her head turned away from him, she closed her eyes and forced her mind to be still.

Chapter Ten

"Nothing typical about this baby," Liam said to Brianna and Mike the next morning. Liam pulled out a square device no wider than a CD case from his jacket pocket and placed it carefully in the middle of the polished mahogany table of the conference room. "I've already checked it for prints," Liam added. "It's clean."

They were at the TALON-6 Building in midtown Manhattan, where earlier Mike and Brianna had met Liam in the coffee shop downstairs. Mike had insisted that Liam show them the latest information he'd put together so far on the case.

"It looks like a worthless piece of metal." Brianna stared at the tiny gadget that Liam had found behind her car bumper. Although Mike had told her about the device, she had wanted to see it. She needed to see it to believe something so small could be so sinister.

Mike picked up the object. "With this tracker in the vehicle, when you're in the car, you appear as an electronic blip on the stalker's video screen."

She let out a whoosh of noise.

Mike studied the device. "This baby was put in by no rank amateur," Mike said, turning it over in his fingers. "This is the same toy the CIA boys use."

She covered her face with her hands. "Dear God, what have I gotten myself into?"

Mike took her hand. "It's all over, Brianna. We've put an end to his games. You're safe here. Liam did a full sweep of your car, your apartment and your office. Everything is cleared of any surveillance bugs."

She pushed the hair from her face. "I can return to my office today?"

"I don't see why not."

"Well, that's a relief." She smiled at Liam. "I'm sorry for being so edgy. I'm very grateful. Thank you. Mike said you had left your sister's wedding party earlier than planned. I'm sorry that you were inconvenienced on my part."

Liam chuckled. "You're most welcome. I'm blessed with six sisters and the last of them has finally tied the knot. But whenever we get together, they gang up and try to marry me off to their friends. I was rather glad to escape, if you know what I mean." His deep laughter was contagious.

"Well, I'll be in my office," Liam said. "Before you leave, Mike, I'd like to go over the rest of my reports. Shouldn't take long." He started to rise, then glanced at Mike, "Or do you want me to stay while you ask her?"

"Ask me what?" Brianna turned to Mike.

Mike gave an uneasy glance to Liam, then turned to Brianna. "Before you say no, I want you to think over what I'm about to suggest."

She tried not to smile. "I might surprise you. What do you want me to do?"

Mike's expression was somber. "What do you think about talking to our profiler about your clients. She's a crack agent for the FBI and we've used her on past cases with great success."

Instead of the immediate refusal he'd expected, Brianna looked thoughtful. "Okay, Mike."

He tried to hide his surprise. "You're agreeable?"

She nodded. "I trust you. Besides, we have to get this guy. He's overheard private conversations, not only from my clients, but my secretary, my partner, even Aunt Nora. Everyone who has been in my office and home." She shook her head. "He's tracked my whereabouts, even when I've visited clients at the hospital and shelters. I'll do anything to catch him." She turned to Mike. "We must catch this guy."

A FEW MINUTES LATER, Brianna put down her athletic bag, shook out her umbrella and hung it on the coatrack inside the TALON-6 suite hallway. When she opened the doors of the chrome and glass reception area, the delicious aroma of Colombian dark-roast coffee greeted her.

The young receptionist looked up from her computer screen and smiled. "'Morning, Brianna." Bailey looked around expectantly. "Isn't Mike with you?"

"Hi," Brianna said. "We met Liam downstairs in the coffee shop as we came in. Mike wanted to introduce me." She picked up her bag and crossed in front of Bailey's desk. "We had no sooner said hello when Mike asked Liam to bring us up to date on his latest reports." She glanced at her watch. "That was over an hour ago." She smiled. "When I left them down the hall a few minutes ago, they were on their way to Mike's office, their heads together, going over more strategies."

"Sounds like business as usual." Bailey got up from her desk and stepped around the counter. "The fax from Erickson, from hospital security, was waiting when I came in. Still haven't found Leonard Braewood, I'm afraid."

Brianna bit her lip. "I was hoping…"

A look of sympathy crossed Bailey's freckled face. "How about some coffee?"

"Sounds great. Thanks."

Bailey disappeared into an alcove where a coffeemaker sat on a counter. When she came back into the room, she held a steaming porcelain mug in each hand. "Finding Braewood may take a while, Brianna, but Mike will get him. Don't worry." Her face shone with a confidence that heralded her unshakable belief.

Brianna felt a surge of respect for Mike and the team who garnered such trust. "I hope so, Bailey." She sipped the aromatic brew. "Mmm, wonderful. Just what I needed." She watched Bailey take her seat in front of the monitor. "Say, what time did you get here this morning?"

Bailey took a gulp from her mug. "During the week, I stay in the TALON-6 apartment one flight down. On weekends, I usually drive to Vermont and stay with my mom. But this weekend I'm up to my ears with finals."

"You go to college here in the city?"

"Yeah. Columbia." Bailey brushed an auburn tendril away from her cheek and rolled her eyes. "Two more weeks and I'll have my degree."

"Congratulations." Brianna was impressed. "Working here and going to school. That's quite a load."

Bailey pursed her lips, her blue eyes narrowing. "I owe a lot to Mike and the guys. Working here is small payment for what they've done for Mom and me."

Although she was curious, Brianna didn't want to appear nosy. "Mike mentioned there was an exercise room on this floor." She pointed toward the corridor. "Is it down the hall?"

Bailey put down her mug. "Here, let me show you."

"The gym has a handball court and swimming pool, too," Bailey said a few minutes later when they came to a set of bronze doors. She pressed a numeric pad that was clipped to the waistband of her jeans. The doors slid open; indirect lighting, hidden along the ceiling, flicked on.

Brianna stepped into the room and gasped in surprise. The room was cavernous; she was sure her voice would echo to the rafters. "Why all this?" she asked. "Why don't the guys go to one of the gyms?"

"Security, for one thing," Bailey explained. "Often we have clients, such as political leaders, celebrities and every-day people, who need a safe-house stay with us. Here at TALON-6, they can enjoy the lifestyle they're accustomed to, yet feel safe.

Brianna glanced around, understanding TALON-6 with new eyes. No wonder Mike showed such empathy and compassion for the work she was doing at the women's center. Their work was very much the same.

"As you can see, this is the rappelling area," Bailey said as they walked past walls of ceiling-to-floor granite. "Great way to keep in shape. Mike and the team have little choice, considering their dangerous professions."

Danger. Challenge. Adventure. Of course, how could she have forgotten? TALON-6 was formed from Mike's Spe-cial Forces team. Even though Mike wasn't officially in Special Forces, she knew he still considered himself a pro-fessional soldier, ready to fight, even kill, if his country called. The thought gave her chills.

"Where does that door lead?" she asked, hurrying to-ward the next set of doors.

"That's the swimming pool." Bailey motioned to an-other doorway. "And over here is the equipment room."

"This is more my speed," Brianna said as she stepped inside the mirrored room and took a seat on a recumbent bicycle. Several treadmills, a StairMaster and three rowing machines stood nearby.

"The air temperature and humidity automatically adjust

to our outer body temperatures,'' Bailey explained. ''Cool, huh?''

''Decidedly cool,'' Brianna agreed, pushing herself off the bike to catch up with her guide.

''An indoor track is on the left.'' Bailey punched a button from the device at her waistband. ''The area lights automatically turn on once you step inside, but I like to play with the gadgets,'' she said with a grin.

''I can see why,'' Brianna said, amazed.

''The weight room is straight ahead, the dressing rooms, showers and Jacuzzi are to the far right.''

''I think I'm lost,'' Brianna said, only half joking.

''No problem.'' Bailey pointed to a small panel along the wall. ''Each room has one of these. It's also a security device, recording movement, sound, temperature and more things than I can remember.'' She glanced back at her. ''Just press this button and...'' Bailey's finger barely touched the panel when a diagram of the floor plan appeared. ''See, you can't get lost.''

Brianna noticed that the route they had each taken was outlined in fluorescent green. She didn't fail to notice that if anyone else had been in the area, the device would have automatically exposed them, too.

''Amazing.''

''Another one of Mike's gadgets,'' Bailey said with a hint of hero worship in her voice. ''And look at this.'' She pressed another button. ''The music panel.'' She grinned at Brianna. ''You wouldn't be a fan of 'N Sync, would you?'' she asked hopefully.

Brianna laughed. ''How did you guess?'' In a microsecond, the room was filled with pulse-pounding music. She shook her head. ''Wow, living here must be fun.''

''It is.'' Bailey returned her smile. ''I'd love to live here full-time but I can't leave my mom.''

Brianna sensed that despite Bailey's outgoing manner,

there was an elusive sadness about the young woman that even her whimsical charm couldn't quite hide.

"Well, I better get started on my workout." Brianna turned toward the changing room then paused. "Say, do you think your boss would mind if you joined me?"

Bailey's face lit up. "Yeah, I'd like that." She clicked a button at the keypad at her waist. "Hey, Brianna. Watch this." A video monitor appeared from a recessed area beside the door. Views of the reception area flashed across the screen. Several seconds later, Bailey's desk area appeared, followed by a view from the hallway outside the TALON-6 suite entrance, then the scene changed to each partners' offices. "Way cool, huh?"

Brianna shook her head in amazement. "Way cool."

MIKE LEANED BACK in his leather chair and propped his long legs on the desktop while he speed-read Liam's report. When he finished the last sheet, he looked up at his partner.

"So you think the stalker lives in the city?"

Liam raked his large hand through an unruly shock of black hair. "He must. The type of tracking device I removed from the bumper of Brianna's car has a range of about fifteen miles." Liam's brogue was always more pronounced after spending a week with his Irish family. "Of course, the stalker might use a mobile receiver in a van."

"Parking would be a bitch. Besides," Mike said, "following her car in and out of traffic would be hard to do in Manhattan."

Liam nodded. "Maybe the stalker works near her building."

"Or he has access to a receiver, one already installed and readily available to him, like a police car, or another municipal vehicle."

"You think this guy is a cop?"

"Ex-cop, maybe. With the skill he's using, I'm guessing

he's ex-military, or maybe he's been in the pen. He'd meet plenty of contacts who could steer him to black-market equipment.''

Liam thrust his hand through his thick hair. ''If he was an ex-con, that would tie into your theory that he's connected with one of Brianna's clients. Has she given you the names of her clients yet?''

''We're heading over to her office from here. I should have them by this afternoon.'' Mike tossed the report on his desk. ''What chance do you think the stalker might be a woman?''

Liam's thick eyebrows lifted. ''Anything's possible. A woman could have knowledge of sophisticated equipment, too. Or maybe the woman's got a boyfriend.''

''Leonard Braewood?''

Liam shrugged. ''I don't think we should rule it out.''

Mike swung his feet to the floor and spun to face Liam. ''Logically, I agree. But my gut tells me it's a man. Don't ask me why. But male or female, the stalker is close by.''

''What do you mean?''

''He's around. I can sense it. He's so up to date on her whereabouts. He must be within eyesight of her every day. Hell, we might have passed him on the street. In the elevator. He might even work in her office building. I think he's someone who's inconspicuous.''

''You won't get an argument from me.''

Mike ran a hand along his chin. ''Dammit, Liam. Ordinarily I can trust my hunches. I also keep my emotional distance while on a case. But this time…''

Liam studied him, his blue eyes glinting. ''She's the one that got away, eh?''

''What the hell does that mean?''

''I've known you since we were in basic training, Mike. I've always thought that there was some woman you'd never gotten over. And one look at the two of you this morning and even Ray Charles could see you're in love with her.''

Mike glared at him. ''Well, the lady isn't interested, if it's any of your damn business.''

Liam held up his hands. ''Look, Mike. You're the guy with the sixth sense, not me. But if those electrical sparks that were arcing between you two had been any hotter, I'd have singed my eyebrows.''

''You're lucky I don't singe more than your eyebrows, O'Shea!''

A soft rap on the door caused Mike to look up. ''Yeah?''

The door opened and Brianna poked her head inside. ''Liam, Bailey's on another line. She asked me to tell you that a courier just arrived. He needs you to sign for a package.''

''Thanks, Brianna.'' He glanced at Mike. ''I'll be back in a minute, and I'll bring a fire extinguisher.''

After he left, Brianna turned to Mike, a quizzical look on her face. ''What did Liam mean by that?''

Mike shook his head. ''Pay no attention to him, Brianna. He thinks he's a comedian.''

She took a chair by the window. ''I think he's charming. I'm a sucker for an Irish brogue.'' She looked over at him. ''He seems so easygoing. He's a nice contrast to your, shall we say, intensity.''

''Not you, too?'' He grinned at her as he broke away from studying the stack of papers on his desk. ''Did you have a good run?''

Her face lit up with pleasure. ''Yes, thanks. I got rid of a lot of tension. You have quite a place here. Bailey showed me around. We'd still be working out, except when we saw the courier arrive on the monitor, Bailey recognized him from the police department. She thought the package might have information about Leonard Braewood.''

"I sure hope so." He let out a short breath that sounded impatient. "We could use a break in this case."

Brianna stood and moved behind him, placing her hands on his back, gently kneading the tight muscles between his shoulder blades. "Bailey said that it sometimes takes a while with a case like this."

Mike huffed. "Bailey believes that TALON-6 is invincible." He turned and smiled up at her. "I'm hoping we never disappoint her." His smile faded. "Or you."

Brianna dropped her hands to her sides. "You won't, Mike."

The door rattled with a loud knock, and Liam called out, "I'm comin' in, ready or not."

Mike gave him a warning look, then his gaze dropped to the package in Liam's hand. "Is that the police artist's sketches?"

"Sure is. Here, take a look at these." Liam pulled the computerized drawings from the envelope and laid them on the desk in front of Mike and Brianna. Liam pointed to the sketch of a close-cropped, white-haired man. "Ever see this man, Brianna?"

Brianna frowned. "No. Should I know him?"

"This is the composite of the priest from Erickson's description." He pushed another drawing beside the first sketch. "Here's another one of the priest drawn from the furniture mover's description."

"The basic features are similar," Brianna said. "But I've never seen this man, either."

The third sketch was Brianna's description of Leonard Braewood. She moved it beside the other two and compared them.

Mike stood up and peered over her shoulder. "Dammit. They're different. I was hoping…" He let the words fade away. Leonard Braewood was younger, beefier. The priest had pale-colored eyes, almost an aristocratic nose, with well-defined eyebrows. His head shape was all wrong, too. And from the physical descriptions given by Brianna and Hershall, Braewood was a much taller, larger man.

"I think this proves there might be two of them working together," Liam said.

Mike shook his head. "Stalkers are usually a solo act. They're like serial killers. Of course there are always exceptions."

"What do you think, Brianna?" Mike asked. "Think the priest looks like Braewood?"

Her gaze remained on the two faces. "Maybe."

Liam straightened, surprised. "How so?"

She ran a finger along the brow line of the priest. "If Braewood had worn a wig and a false beard, the hair would have concealed a high forehead and a square jaw."

Mike shook his head. "The body build is different. Erickson said the priest was of slight stature."

Liam looked up and crammed his fists in the pockets of his jeans. "Let's say he stuffed a big pillow in his gut and he wore shoe lifts."

Mike sat back in his chair. "It's possible."

"But not impossible, especially if he has an obsessive personality," Brianna finished for him.

Mike and Liam remained silent, studying the sketches.

Liam scratched his head. "After we run your clients' names through our computer bank, we'll get a better handle on him." Liam picked up the report and leafed through the first few pages. "Let's see what we do know. This guy is smart enough to use general photographic paper and supplies. Nothing traceable in those black-and-white glossies he sent. Nothing criminal about their content, which eliminates the police." He looked up, his gaze on Brianna. "Mike thinks he lives close by, maybe Upper East Side. He might have a law-enforcement or military background.

Does that ring any bells with any of your clients, your neighbors or casual acquaintances?''

She shook her head. "I'll have to think about it."

"He possibly works or worked for the FBI or CIA," Mike added.

"Definitely knows his stuff when it comes to electronic surveillance equipment," Liam said, his eyes fixed on the report.

"That description could be anybody," she said.

"What about the furniture mover, Gary Hershall?" Liam asked Mike, his finger holding his place on the page.

Brianna looked questioningly at Mike.

Mike shook his head. "Hershall was waiting with the priest for the elevator when Erickson arrived on the sixth floor. From his statement, Hershall had been moving file cabinets all afternoon. From 1:00 p.m. until 4:00 p.m. to be exact."

"Do we have a picture of Hershall?" Brianna asked. "How do we know he's not Leonard Braewood?"

"His description doesn't fit the description of Braewood that you gave Erickson," Liam answered. "Besides, I checked Hershall out. He's so clean he could be Man of the Year."

"So where did Leonard Braewood disappear to?" Liam asked, his expression open with possibilities. "We know the elevator stopped with him on it at the sixth floor. He could have gotten out, taken the stairs—"

"No. I was coming up the same stairwell," Mike said. "I would have seen him."

"Okay." Liam pointed a finger. "Braewood gets off at the sixth floor, which Brianna verified by watching the elevator dial."

She nodded.

"And Braewood picked the sixth floor," Mike said, his attention on Brianna, "because he knew the patients and nursing staff had been vacated. The only people left were the moving guys. So Braewood goes to the empty linen closet where he's previously stashed a disguise." Mike pulled out a paper tube from the stack on his desk and unrolled the blueprint. Spreading the sheet across the top of his desk, he leaned over it. "Here it is," he said, running his finger along the floor layout to point out the small supply closet adjacent to the nurse's station.

Liam folded his arms. "Then our orderly changes out of his scrubs and puts on the priest habit."

Brianna picked up the priest sketch in one hand, and the composite of Leonard Braewood in the other, her face grim.

"Then the priest slips through Erickson's net," Mike adds, "because they were looking for a large, bearded man dressed in scrubs."

"And the priest rides the elevator to the main floor where he walked out, pleased as punch with himself." Liam shook his head and slumped in the chair across from Mike. "It's a possible."

Brianna frowned as she put the sketches on top of the desk. "Whoever he is, the stalker is a very tormented soul. I saw the hate and rage in his eyes when he looked at me. If we knew what caused his problem, it might give us a clue. Maybe his mother abused him. Some female in his past must have done something horrible to make him transfer that rage toward me."

Mike straightened. "I recognize that tone, Brianna. Don't try to cure this guy. Some people are beyond help. Don't even go there."

Her shoulders stiffened and her eyes shone with exasperation. "Don't play mind reader with me, Michael. You have no idea what I'm thinking."

"This guy is a loony," Mike retorted. "He's a very dangerous man. He's not some misguided soul who was frightened by his potty chair when he was two." Mike grimaced, then shook his head. Dammit, why did I say that? He glanced at Brianna. "Honey, I'm sorry. I didn't mean that."

Brianna cast a shuttered look at him. "If you'll excuse me," she said, her tone cool, "I think I'll see if I can help Bailey or something." She turned and strode from his office.

Liam looked at the closed door, then back to Mike. "I think you've just lost your objectivity, partner. What in hell got into you?"

Mike rubbed his face. "Dammit, Liam, I know that I-want-to-save-the-world look of hers. If she starts thinking that maybe she can save this guy, she won't take him seriously. He's dangerous, and she's got to be made to understand that."

"Okay, okay. She's a smart lady. She knows the stalker can be dangerous. She was the one who went eye-to-eye with the orderly, remember?"

"My point exactly. Brianna went eye-to-eye with him before she knew he might be the stalker. This guy *is* dangerous. He's close by, and I think she sees him or passes him every day. Which means he's in a position of harming her before she can call out for help." He pounded his fist. "And if I'm right, I may not be able to keep him from her."

Liam stood up and leaned his hip against the corner of the desk. "Okay, Mike. What do you want me to do?"

When Mike looked up, all tension was gone. In its place was a cold, frosty stare. "Once you install the new deadbolt lock on her waiting-room door. I want you to install a video camera inside her office."

"Do you think the lady will sit still for having her clients taped?" Liam's mouth tightened. "We could lose our license over this, not to mention a host of lawsuits if anyone found out. And they will, you know."

Mike's jaw clenched. "I'm not suggesting something illegal. We have enough evidence in your report to get a judge to sign a court order. Lieutenant Mercer owes us quite a few things. See if he can hurry this through to someone who can get the necessary legal orders so we can install that camera."

"What good will the camera do?"

Mike leaned back and crossed his long legs. "The stalker has lost complete contact with Brianna. He must be getting desperate by now. He doesn't know where she's staying, but he does know that she'll be in her office, like a sitting duck. It's my guess this is where he'll strike next. He'll try another bug, maybe."

"Okay. I'll check with Mercer over at the police department. He'll know a judge who'll cooperate. He's never failed us yet."

"Good. You can install the camera so it shows only the front of the office. It will capture whoever enters, but what goes on inside Brianna's office will remain private."

"You're going to have to tell her about this, you know."

Mike looked up. "And I will. But I'll tell her in my own sweet time, and not before."

Chapter Eleven

"I didn't mean what I said," Mike told her ten minutes later when he'd caught up with Brianna at the front desk. She was alone, perched on the side chair beside the desk, sipping a steaming mug of coffee.

She peered at him from over the rim, then put the mug down. "Yes you did," she said, her eyes bright with hurt.

Mike came toward her. "I respect your work and what you do. I didn't put into words what I really meant—"

"No need to explain, Mike." Her tone offered no easing of tension. "We've had this conversation before. Seven years ago, if memory serves."

"Dammit, Bria, I spoke out of fear." The admission brought a flash of surprise to her eyes. "Yeah, I'm scared. Do you know how I felt when I got your call from the hospital and knew the stalker had had you alone in the elevator?" He looked away, his easy self-confidence suddenly deserting him. An overwhelming uneasiness took over; he felt unsure how to proceed. He wasn't used to admitting his feelings, especially feelings he wished to hell he didn't have. But how could he admit to the woman he loved that with all his experience, his know-how, he was afraid he couldn't protect her?

"Michael," she said in a sexy whisper. She stood and came to stand beside him. "I think we really need to talk."

He nodded solemnly and glanced at his watch. "Over lunch. Let's get out of here."

For the next twenty minutes, neither one of them spoke until they were seated at a quiet booth inside Clancy's Pub. After Ben took their orders, Brianna unfolded the napkin in her lap. She was still stunned at the pain in his voice at the admission of feeling that Mike had shared with her. Never had she heard him divulge a weakness in himself. Before today, she wasn't sure he was capable of such a feat, but a little while ago, Mike Landis had admitted that he was frightened. She was filled with a mixture of joy at the breakthrough and bittersweet longing to comfort him. But to do so might close him away forever. Instead, she took a sip of water and waited for him to speak first.

He cupped her hand, caressing her fingers as he gazed at her. "I appreciate you, Bria. I'm so proud of you and what you've done for the women's shelter. I didn't mean to sound as though I discounted your work."

She tried not to shiver with the sensations his fingers elicited. She forced her attention on to the subject. "When Bailey showed me the exercise gym and explained the need for security, I realized that, in a way, you and I have the same professional goals. You protect people from those who wish to do them harm, so do I. Our client base might be different, but we strive to help others."

His fingers stilled. "I respectfully disagree. To do your job, you need the help of lawyers, police and other agencies for protection. You can't protect yourself, regardless of how right your cause."

She pulled her hand away. "I never said I could. But understanding the sick mind is a tool, as well. If we know how the stalker thinks, it will help us know what he's going to do next."

"Brianna, I need you to promise me you'll not go off on your own. Promise me, okay?"

"There you go, treating me like a fool."

"Promise me, okay?"

"Of course I promise." Any further conversation was halted when the waiter approached with their salads. After he left, she leaned forward and stabbed a fork into a small wedge of tomato.

"Am I forgiven?" Mike asked, grabbing his goblet of water.

She twisted her mouth. "For the time being." She caught his look and was surprised that instead of the lighthearted grin she'd expected, his eyes were dark, his mouth serious.

"Yes, I accept your apology," she said barely above a whisper. *Oh, Mike, don't you know it's okay to be scared? Okay not to be perfect?* The words edged in her tight throat. She pushed an arugula leaf around the gold border of her plate. *Now who's not communicating? Why not tell him that being frightened is perfectly natural?*

Because he had turned the tables on her again, and she didn't know how to handle this sudden change in him. So what if he'd changed? Really changed? Could she risk her heart to find out? No, it was easier to blame him, put the fault of their failed relationship on his inability to confide his feelings to her.

What if she needed a man to turn away from her? What if she was so afraid of being hurt that she'd rather be alone, unhappy, than to risk opening herself up to him?

When she glanced back at her plate, unshed tears stung her eyes. She put down her fork. "I—I guess I'm not very hungry." She didn't look at him as she grabbed her bag and headed for the powder room.

When she returned to the table a few minutes later, he was on the cell phone, talking to Bailey.

"Anything new?" she asked, noticing Mike's serious expression. He broke off the call and slipped the phone into his jacket pocket. Leaning forward, he put his forearms on the table. "Bailey ran a check on some of the people from your list. Did you know that the doorman at your apartment house has a criminal record?" He noticed the surprise light her eyes, but she recovered quickly. "Has he ever said anything or done anything—"

"I didn't know about his record, that's true. But lots of people make mistakes, Mike. That doesn't make them criminals. In fact, I remember when you were sixteen. If you hadn't had the good luck to come before a judge who saw in you a decent boy who just made a mistake, you would have a criminal record, too."

"I've never forgotten what your uncle did for me, Brianna. Okay, I agree with you. But I wouldn't be doing my job if I didn't check out everyone with whom you come into contact."

"My doorman, Mr. Farentino, has always been polite, with impeccable manners. His daughter is a senior in high school and makes Christmas wreaths. I buy one every year." She shrugged. "Checking everybody with whom I come in contact each day is going to take years."

"Not with our contacts. Once you give me the final list of names, it will be a matter of hours before we have them processed." He leaned back and studied her. "Bailey also mentioned that your secretary's ex-husband has a criminal record."

Brianna shot her head around. "Yes, that's why he's Simone's ex." She took a deep breath. "Mike, I've known her for four years. She was volunteering at the women's shelter when I first met her. Her ex had done everything he could to destroy her self-confidence. After much therapy and dating more Mr. Wrongs than you can imagine, Simone has her life straightened around and she's just recently met a man. He's moved into her apartment building. He has a cat, like she has. He's Lithuanian, like she is. They love opera. He makes her potato cepeliniai…" She saw Mike's eyebrows arch in a puzzled look. "Potato pancakes," she explained. "His mother's recipe."

"I'd like the name of this new boyfriend."

"Oh, Mike!" She shook her head. "It's not that I don't want to cooperate, but I don't want to alarm Simone. She's finally met someone who—" She waved her hand. "Oh, never mind. You're the professional. If you think we need to drill her about her friend, fine."

Mike gave a relieved sigh. "It's for Simone's own protection, too."

Brianna jotted another line in the small notebook in front of her. "Okay, so far you want a list of my clients who have had violent partners, a copy of my appointments for the last three months, a list of all people with whom I come in contact during the day. And I shouldn't mention to Simone about the listening devices." She looked up. "Anything else?"

IN THE ELEVATOR on the way up to her office, Brianna tried not to think of the stalker or that he'd ridden the same elevator she and Mike were now on, but she couldn't erase the face of Leonard Braewood from her mind. "I know it's good for me to confront my fears, but I can't help thinking about him whenever I'm in an elevator," Brianna whispered to Mike.

"Remember, I'm here, honey. That's what's important."

"I know, but…" She drew her hand through her hair. "He hasn't given us so much as a clue as to why he's doing this. Not that it would make any difference. But it all seems so crazy."

He squeezed her hand. "I promise you, we'll get him."

She looked up at his handsome face and smiled. "I don't know what I'd do without you."

The elevator stopped with a soft thud and the doors

whooshed open. As they stepped into the corridor, they heard voices at the end of the hall.

"...or should I meet you at your place later?" Simone was smiling at a tall, distinguished-looking man with a touch of white at his temples. When they approached, the man adjusted his silver-rimmed glasses and smiled a greeting. He turned back to Simone. "Why don't you meet me at the coffee shop," he said, his voice heavily accented. Then he brought his attention back on Brianna and Mike.

"Oh, Dr. Kent." Simone turned toward her, smiling. "I thought you were in court today. I'm so glad you stopped in. I'd like you to meet my friend, David Malden. David, this is my boss, Dr. Kent, and her friend, Michael Landis."

Brianna shook David's offered hand then watched as Mike exchanged handshakes with the older man. "Glad to finally meet you, David," Brianna said. "Simone has told me so many nice things about you."

"Congratulations on your recent award, Dr. Kent." He glanced at Simone. "I'm sorry I couldn't attend the ceremony. Business, you know."

"Yes," Simone chimed in. "David is in charge of financial investments for Pierce, Alcott and Barney. He had to take a late flight to Chicago to oversee an important insurance merger."

The man almost blushed. "I was waiting for Simone to finish up, then we were going to dinner." He glanced at his watch. "But since she's not quite through, maybe I should wait downstairs in the coffee shop."

Brianna glanced at her watch. "Why don't you call it a day, Simone. I'm not expecting any clients, and the transcription tape can wait until tomorrow."

Simone grinned with pleasure. "Very well." She blushed, then looked at David. "I won't be a minute," she said, straightening her desk. "And thank you, Dr. Kent. Have a lovely evening, you two."

Brianna exchanged a smile with Mike as she strode across the waiting room and withdrew her key. When she unlocked her door and walked into her office, the memory of the surveillance bug that Mike had found in her phone came back to haunt her. She stared at the phone sitting at the center of her desk. When Mike came inside, he closed the door, and took a seat beside her desk.

She pulled a chair over to the file cabinets and pulled out the top drawer. Her fingernails flicked through the tabbed folders, withdrawing several files. By the time she'd finished going through all the drawers, she had almost twenty folders in her lap. "These clients have had at least one male batterer in their histories," she said grimly. "Four of them have left town and are living safely under a new identity. Some aren't so lucky." She handed Mike one file, her face drawn. "This woman's ex-boyfriend murdered her before she had finished packing. We warned her not to return to their apartment, but…"

"Where is the man now?"

"He's in prison. He'll be out on good behavior in a couple of years."

He understood how someone with Brianna's intense dedication to her clients would feel their loss. He wished he could say or do something, but all he could do was say, "I'm sorry."

She looked up at him. "I am, too." She pulled several more files from the drawer. "Not all batterers are male. Here's a woman whose husband came to me. Her husband wanted to save their marriage, and his wife, thank God, was willing to go through therapy. They both worked hard to get to the root of their problems. When she was stronger, she left him."

"How did her husband take it?"

"He seemed to have adjusted to her leaving, then a few months later, he killed himself." She slapped the file on top of the others. "Not many happily-ever-afters in this business."

That, plus our own failed marriage, he thought with regret. He took a stack of folders from her. "We'll run a check on these people, then we'll check their siblings or parents just to be sure no one else in their background might be nursing grudges against you."

She walked to a small closet and drew out a folded storage box. "I think the files will all fit in here," she said, placing the box on top of her desk. "Why don't we pack them up and work on them at the Crib."

"Sounds good to me." As he finished the task, he wondered if Bailey had finished running Larry Cunningham's name through their files. "Is Cunningham on call this evening?"

"No, I am. Why?"

"Hmm. Just wondered."

She got to her feet and pulled the stack of files together. "Might as well take these for starters."

She was about to leave, when she noticed the mail stacked in her in-basket. Simone must have brought it when she had first come in. Brianna sifted through the first few business letters, then she stopped. "Mike, look."

He turned around. He knew by the size of the envelope and the lack of a return address that it was from the stalker.

"Want me to open it?" Mike asked.

She shook her head. "No, no, I'll do it." She turned it over and lifted the back flap from the envelope. As before, the stalker had used a self-adhesive mailer. She slid the photo out onto the desktop, making certain not to touch the picture in case Mike wanted to dust it for prints.

A cold shiver coursed through her as she stared at the black-and-white enlargement. "It's Kristi!" The teenager was laughing at someone or something out of camera range as she strode down the stairs of a brownstone apartment building. "Dear God, Mike. You know what this means, don't you?"

"Brianna, he's trying to scare you. That's all." He put his arm around her. "We can't tell by a photo what he's intending to do."

"Yes we can." She dug her fingers into his forearm. "He's telling me that if he can't get to me, he'll get to Kristi."

MIKE CLOSED A HAND over hers and linked fingers. "I've just called Liam and he's putting a twenty-four-hour surveillance around Kristi. She'll never guess a thing. Now, don't worry."

"Dammit, Mike, how can I not worry?" She stared down at their joined hands. They were back at the Crib, and Mike had spent the last hour on the phone, calling and checking contacts, all the while reassuring her that he'd protect Kristi from the stalker. But the morgue was filled with victims who thought they were safe from their attackers.

"Bria," he said, his words gentle. She couldn't quite look away from the burning intent in those blue eyes, yet she wanted to. She pressed her palms flat against his hard chest. "I need to walk around. I can't stay cooped up like this—"

"Maybe what you need is a little exercise." He was sitting so close to her, so very close. She looked away but didn't make any move to leave. "You need someone to take your mind off…" His words whispered in her ear and she felt a jolt of electricity that had nothing to do with Consolidated Edison.

"Mike, I don't think that would be a very good idea…"

"Hmm. Why not?" He brushed a strand of hair from her lips.

"Because…" His gaze remained on her lips, almost intense, and she felt a strong desire to draw him to her. Maybe Mike was right? Harmless sex with her ex-husband? Like hell. There was nothing harmless about Michael Landis. And sex with him would leave her remembering what was missing from her life. Maybe a few hours of incredible sex would cut the anxiety from his life, but loving Mike had never been a casual thing for her.

She watched his eyes darken with need. His breathing was as rough and ragged as hers.

I walked away from you once, Mike. I don't think I could go through that again. The truth struck her as hard as a direct blow to the sternum. She wanted a man who came home every night, a man who didn't feel he had to save fledgling nations' dictators, or head up a covert team of special military maneuvers at a moment's notice. No, she deserved a man who would put her and their children first. She wouldn't settle for anything less.

She forced herself to stand, willing her legs to carry her to her room. "I'm going to turn in early," she said, not looking at him. For if she as much as stole a glance at the hunger she'd see in his eyes, she'd be gone. And once she gave in, she'd be lost.

"Dr. Kent, help me!"

Brianna stumbled along the dark hospital corridor, her feet sliding on the warm, thick oil covering the floor. "Kristi? Where are you?"

"Help me, please!"

Panic welled in the back of her throat. "Tell me where you are?" Brianna peered wildly through the growing shadows. Where was the light switch? Why was it so dark? "Kristi? Tell me where you are and I'll come—"

"She's here," a deep male voice called out from behind her. Brianna twirled around. Leonard Braewood grasped

Kristi by her bloody throat, the knife clenched in his fingers dripped with blood.

"Help me," Kristi cried, her white face grotesquely contorted. "I don't want to die." But Brianna knew the girl was already dead. The metallic smell of blood was everywhere, Brianna didn't have to look down at her feet to know she was standing in a river of Kristi's blood.

Brianna jerked awake, tears of terror swelling over the dam of her lashes. She reached across the pillow for Mike, but he wasn't there. Of course he wasn't there. She was alone.

She sat up, fighting away the nightmare as her mind strained to remember what was real. Yes, she was safe. She was at the Crib, with Mike sleeping in the bedroom across the hall. Kristi was safe, too. She had phoned the girl late last night, heard her sleepy voice stirred from sleep. It was only a dream.

But that didn't stop her shaking, or her heart hammering or the cold sweat filming her skin. Leonard Braewood wasn't a figment from a nightmare. He was real. The hate she'd seen in his eyes had been real, too. She'd seen something else crack through the animosity in those brown eyes. *Insanity.* She'd blocked the truth from her consciousness until now, but she'd seen that look in the criminally insane too many times not to recognize a sick mind.

Leonard Braewood, or whoever the stalker called himself the next time they met, was a sick man. And they would meet, if he had his way. He was out there, waiting. And he wouldn't stop tormenting her until he got what he wanted.

Hot tears formed against her will. Damn, she was tired of being so afraid and pretending to be brave. She lay back against the pillows, fighting a sob as recent events caught up with her. The exhaustion of the past weeks, the terror of facing the man who was obsessed with making her life a living hell, the futility of keeping her clients safe, and the painful and sweet memories of Mike and the feeling of inadequacy they prompted.

She covered her wet face with her hands. In the darkness, she didn't have to be brave. But she was so sick to death of being frightened. She was tired of being alone. She wanted... She needed...Mike.

She swung her legs over the side of the bed. *You're going to regret this,* a little voice warned, but she didn't care. She needed Mike. She needed his strong arms around her. She needed to feel safe. If only for tonight.

MIKE DIDN'T KNOW if he had sensed her coming, or if he'd heard the click of her bedroom door as it opened. Whichever it was, he didn't care. She was here, eager to let him love her.

Without a word, he opened the covers and drew her into his arms. Her hair was damp as he brushed it from her face. Her lips tasted like tears, and something akin to helplessness descended upon him. He remembered one other time when she had cried and he'd felt helpless.

They had only been married a month when she thought she was pregnant. Despite the financial problems a baby would have brought into their lives, they'd been head over heels delighted with the possibility. Arm in arm they'd window-shopped for stuffed bears, frilly organdy bonnets and a tiny football in case the baby was a boy. But a few weeks later when she discovered that she wasn't pregnant, he had held her, like now, while the tears flowed.

He had felt more than helpless. He knew what she'd wanted him to say, but he was too practical to say they could try to have a child. Not until they had some financial stability. He'd be damned if they'd live on her inheritance, and with his minimum-wage jobs, financial security would have been highly unlikely. But who would have believed that his invention—his new design of a semiconductor for computer modems—would be purchased the year after their divorce. How could he blame her for not believing in him. Without her, he'd lost faith in himself, too.

"Make love with me," she whispered. He held her, knowing that he'd dreamed of this moment for so long. But did she want him or only need him to make her feel safe?

"Bad dream?" he asked.

"Mike, I was wrong."

"Wrong?"

"You were right when you said we may only have today. Who knows what tomorrow will bring?"

He bit back the feeling of regret. "No strings. Is that what you're saying?"

She sat up, propped herself on one arm and pushed her hair from her face as she looked at him. "Isn't that what you want?"

He took her mouth, avoiding the answer. She moaned, softening against him as their kiss deepened. He wanted strings. Plenty of them where she was concerned. He also wanted to hear that she loved him. But if she said those words now, he wouldn't believe her.

Maybe he'd been right. Maybe they only had today.

Chapter Twelve

Brianna's hair trailed across Michael's cheek, the sensation waking him. For a moment he listened, treasuring the sound of her soft breathing. He smiled, watching her asleep in his arms, his heart full in the afterglow of their long night of lovemaking.

He glanced at the neon-blue numbers of the bedside clock: 4:12 a.m. He wanted her again. He was ready. But she needed her rest. He grinned, remembering how eager she'd been, how eager they'd both been…to start something that had nowhere to go.

He wouldn't worry about that now. He brushed the top of her silky head with his lips, pushing away the memories of long-ago mornings that began with waking up with Brianna in his arms. That was another lifetime ago. Now he was older, smarter, or sure as hell should be. She's a client first, his ex-wife second. You don't go to bed with a client. Never. No exceptions.

He stared at the ceiling and took in a long, deep breath, careful not to disturb her. Brianna would wake up with regret, no doubt about that. If she didn't say so, he'd read it in those greenish eyes that reflected deep within her soul.

She'd feel responsible, too, but he wouldn't allow her to bear the guilt. But if he said she shouldn't feel guilty, would she think he wasn't taking their going to bed seriously enough? Or would she prefer that he take their lovemaking lightly? Yes, maybe she'd want him to think that their love-making was nothing more than just physical need.

Physical attraction, she'd called it.

Hell, he couldn't second-guess her seven years ago, and he still couldn't. No wonder he was afraid to share his feelings. He was afraid to feel, where she was concerned. For below the scab were feelings he didn't want to probe. Scary thoughts of involvement, commitment and connection for the long haul. Scary things that a guy like him—the original rolling stone—had no right to be wanting.

The cell phone on the table beside the bed sputtered a soft ring. She stirred slightly. His hand reached the device and clicked the on button before the phone rang again and woke her.

"Hmm."

"Mike? It's Liam."

"What?"

"You and Brianna better get down here. I'm at Kristi McFarland's apartment building. Her boyfriend just left. They apparently had a fight and she's hurt. Looks like she's taken a nasty tumble down the stairs. I've called the police and an ambulance. I thought you and Brianna would want to know."

"Stay with her. We're on our way."

"W-what is it, Mike?" Brianna said sleepily.

"Get dressed, honey. That was Liam. He's with Kristi. There's been an accident."

"The stalker?" she said, instantly awake.

"Not this time. I'll tell you in the car.

REFLECTED RED LIGHTS from the ambulance ricocheted off the gawking faces of tenants and neighbors who lined the sidewalk leading to the corner brownstone apartment building. A police cruiser, its blue flashing lights rotating, angled in front of the curb. Liam was talking to several police officers at the sidewalk. When he saw Mike's SUV double-parked, he came toward them.

Brianna unlocked her seat belt and dashed from the passenger-side door before Mike had brought the SUV to a complete stop. By the time Mike and Liam caught up with her, the entrance door swung open and a team of paramedics hefted a stretcher down the steps.

"What happened?" Brianna asked Liam when he came beside them.

"Kristi and her boyfriend started arguing. The windows were open, most of the neighbors heard their fight." He shook his head. "Something about the boyfriend taking her money. The guy left, mad as hell. He didn't even shut the front door. All was quiet for about five minutes, then I heard a scream and I ran inside and found her at the bottom of the stairs. I heard her before I saw her. The hallway light was burned out."

"So it was an accident?" Brianna asked.

"She said someone pushed her. But if she's covering for her boyfriend, he might have pushed her and she was knocked unconscious for a few minutes. Then when she came to, she saw she was injured and decided to scream for help. She might be lying about the strange guy lurking in the hallway who pushed her."

"Did you see anyone?" Mike asked.

"No. By the time I found her, called 911, enough time had passed for someone to get away, if there was somebody."

"If?" Brianna's eyebrows lifted. "Maybe she's telling the truth."

"I'm considering every angle, Brianna." Liam looked at Mike and shrugged. "There was time for someone to head out the back window and go down the fire escape then beat it down the alley."

"So you don't think her boyfriend did it?" Brianna asked.

"I'd rather wait until I see what the police turn up," Liam answered.

When the gurney wheeled past, Brianna rushed along the side. Mike tried to hold her back. "Let's get in the car. We'll follow the ambulance to the hospital," he said, not wanting her to witness any more unpleasantness than necessary. He should have known better. She jerked free and was at Kristi's side before he could stop her.

"Dr. Kent," Kristi murmured when she saw Brianna. The teenager appeared to be under the effects of the medication that was being administered from an IV pole carried by the EMT at her side.

"I'm here, Kristi." Brianna jogged alongside the gurney. "Don't worry, dear. I'll meet you at the hospital."

Mike stepped back and turned to Liam. "Do you think there was someone in the hallway?"

"I'm not sure. I do know the girl doesn't want to involve her boyfriend. She didn't want me to call the police. She thinks he might be arrested. She's banged up pretty good. She might invent a story to keep her boyfriend safe."

Mike swore under his breath.

"Step back, please," the burly EMT said as he helped hoist Kristi into the back of the waiting ambulance.

Kristi's face twisted with a wrench of pain as she was lifted and placed inside. The doors slammed shut and the siren screamed to life.

Brianna felt Mike's hand on her shoulder as she watched the ambulance move past the corner and race down the street.

"I KNOW YOU'RE WORRIED about Kristi," Mike said to Brianna as they waited in the E.R. waiting room. "Why don't I drive you to the Crib. You can rest then come back later after Kristi gets out of recovery.''

They had been waiting over four hours. From the E.R. doctor, Brianna had learned that Kristi was undergoing surgery. She'd suffered a broken pelvis, several broken ribs, a possible concussion, numerous bruises including a ripped eyebrow. The good news was they were able to save the baby.

From what little that Kristi had told Brianna, and from Liam's report that he'd given Mike, Brianna was able to piece together some idea of what had occurred. Liam said he'd followed Kristi and her boyfriend, Kevin, back from a party to Kristi's second-floor apartment at 3:48 a.m. Through the open windows, Liam saw the apartment lights turn on, then a fight broke out. From the yelling and accusations, Liam heard that Kevin had taken Kristi's savings, money he'd found in her jewelry box. One thing led to another, and at a little after 4:00 a.m., Kevin left on foot, leaving the front entrance door wide open.

Mike sat quietly beside Brianna, scanning a dog-eared copy of *Time* magazine. She knew he was giving her the time she needed to absorb everything that had happened to Kristi. Although Brianna had at first been terrified that the stalker had caused Kristi's injuries, something wasn't right about her story. Liam had suggested that a homeless person might have curled up in the doorway for the night, then when Kristi stepped into the hall he attacked her, thinking she was an assailant.

No, that didn't make sense. Then why hadn't Kristi's boyfriend run into the attacker?

''I wonder where Kristi was going?'' she said as much to herself as to Mike.

Mike looked up. ''Going after her boyfriend?''

''But Liam said five minutes had passed between Kevin's leaving the building and Kristi's scream.''

"Maybe it took that long for her to pull herself together." He gave her a reassuring smile. "In a little while you can ask Kristi herself."

"Hmm." Brianna sat back, still not convinced. "While I was with Kristi, did Liam tell you anything else that you haven't told me?"

Mike folded the magazine and placed it on top of the side table. "He's not totally convinced Kristi is telling the truth."

"He thinks she invented the man who pushed her down the stairs?"

"Yeah. Liam thinks her story will save Kevin from facing possible charges. What she didn't expect was Liam charging in, calling the police. That's when she realized that Liam saw Kevin run out the door." He gave her a serious look. "Has she ever lied to you before, Brianna?"

She couldn't deny that Kristi had lied in the past to protect Kevin. There was a grain of truth in what Liam thought. She sat back in the chair, silent.

"Liam is trained to think of all the angles, Brianna."

She nodded. "And what do you think?"

He shrugged. "I'm more interested in what we can prove. Do you think Kristi would take a polygraph test?"

She covered her eyes with her hands. "Probably not, if she's lying to protect Kevin." She shook her head. "Damn, I feel so angry, so frustrated. Angry that Kristi would throw herself away on a worthless man like Kevin, and frustrated because there's so little I can do to help her." She looked up at the ceiling as she spoke. "I knew this was going to happen. As soon as Kristi's boyfriend found out about the baby, I knew he'd react violently. But I could never get that through to Kristi. It seems when these things happen, I just…" She tossed up her hands. "I feel so helpless."

He took her small hand. "I wish you'd come back to the Crib and rest."

"Mike, be reasonable. Kristi is my client. This is my work. I have to be here with her."

"You can't forget about the stalker, Bria. He practically told us he was planning to harm Kristi when he sent you her picture." His words trailed off when he saw her bite her lower lip and bravely face the truth.

She took a deep breath. "I know what you're saying is true. But I hate that he can manipulate us like this." She glanced down at her hands in her lap. "Let's compromise. Stay with me until Dr. Andrews comes out of surgery. I'll leave as soon as I talk with him."

Mike sighed. "Honey, the stalker is probably somebody you see every day as you go about your routine. Somebody who knows how hands-on you are with Kristi—"

"I resent your saying that. I'm not hands-on."

"I'm sorry if that's not the right term. But I can't think of many psychologists who would be sitting in a waiting room while their patients were in surgery."

"First of all, there will be an armed guard at Kristi's room. She's only seventeen years old. She's alienated from her parents. Her boyfriend has managed to isolate her from all her friends and family. All she has is me. It's a miracle she hasn't given up on therapy, too." She leveled her gaze at him. "If you're asking me to run and hide, Mike, I won't do it."

"Okay, but you're making my job that much harder."

She shrugged. "I can't help that."

"That may be exactly what the stalker wants."

Just then the double doors of the E.R. opened and a gray-haired man wearing a white lab coat strode into the room. His shoulders slumped with fatigue. "Dr. Kent," he said as he swung his hand and gave her a tired handshake.

"Dr. Andrews." Brianna turned to Mike and briefly introduced him.

"She's a strong young woman," Andrews said, gazing

at them over his bifocals. "Her bones will mend quickly. She didn't lose a lot of blood, and the fetus remains stable. We've sutured her face as good as new, and she won't have any lasting scars. We're giving her something for pain, so she'll be groggy when she comes out of recovery. Why don't you go home for a while, Dr. Kent. Come back in a few hours. You can see her then."

"That's what I've been trying to tell her," Mike added.

"Okay, I might do that." She smiled, then asked, "Dr. Andrews, was there any residual damage...I mean—"

"She'll be fine." He smiled.

Brianna let out a whoosh of relief. "Thank you, Doctor. Have Kristi's parents been notified?"

"No. You're the only name listed on her medical release. She told me again that she doesn't want her boyfriend to be allowed to visit her."

Brianna couldn't help but wonder if Kristi had finally given up on him or if she was afraid that Kevin might be arrested if he came near her.

The doctor took off his glasses and wiped his eyes. "I'll be interested in your psychological evaluation, Dr. Kent."

"Thanks, Dr. Andrews."

After he left, Brianna drew a shaky hand through her hair. "Let's go back to your office, Mike. I'd like to ask Liam some more questions." She had no sooner stepped into the hall when her name was paged over the P.A. system. She glanced at Mike, then they both hurried to the nurse's station at the end of the hall.

"I'm Dr. Kent," she said to the smiling, round-faced nurse at the desk.

"Oh, Dr. Kent. This just came for you." She swiveled in her chair and returned with an envelope. "If you'll sign on this line, please." She handed Brianna a clipboard with a pen attached to a chain.

After she scribbled her name, Brianna glanced at the

business-size white envelope. Before she had a chance to turn it over to lift the flap, Mike grabbed it from her fingers.

"Mind if I open that, Brianna?"

"No, but why?"

Mike took the envelope, realizing there was a small bulge in the corner. He lifted the flap and glanced inside. A folded slip of blue-lined, yellow paper contained what looked like a small silver hoop. A delicate initial K hung from a hook on the post.

"An earring?" Mike asked.

Brianna gasped. "No, it's a captive-bead ring. Kristi wore it in her pierced eyebrow."

Mike watched her pale as she saw the typed note he'd already read:

NO MORE GAMES, BITCH. YOU'RE NEXT!

"WHERE'S LIAM?" Mike asked Bailey when he and Brianna returned to the TALON-6 office a half hour later.

"He got a call about an hour ago. As he was leaving, he told me to say that he'd call by 2:00 p.m." She glanced at her watch. "He should be calling any minute."

"Bailey, why don't you take Brianna downstairs to your apartment. She needs to rest—"

"Dammit, Mike. No!" Brianna's eyes glittered with defiance. "I need some answers, not rest. Liam must have seen someone. He's been following Kristi since yesterday afternoon."

"Brianna, listen. I'd like you to wait here with Bailey until Liam calls. When he does, ask him whatever questions you want. Meanwhile, there's something I need to do—"

"Michael Landis, don't you dare leave me here. If you're going someplace, I want to go, too."

He let out a long breath. "I want to go back to Kristi's

apartment building. In the daylight, maybe I can find something.''

Anything, dammit, Mike thought to himself. Whoever this stalker is, so far he's only been playing with us. But kicking an innocent teenager and ripping her ring from her eyebrow as proof that he was her attacker was sadistic as well as barbaric. This wacko was showing all the signs that he was at the end of his rope. If he wasn't caught soon, then… Mike refused to think of the alternative. He frowned at Bailey.

''When Liam calls, have him get back here and wait for us. I want to stop at police headquarters first, then I'll check out the grounds and hallway of the victim's apartment.''

Brianna dashed toward the door. ''Wish us luck, Bailey.''

Mike pushed the door open as she stepped into the hall. ''Wish us luck, hell. We'll make our own luck!''

''WELL, THAT WAS a wild-goose chase,'' Mike said as he slipped the Escalade into a vacant space at St. Luke's Hospital's parking lot. The police detectives assigned to the case had turned up nothing, which was no surprise to Mike. And for the past two hours, he and Brianna had combed every inch of the grounds at Kristi McFarland's apartment building and they'd found nothing out of the ordinary.

Brianna smiled across the small space between them. ''Something will turn up, Mike. Don't worry.''

He shot her a look of mild surprise. ''That's my usual line to a client, not the other way around.''

''Well, maybe you need a little reassurance now and then, too.'' Her gentle hand cupped his fingers that were still resting on the gearshift.

He lifted her hand and placed it against his sternum. ''When you look at me like that, my heart beats like a primitive tribal drum. Feel it?'' He grinned when he saw her blush, and he knew they were both thinking of other parts of his body that were affected by her. ''I can think of more pleasant ways to spend a few hours with you than retracing a crime scene,'' he added.

''Maybe so, but right now I have to see my client.'' She leaned over and brushed her lips against his. ''Happy drumming,'' she said against his mouth.

His hand clamped hers as he pulled her closer. ''Not so fast.'' He drew her to him, her lush mouth giving in to him. His fingers twisted into the shimmering sunbeam of her hair as she opened for him. His tongue plunged into her, savoring her sweetness. She sighed with a purr of pure female triumph as she arched against him.

''Oh, Bria.''

He heard her catch her breath. ''I-I've got to see my client,'' she said, her voice husky.

He let her go, and for a stunned minute realized that he was staggering on the edge of control. His hand was shaking as he turned off the engine. He heard the click as she unbuckled her seat belt. The car door opened and the burst of hot, humid New York City afternoon heat felt cool on his skin compared to the fire in his veins.

Damn, it was going to be a very long afternoon.

They had no sooner reached the fifth floor of the East Wing and greeted the police officer standing guard in front of Kristi McFarland's hospital room, when Mike's pager buzzed. He glanced at the digital readout. ''It's Bailey,'' he said to Brianna, who waited for him at the door. ''I'll be down the hall at the pay station,'' he whispered.

Brianna nodded before stepping inside Kristi's room and closing the door.

Mike hurried to the phone booth across from the public rest rooms. After he punched in the TALON-6 phone number, Bailey answered.

"Liam's in the lab," she said. "I'll switch your call downstairs to him."

"What's up?" Mike asked when Liam came on the line.

"I just came from Brianna's office," Liam said, his voice grave. "I got a call that a security break occurred this morning at 9:37 a.m."

"Someone broke in?"

"No. A man entered her office with a key. We've got it all recorded on the security video camera I installed yesterday."

"Do you recognize him?"

"No, but Brianna might. There's more. He screwed a listening device inside the ceiling-sprinkler head."

"You didn't deactivate it, did you?" Mike asked.

"No. Figured we need it for evidence."

"Yeah, and for the time being let him think we don't know about it. Might come in handy later."

"I enlarged a clear negative of the man's face from the tape. I'm developing a print from it now. Want me to bring it to you when it's dry? I know you'll be anxious for Brianna to see him."

Mike let out a deep sigh. "Yeah, but I'll need to explain a few things to Brianna first." He rubbed his darkening shadow of a beard. "Wait for us at the lab. When Brianna finishes with her patient, we'll head back to TALON-6."

Damn, he should feel elated, Mike thought as he strode back toward Kristi's room. Finally they had a picture of the stalker, and with the evidence of the newly installed bug, he'd be sent up for good.

Would Brianna understand that he had to install that camera in her office? Maybe she'd be so relieved to know they'd caught the stalker on videotape that she wouldn't care. He could only hope.

BRIANNA CLOSED the hospital door behind her and tiptoed to the edge of the bed. Kristi's eyes fluttered open. Without her black-lined eyelids and spiked, moussed hair, she looked younger, almost like an innocent child. A thick bandage covered her left eyebrow. The thought of the silver eyebrow ring delivered in an envelope by private courier, like a barbaric war token, made her skin crawl. *Whoever did this to you, Kristi, so help me, I'll make him sorry!*

"Hi, Kristi. How are you feeling?"

"I—I never want to see Kevin again!" Kristi's words broke off with a sob.

Brianna listened, holding Kristi's hand as the girl explained everything that had happened after she and Kevin had returned from a party. When she finished, Brianna realized that Liam's account of those early-morning hours had been accurate. She shivered with the thought of the stalker, lurking in the darkened hallway, waiting to harm this innocent girl.

Dear God, would this never stop?

"I couldn't believe Kevin would take my savings!" Kristi's eyes rimmed with fresh tears. "All my money. My money for the baby. Gone."

"Shh, we can talk later. Right now you need to rest. You need to rest for your baby's sake." Brianna knew only too well how many times she and Kristi had played this scene before. Since she was thirteen, Kristi had been dependent on her relationship with Kevin. During their bad times together, Kristi would vow never to see him again. Yet the minute he curled his little finger at her, she'd fly back with him, ready to forgive and forget.

Brianna stood, still holding the girl's hand. "I want you to think about how lucky you were this time. You might have lost the baby. You need to get away, be with people who love you. I want you to think about calling your parents. You know they're worried and would love to hear from you. I want you to think about this, okay?"

Kristi said nothing, but a fresh welling of tears brightened her eyes.

"Maybe visit them for a weekend, for a start," Brianna said. "I'll make the arrangements."

Kristi remained silent, her mouth trembling slightly. Brianna wasn't sure if she was quietly refusing or if the pain medication was making her drowsy.

"Thanks," Kristi said thickly. "I'm getting a bit sleepy."

"I'll call you this evening." Brianna turned and smiled before she left the room.

When she came into the hall, Mike lifted his head from the folded crossword puzzle in his lap. A paper container half-full of black coffee sat on the floor beside his chair. "How's she doing?"

Brianna nodded. "Physically she'll be okay. But I won't know the effects of her attack until she's had a chance to think through her options." She crossed her arms and walked down the corridor, Mike following in step. "She needs sleep. I thought in the meantime we might go to my office. I'll make a few calls, then head back here for when Kristi wakes up."

"Brianna, we need to talk first." The somber tone in Mike's voice caused her to look up. His deep-blue eyes were shuttered from any emotion.

"Sure. Why don't I see if there's a vacant room available?"

Five minutes later they were seated in a small conference room on the first floor. "I was going to tell you, but I didn't think things would happen this fast," Mike said.

She waited, a thread of worry forming in the pit of her stomach. "Tell me what? What's happened? You're scaring me, Mike."

"I ordered a security camera to be installed in your office." He ignored the surprised look on her face and went right on talking. "Liam did the work right after you found the photo of Kristi in your office."

"A security camera?" she asked. "You mean a video camera that records everything that goes on in my office?"

"Yes. The camera is triggered by motion." He could see the anger in her eyes, but she remained silent. "I have a judge's signed warrant," he said defensively. "And I'll be honest, Brianna. I didn't ask your permission and I didn't tell you about the camera because I knew you'd fight me. I didn't want an argument. But it was the only way to protect you. I knew the stalker needed to reconnect with you and he'd do it at your office. This morning, Liam found the camera tripped. Someone went into your office last night and put in another listening device. Only this time, we've got the guy on tape."

"You know who the stalker is?"

"Liam said we've got a good image. He's processing a print from the video. We're hoping you'll be able to identify him."

"Good. Then I can get my life back to normal." She turned and moved toward the door.

"I knew you'd be angry. This is why I didn't want to tell you. Dammit, Bria. I'm trying to save your life."

She stopped and whirled to face him. "How could you think I wouldn't know that. And yes, I'm angry. But I'm not angry about the camera. I'm furious that you wouldn't trust me enough to tell me. Instead, you went over my head, without even giving me the courtesy of telling me, for God's sake." She put her hands on her hips and turned to face him. "Just when had you planned to tell me?"

"When the opportunity presented itself."

She raised an eyebrow. "Let me get this straight. You planned this all along, but you just never got around to telling me?" She narrowed her eyes. "Because if I knew, maybe I wouldn't go to bed with you?"

"Brianna, that's not fair."

"I notice you're not denying it." She turned and grabbed the doorknob.

"Go ahead. Run away. You're good at that. Just don't storm back here, blaming me for not communicating."

Her hand froze on the door. She edged a look back at him. "I wasn't the one who ran away," she said, the anger in her voice matching the fury in her eyes as the memory of that night, seven years ago, came alive as if it were yesterday.

"The hell you didn't." Anger made his voice tremble. "You didn't put up much of a fight, if I remember."

"How would you know? You weren't there." Her words rang with accusation. "I paced the length of that tiny apartment, frantic when you didn't come home from work. You always called, even if you were only a few minutes late. I'd begged you not to take that bartending job in that dangerous part of town. But no, you wouldn't listen. You wouldn't take a cent of my money. You and your damn pride."

She stabbed at the tears that glistened in her eyes. "But instead of your Thunderbird roaring up the driveway that evening, it was my father's Mercedes that pulled up to the door. He wasn't alone. He brought Marcus Boynton, the company lawyer, who showed me the divorce papers that you'd signed earlier. The ink was barely dry before you left town and never once looked back."

"Is that what you believe?"

"It's the truth, isn't it?"

"Do you deny that you married me to show your old man you'd finally grown up and could do whatever you wanted? You lost no time in returning to your fancy life. School in England, or was it France?"

"I couldn't believe you would sign those divorce papers." She glared at him, feeling all the confusion and betrayal of that long ago night. "How could you just leave, without standing up to my father?" Her chest tightened with pent-up fury.

"What good would it have done? Come on, Brianna. Everyone in town knew you married me to flaunt the most unacceptable choice in your father's face. It was only a matter of time—"

"If you thought that, then why did you marry me?" The question hung between them. She studied his eyes and wondered if her own heartbreak and disillusionment showed as openly as his. "Why, Michael?"

He swallowed. "Because even though the whole town didn't think our marriage had a chance, I wanted to believe we could make it. I loved you. I loved you so much. But when your father and his hotshot lawyer came barreling into the mill office, armed with a briefcase of legal mumbo jumbo, I wanted to fight them. I wanted to tell him to go to hell. But I realized that what he'd said was true. You weren't happy. You never liked it that I was always gone, leaving you while I worked double shifts."

"I never asked you to. I had my mother's inheritance—"

"We've been down this road." His voice was cold and hard like steel. "Whatever my faults, you can't say I didn't love you."

Her chest ached with loss. Fighting to keep her voice steady, she murmured, "Love is nothing without trust."

"Come on, Brianna. Quit the platitudes. I noticed you didn't answer my question. Admit it. You married me to show your old man that his little girl had a mind of her own."

You're so wrong, Michael. Why won't you believe me? She felt her control slipping and her breath quickened. If she blinked, hot tears might pool at her eyes. She drew herself up.

"You can keep accusing me, Michael, but it simply isn't

true.'' All anger was finally spent from her voice. All she felt was a deep sadness. ''I really wouldn't have been angry about the video camera, Michael. But I'm mad as hell that you didn't trust me enough to make the right decision.'' She gave him a lingering look before she opened the door and left the room.

Chapter Thirteen

"David Malden! There must be some mistake." Brianna stared at the grainy, black-and-white photo Liam had placed in front of her.

Behind her she heard Mike swear and punch the conference-table top with his fist. "Damn! Your secretary's boyfriend! He's been right under our noses. I'll bet that's not his real name, either!"

Liam's gaze lifted from Brianna to Mike. "You'd said that it might be more than one person working together."

Brianna spun in her chair to face Liam. "You can't think Simone knew about this?" She jumped up from the table, skidding her chair. "Mike, there must be some other explanation. I—I can't believe—" She glanced down at the picture of David Malden in her hand. Any further attempt at denial died in her throat. How could she ignore the evidence? He was caught in her office, screwing another listening device into the ceiling-sprinkler head. How much proof did she need?

Liam looked at Mike. "If the secretary is innocent, there's still a chance she could be charged as an accomplice. We need to find out whose side she's on."

Mike's blue eyes flashed dangerously. "For Brianna's protection, we'll assume Simone is guilty until proven otherwise." When his gaze turned to her, the fury she thought she saw disappeared from his face, locked away behind an expressionless mask. Had she only imagined it?

"What exactly have you told Simone about our investigation so far?" Mike asked her gently.

"Exactly what you told me to tell everyone. I told her I was taking some time off from work for a few days. She expects to report for work this Thursday, when I told her I'd be back. Simone also knew I was having all the locks changed at the end of this week."

"Is that all?" Liam asked. "Did she know about the stalker, the photos?"

"No. I didn't want to upset her. I thought if she knew, she'd worry herself sick like my aunt Nora did." Brianna stood and stared out the window, then pivoted toward Mike. "Dear God, I refuse to consider that Simone knew David was stalking me."

"We'll sure as hell find out." Mike spun around and punched a button on the intercom. "Bailey, bring in all the info we have on Simone Twardzak," he ordered. "Plus David Malden. And bring in all the info on outstanding requests you're waiting on for answers, okay?"

"It'll take a few minutes," Bailey said over the speaker.

Mike clicked off the intercom and whipped out his handheld computer from his jacket breast pocket.

Brianna leaned against the table and picked up the photo of David Malden. She recognized the high forehead and thin, cruel lips of the priest. "Yes," she said finally. "And with a wig, a false beard and body padding, he could look like Leonard Braewood."

"He could look like the priest, too." Liam added.

She pulled out a chair and folded herself into it. "Dear God, what does he want from me?"

"Good question," Liam said. "If Simone is in on it, Malden could easily get any client information he wanted."

Brianna nodded. "Simone has access to all the files. Both

open and archive cases.'' She rested her gaze on Mike and wrapped her arms around herself. "I can't believe Simone knows that David is the stalker. And if I'm right, Simone may be in mortal danger if David finds out we're on to him.'' Her chest tightened. "He might even kill her.''

She stood and started to pace back and forth. "It's me he's after. He said as much in that note. 'No more games.' I'm his next victim.'' She winced. "Unless Simone accidentally stumbles onto the truth.''

Mike leaned his hip on the edge of the desk. "I'm giving you an order, Brianna. You'll treat Simone as if she's working with Malden. No warning her, no information. Nothing. I want your promise, okay?''

"But what if Simone doesn't know anything about him? She's in grave danger.''

"I'll hire a team of bodyguards to watch over Simone. She won't know she's being tailed. Round the clock, like we did for Kristi.''

"Look what happened to Kristi!'' she retorted. "No offense to you, Liam, but even you couldn't keep watch over her every minute.''

Liam spoke up. "Mike is right, Brianna. We can't jeopardize catching this guy by tipping off Simone. Bodyguards pulling 24-7 surveillance can be extremely effective.''

She bit her lip but said nothing.

Liam's eyebrows drew together as he looked up at Mike. "Should we call in Clete or Russell? Who knows how wide the net will be before this case is over.''

"They're on assignment in Saudi,'' Mike said. "I'll check with Ben at Clancy's to see about using a few freelancers. Or we could see if Jake is out of the hospital yet.''

"If the stalker wants me, why not set a trap and draw him out?'' Brianna said suddenly.

Mike spun his head around. "What do you mean?''

"Regardless of what you say, I know Simone is loyal.

She'd never condone what this stalker has done. If he is learning my whereabouts from Simone, he's doing it without her knowledge. So let's set a trap for him.''

''Not with you as bait,'' Mike said.

Liam leaned back in the chair, his fingers tented, as he silently listened.

''Mike, hear me out,'' she countered.

''No. End of discussion.''

Brianna turned to Liam. ''What do you think?''

He studied her from behind his arched fingers. ''I appreciate where you're coming from. You've just found out that your employee is, whether knowingly or not, providing information to a very dangerous man. You're angry. You're frightened. You have a right to be. But I'd listen to Mike. You've hired the best. Let Mike protect you.''

The door opened and Bailey entered with two piles of folders. She dropped the reports on the table, and gave the top clipped file to Mike. ''The fax on top came in a few minutes ago.''

Mike's expression remained neutral as he glanced at it, then handed the fax to Liam. ''According to the DMV and the Bureau of Vital Records, no David Malden exists,'' he directed at Brianna. ''Now, why am I not surprised?''

''Hmm,'' Liam said after he scanned the fax. He unfolded his lean frame from the chair. ''Looks like I've got a job to do.''

''What do you mean?'' Brianna asked, bewildered.

''It means, my fair colleen,'' Liam said, ''that I'm going to lift a set of fingerprints from Simone's boyfriend.'' He raised his eyebrows and chuckled. ''Just one of my many talents.''

''You'll find Simone's home address in this file,'' Mike said as he slid a blue folder across the table at Liam.

''Mike, would you care to explain what Liam means?'' Brianna repeated.

"That I would," Mike said as he came around the table and wrapped his arm around her waist. "I'll tell you all about it over a loaded pizza at Clancy's." He led her toward the door.

"Give Clancy my regards," Liam said with a smile, his gaze never wavering from the pages inside the blue folder.

"MIKE, YOU KNOW THIS is the chance we've been waiting for," Brianna said after she watched Mike finish the third piece of pizza and reach for the dimpled-glass mug of nonalcoholic beer beside his plate. They'd been in Clancy's Pub for over an hour and neither one had broached the subject of setting a trap for the stalker.

He took a gulp, then plunked the mug on the shamrock-shaped blotter. "I agree completely."

"You do?" She was genuinely surprised.

He nodded, then took another swallow of beer, eyeing her over the edge of the mug.

"Here's what I think might work." She was encouraged by his willingness not to interrupt her. "I'll go into the office tomorrow and call Larry on the pretext that I need more time away. I'll need to confer with him about taking over some of my caseload. If he asks why, I'll say that I've been under a lot of stress lately. David will believe the stress angle," she said derisively.

"Let's not forget about Simone," Mike said. "I know you don't want to believe it, but you can't rule out that she's involved."

Brianna knew in her heart that Simone could never do such a thing. She also knew that Mike was only doing his job. "You'll be with me all the time, Mike. I'll be safe."

He said nothing, but a muscle above his jaw ticked.

"We'll go over beforehand what I'm going to say. From my conversation, the stalker will hear where you're taking me and when. Someplace he'll believe. An isolated area, out of the city. We'll specify the time. When Malden comes after me, you and the police will be waiting.''

Mike leaned back and wiped his chin with a napkin, his face expressionless. ''Okay, with one small change.''

She leaned closer. ''What?''

''I've been thinking of a similar plan all along. After all, Malden installed this bug, expecting to hear something. Yeah, we give him something all right. Only, after that, you'll be far away from the designated target sight. No one but the TALON-6 team will know where you really are.''

''Okay, but you've said all along that the stalker has access to sophisticated surveillance equipment. What if he watches and knows that I'm not where I said I would be?''

''Let me think about it.''

''Mike, what's to think about? Do you remember Aunt Nora's family estate in the Catskills? It's over two hundred acres of woods, very isolated. Simone spent several weeks with us there last October. She'd be able to answer any questions if David asks her about the place.''

Mike leaned his arm across the table. ''Do you think Simone can give this jerk accurate enough directions to find it?''

''I'll make sure she can.'' She felt a rush of hope. ''Mike, it will work.''

He leaned back, thoughtful. ''Let's see. David hears the plan, then makes his move. We'll know where and when and we'll be ready for him.'' He paused a minute. ''If I remember, the estate is located on an unpaved camp road near a river.''

''Norton Hill Stream,'' she said. ''It feeds into the Catskill Stream.''

''I'll check out the area ahead of time,'' he said. ''We can bring in our equipment and set up before Malden hears of the plan. TALON-6 will take care of him then turn him over to Detective Sanchez.''

He leaned back and studied her. ''Yeah, I think this will work.'' He smiled, the first time she'd seen any humor from him since they'd identified the stalker as David Malden.

''But once we pick up the bastard,'' Mike said, ''we'll have enough to put him away for good.''

LIAM HAD BEEN SITTING at the bar watching Simone Twardzak and David Malden hold hands and gaze at each other over a leisurely dinner and drinks for over an hour. Damn, he wished he'd had time to grab a hot dog from the corner stand before he hopped a cab and followed them to the upscale restaurant.

Liam's stomach grumbled and he fished another handful of peanuts from the bowl next to his club soda. With a twist of lime, for show.

Just then, David stood up and Liam watched him move around the table to escort Simone to the dance floor. Finally, here was the chance Liam was waiting for.

The pretty red-haired waitress, who he had been giving the eye all evening, sauntered toward Malden's table, swaying her hips provocatively. She leaned over and gave Liam an eye's worth of cleavage as she picked up the empty glasses and placed them on a tray. He trained his eye on her, and sure enough, she met his eyes and winked.

He winked back, then gave her a slow smile, watching her pick up the tray and move toward him. She threw her shoulders back as she strolled in front of him.

''Hi, love,'' he said to her with a killer smile.

She stopped, turning back toward him. ''Would you like a table?'' she asked, her green eyes taking him in with one practiced glance. Her inviting smile told him she approved of what she saw.

He flicked a crisp twenty-dollar bill at her. ''Another time, sweetheart. What I'd like now is to borrow a glass.''

Her heavily mascara-lashed eyes widened with surprise. "A glass?"

He grinned as he stood from the stool. Carefully he picked up the stemmed wine goblet David Malden had been drinking from and slipped it into the plastic bag he'd pulled from his suit jacket breast pocket. Then he pressed the bill into her palm.

"I'd appreciate you not saying anything about this, sweetheart," he whispered in her ear. "Say, I didn't get your name."

"Stephanie." She gave him another head-to-toe, blatant look.

"What's it worth to you?"

Liam smiled. He had a weakness for redheads, especially green-eyed redheads with freckles. He wondered if she was freckled all over. "When do you get off work?"

"Midnight." The smile she gave him was filled with expectation.

"Write your number on the back of this," he drawled, picking up a book of matches from the bar top. "I'll call you later and we can talk about it."

She grinned, jerking the matches from his fingers. She jotted a number on the inside cover, then handed it back to him. "Mister, you've got the most original come-on line I've ever heard, and baby, I've heard 'em all."

He smiled as he picked up the matchbook, then gave her an open kiss on the mouth. Before she'd opened her eyes again, Liam had disappeared into the crowd.

Chapter Fourteen

Later that night, Brianna hung up the phone after talking to her aunt Nora and looked out the living-room window of the Crib. Across the river, Manhattan's colored lights glittered against the black-velvet sky. "There's no reason to worry about the stalker. Mike had everything under control," she'd told Nora only a few minutes ago. And that was probably true—for her own well-being. But what about Simone? Out there in the city, Liam was tailing Simone and Malden, the man who had cold-bloodedly pushed Kristi down the stairs. How could she not worry, with her secretary on a date with a man capable of anything?

She turned away from the window. Mike was right. There was nothing she could do. Besides, Mike had hired one of the best undercover freelancers to act as Simone's bodyguard.

Nervously, she bit her lip. She worried about Mike, too. He would do anything to protect her, and if his thoughts were preoccupied with her, his concentration might be impaired. Since seeing the stalker's face, Mike was more intense, more focused. Gone was the twinkle in his eyes and the quick, easy grin. If something were to happen to him, how could she live with herself?

Dear God, she'd go mad if she kept this up. Maybe if

she spoke to Liam about Mike, he might know what to do. It was worth a try.

She crossed the room to the hall, on her way to check on Mike. He must be finished with the seemingly endless phone calls he'd made since they'd returned to the Crib over three hours ago.

As she passed the wall of security monitors, her gaze flew to one of the six screens that scanned various positions outside the building perimeter. The last screen fixed at the corner of the roof facing the street corner revealed a man walking a white Pekingese on a leash. His face and hair were hidden beneath a baseball cap. Her heart tripped. What if he was David Malden, alias Leonard Braewood, alias who the hell knows?

The man paused, glanced covertly over his shoulder and pulled a pack of cigarettes from his shirt pocket. She held her breath. Slowly, he flitted one to his mouth, then flashed a lighter from his pocket. A small glow sparked the end, a puff of smoke haloed over his head, while the dog yanked at its lead.

The rush of adrenaline made her hands shake as she watched the monitor, fear coiling inside her stomach.

Suddenly a shadow crossed the wall in front of her. Startled, she jumped.

"Hey, take it easy," Mike said, reaching around her waist to steady her. "Don't worry. That's Joe, a regular in the neighborhood. He's trying to stop smoking but he sometimes sneaks a puff when he walks the dog." He pointed to the monitor just as Joe stomped out his cigarette and continued down the street.

She felt foolish. "Guess I'm a bit tense."

"It's understandable." He was standing so close that she could feel his body heat. "You need to relax," he said. "Would you like a glass of wine?"

"I didn't think you drank."

"I don't but my guests do. My kitchen may be bare, but you'll be very impressed with my wine cellar."

She shook her head. "Thanks, but I thought I'd soak in a warm bubble bath."

"Hmm. Want me to wash your back?" His eyes danced. "Like I used to?"

"Hmm," she mimicked. "As I remember, that's not quite what you did," she said with a quick smile.

He brushed her hair away from her ear and kissed her earlobe. "Hmm, seems I don't ever remember you complaining." His tongue lingered in that special place he knew could drive her wild.

Her eyes closed, then opened. *What was she thinking?* She swung away, but his hand remained at her waist. "I don't think that's wise, Mike." Her voice was almost wavering.

"Then don't think." He pulled her close again, his mouth in her hair. He cupped her breast, and she knew she wanted more. So much more. His thumb flicked over her nipple. Pure pleasure ricocheted throughout her body.

She could feel her willpower slipping and she managed to push him away, needing to take control. "Stop it, Mike." Her voice was breathy. "I don't want to go back down that road again."

He caressed her face and studied her. When their eyes met, the laughter was gone from his eyes. "We're not going back, honey," he said, his voice soft. "We're forging ahead, making new memories."

"That path leads to a dead end, remember?" She was surprised by how angry she felt.

He released her, frowning. "Is this about the video camera? Are you still mad?"

"Shouldn't I be?" She fought to control her temper.

He studied her face, her eyes. "Okay, I'm sorry I didn't talk to you before the video camera was installed in your office.'' He took a deep breath, his eyes shuttered. "You're right. I didn't trust you enough, and I'm sorry. I really am, Brianna.''

She turned away, determined to be cool. "It's over and done,'' she said. "And forgotten.''

"Like hell it is. You'll remember that incident every time I stumble, and you'll bring it up every time to distance yourself from me.''

She hugged herself, refusing to look at him. "Mike, let's not have this discussion.''

"Discussion, hell. We're having a fight!''

She huffed derisively. "*You're* having the fight. I'm not.''

"Oh yes you are. And you fight dirty.''

She spun around at him, hurt and anger flaring inside her. "What is that supposed to mean?''

"It means that on the outside you fool most anyone with that ice-princess demeanor. But you can't fool me. I've had you, remember? You're a passionate, erotic woman, Brianna Kent. Down deep you're a volcano.''

For one long moment their gazes locked. Instead of the anger that she expected, his blue eyes were dark with a yearning so great it took her breath away. Dropping her lashes to hide her reaction, she quickly turned away.

"Don't run from me, Bria. Don't be afraid of those feelings.'' He closed the distance between them with one quick move, and before she knew it, she was in his arms.

SHE LAY in the crook of his arm, her fingers idly toying with the black curls on his chest. She felt at a loss for what to do. In his arms like this, it was so easy to fool herself into thinking that maybe…yes, it could work between them. But down deep, in what Mike had called a volcano, was also a core of reason, of logic, a practicality that wouldn't go away. Damn, she almost envied those Pollyannas who could stumble into bed with their lovers, so confident that things would work out.

Mike had hit a chord when he'd accused her of distancing herself from her feelings for him. Her excuse, that from their history they were still wrong for each other, simply wasn't true. He'd changed, and so had she. But dammit, she was so afraid to drop that last shred of defense. Terrified to even hope they could be happy together for the long haul. Tears welled in her eyes and she was glad for the darkness in case he suddenly awoke. She laid her head on the bristly mat of his chest, listening to the steady beat of his heart. Maybe they would have no future, but Mike would always have her heart.

THE NEXT MORNING, Mike looked up from his reading to see Liam lumber into the kitchen of the Crib.

"Tofu cream cheese for Brianna," Liam said as he removed the first of three small deli containers from the bag in the crook of his arm. "Peanut butter for Mike and lox cream-cheese spread for yours truly."

Mike ignored him as he leaned a hip against the kitchen counter and studied the last page of the report Liam had brought him before heading out to pick up breakfast.

The file contained the CIA report of the man whose fingerprints Liam had lifted from David Malden's wineglass the night before. With his foot, Mike dragged a chair out from under the table, his gaze never leaving the page.

"You said this was good news?" Mike remarked a moment later, taking a seat and crossing his legs. He looked up and frowned as he watched his friend unbox a half-dozen assorted bagels, then remove three disposable coffee containers from a pulp-board tray.

"We've finally got his real name," Liam said. "We've got his description and complete history." The tall Irishman eyed Mike narrowly as he set the cups atop the paper place mats and flatware he'd brought from the breakfast deli around the corner. "What's the matter, Mike?" Liam asked. "I thought you'd be pleased."

"Liam, you've done fabulous work, as always," Mike said, putting down the report. "But have you read this guy's background?"

"Not completely. I just got the call that the computer file was ready to download as I was coming in this morning." He smiled. "An unexpected date." His smile widened. "Anyway, when I saw what the file was, I brought it right over. I eyeballed it while it was printing, to be sure the file was complete." He reached for a bagel. "A blue-ribbon winner, if I say so myself."

Just then Brianna stepped into the kitchen wearing a white Turkish bathrobe, looking as if she'd come straight from the shower. Her hair was damp and a towel draped loosely around her neck. "I thought I heard…" She glanced at the kitchen table, then at Liam.

"Hi." She smiled warmly, peeked at the bag of bagels, then back at him. "You're gorgeous and you bring food, too?" she teased. "A man after my own heart."

Liam chuckled. "I know how hard you're both working," he said, his grin a mile wide. "I thought you should eat to keep up your strength."

Brianna blushed, remembering how Liam, earlier when he'd first arrived, had interrupted her and Mike in the shower.

"Thanks a lot, pal," Mike grumbled.

"Only doing my part," Liam said, then pointed to the cluttered assortment of paper bags, cardboard cartons and food containers that littered the table. "Breakfast is ready and it's on me, mates, 'cause we've got plenty to celebrate." He turned to Mike and waved dramatically. "Go ahead, tell her." Liam sat down and started to smear lox spread on a whole-wheat bagel.

Brianna came behind Mike's chair and peered over his shoulder. "Tell me what?"

Mike scanned the report. "The stalker's real name is Reginald Fox. Forty-eight years old. Ex-military. Awarded for distinguished service. Ex-CIA. A rogue."

"A rogue never retires," Liam muttered.

"Listen to this," Mike continued. "Later he joined the police force. Retired. NYPD."

Liam whistled. "That means he still has connections."

"There's more. Fox is employed at Spender Electronics and Surveillance Equipment."

Liam's gaze met Mike's. "I've heard of them. So that's where he's getting his stuff—"

"Hold it right there," Brianna said. "Why would someone like this be interested in me?"

"The answer is in this report," Mike said, slapping the pages against the tabletop. "We just have to find it."

"What about his relationships?" she asked. "Is he married? Kids?"

Mike scanned the last page and pulled it out for her. "He's divorced. A kid who lives with his ex." He handed her several sheets from the report. "See if you recognize any names or any connections. His wife, kids, relatives, anything."

She took the pages from him as she took another sip of coffee.

Liam broke another bagel in two. "We've handled worse cases, Mike. This guy doesn't sound so tough."

"Never underestimate the enemy," Mike said. "I'd like to dig deeper on a few things. Check his record with NYPD. His military records."

Brianna took a bite from a cinnamon-raisin bagel. "You didn't read down far enough, Mike," she said, wiping a crumb from her lip. "His son doesn't live with the wife.

He died in prison.'' She lifted her head and met Mike's gaze. ''I wonder...?''

''Does the name mean anything to you?'' Mike asked.

''No, it doesn't give the son's full name. He might have retained his mother's name.'' She gazed back over the report. ''I'll check my files. There must be a connection.''

Mike yanked the lid from one of the coffee containers and took a swallow. His forehead creased as he looked at Liam. ''Run this by Detective Sanchez. See if we have enough for a warrant.'' Mike was aware that Brianna was studying him.

''What's worrying you about this case, Mike?'' she finally asked him.

''I'm not worried, sweetheart, just cautious.'' Mike knew she didn't believe him. He rose from the table, collecting the sheets from the file report. ''I think I'll run some ideas I've got through the computer.'' He bent over and kissed her, his mouth lingering on hers, then he turned and headed for the stairway.

When the echo of his footsteps faded, she turned to Liam. ''I think Mike is terribly worried. Ever since we've seen the videotape of the stalker, he hasn't been himself. That quirk of a grin is gone, and his eyes have lost their twinkle. And I'm afraid it's because of me.''

Liam uncapped a small see-through cup of orange juice. ''That's to be expected, isn't it? He's serious about catching this guy.''

''Not if it might get him killed.'' She surprised herself at the emotional tone in her voice.

Liam snorted. ''I think Mike's a big boy. He can take care of himself.''

''You know what I mean. I'm not just another client to protect. I'm...'' She paused when she saw the empathy and understanding fill Liam's eyes.

''Aye, I know what you are to him. He's a lucky man.''

"And because of that, I'm jeopardizing his safety. I'm afraid he'll try *too* hard, take risks that might…"

"Now, Brianna." His tone was gentle. "When I got here this morning, Mike told me about the plan you've cooked up. I think it's fine. I didn't say anything to him, but I think he's spreading himself a bit thin. He wants to spearhead the Catskill operation, and he wants to come back here and stay with you until you're airlifted to a safe place." He glanced at her bagel. "If you don't want that, I'll eat it."

She shoved it toward him. "You're saying that Mike is doing too much?"

Liam scraped out the cheese container with his knife as he talked. "I'm saying that back when we were in Special Forces, we had what was called the seventy-two-hour lockdown. Time can vary, but what it meant was that before a man went on an op, he was quarantined from his family, his loved ones. He was geared to the task, insulating himself from everything personal in his life except the op plan." When he looked at her his expression was serious. "That's what Mike has to do. I think he should spearhead the Catskill operation and stay there until we catch this bastard. We can have Bailey stay here with you and I'll tailgate the operation from here."

"Sounds like a good idea. Can you persuade Mike?"

He huffed with laughter. "Not on your life. But you can."

She wasn't quite sure, but she kept it to herself. She smiled at him as she leaped to her feet. "Maybe I should go and test your theory."

"Good girl! Oh, you better take a bagel with you," Liam said, wielding a cream cheese-tipped knife at her. "Or I can't guarantee there'll be any left when you come back."

"Thanks. For everything," she said as she wrapped two bagels in a paper napkin and headed toward the stairs.

The Crib's war room was exactly what she'd expected.

Computer monitors, maps, overheads and as many gadgets as she'd expect to find at the CIA.

Her heart leaped when she saw Mike. His long denim-clad legs sprawled in front of the computer, his eyes concentrating on the monitor. His hair was tousled, his black T-shirt stretching across his broad shoulders. When he saw her, his mouth quirked.

"Hope you're coming down here to seduce me," he drawled.

Her mouth twitched. "First you'd better eat." She stuffed a bagel into his mouth. "To keep up your strength."

He laughed, half choking, then shook his head. "That Liam!"

She rolled a desk chair up to the console. His tanned hands splayed across the keyboard as he punched up another screen. "Come see what I've found."

She peered at the large monitor. "What is it?"

"It's the police record of the stalker's son. The kid took his mother's name, just like you thought. Reginald Dysart."

"Reginald Dysart," Brianna repeated, the name sounding very familiar.

"The boy was hard to control after the divorce. Most of his early life was spent in juvenile when his mom had custody. When he was seventeen, he joined the navy, left after a few weeks." Mike sniggered. "Bet that made his old man choke on his army medals."

Mike punched up a new screen. A police mug shot of a tattooed, shaved-headed young man filled the screen. His face, gaunt to the point of haggard, sported over twenty jewelry piercings.

"Sonny Dysart." Brianna said. "Now I know who he is. His girlfriend, Bonnie, was my client. She always called him Sonny." A chill coursed down her spine as she remembered the small, wiry man, not more than a boy, who severely battered his girlfriend and her little daughter.

"It was my testimony that sent him to prison," she said softly. "I remember when the judge read the sentence a disturbance broke out in the back of the courtroom." She turned to Mike but in her mind she saw the man's red face, his angry clenched fists, heard him shouting threats when he had to be physically removed from the courthouse. "I never got a good look at Sonny's father, but I think his face and build are similar to David Malden's." She blinked away the memory and looked at Mike. "How did Dysart die?"

"He was beaten to death in the prison yard."

Her stomach clenched. "Oh, how horrible." She shut her eyes, then opened them. "And Reginald Fox blames me for Sonny's death."

"I'LL BE RIGHT WITH YOU, honey," Mike said as he helped Brianna from the cab. "Just relax and you'll be fine."

She stepped onto the curb, the heat from the pavement welcoming as she waited for Mike before entering her office building. "I hope so. I'm so nervous, I'm shaking," she said, rubbing her chilled fingers.

He put his arm around her and took her hands and rubbed them within his palms. "Want my jacket?"

"No, no. I'll be fine," she said, feeling that was a lie, too. Most of everything she was going to tell Larry would be a lie, and she never was good at telling fibs, even as a child. What if Reginald Fox could tell that they were laying a trap for him? Lord, she would never be able to pull this off.

"Ready?" he said before they entered the revolving door of the building. Mike had warned her that he and Liam had determined the bug could pick up their conversations as far away as the elevator, if they were alone. Crowds and noise were in their favor.

"Ready as I'll ever be," she said, then took his arm as they headed toward the elevators.

"I SHOULD BE BACK in a week," she told Larry. Her fingers twisted the telephone cord as she spoke. "The Shapiro file and the Parker file are the most urgent. Yes, I'll leave a note for Simone. You can get them from her."

Mike stood by the window, silently looking at the view of skyscrapers. She wondered if he thought she was acting convincingly or not. No, she needn't worry. He said he would write her a note as a means of communicating with her. She must stop worrying.

"It's the old family estate," she said after Larry had asked about her accommodations. "Isolated. Down a dirt road, in the heart of the Catskills."

She took a gulp of water. "Yeah, the property has been in the family since my grandfather built it back in the fifties. He and my dad and uncle used to go fishing there. You should ask Simone about the place. She and I visited my aunt Nora there last October." Her heart was beating so hard she was afraid Reginald Fox could pick up the sound over the bug. Mike had thought it would be a good idea to plant the info that Simone had visited the property. But when Brianna just said it, she thought it sounded staged.

Larry rambled on about the upcoming July the Fourth holiday plans at the local country club. She had to be polite and listen, but she felt like bolting from the room. Instead, she leaned back in her chair and sipped her water. Mike had mentioned that all the normal room noises could be picked up. She needed to sound as normal as possible.

"Promises to be a lovely affair," she said and managed a laugh. "Thanks again, Larry. I'll see you when I get back."

Her hands were slick when she put the receiver back on

the cradle. Mike turned from the window and winked, giving her a thumbs-up sign.

She returned a weak smile, picked up the receiver again and punched in the numbers of her secretary's apartment.

Dear God, what if Reginald Fox answered the phone?

The number rang and rang. After four long rings, Simone's answering machine clicked on. For a moment, Brianna panicked. She and Mike hadn't rehearsed what to say if Simone wasn't home.

"Hi, Simone," she said lightly. "It's Brianna. Say, how would you like another week off? With pay, of course. I'm extending my vacation for another week. Thought I'd spend some time at Nora's estate in the Catskills while she's in Denver. Mike is flying me up there on Wednesday morning. I should be there by noon. I've left a note of instructions for you on your desk.

"Nothing urgent, just the phone and page numbers of people I thought you and Larry might need while I'm away. I'd like you to come into the office on Tuesday to give Larry the files I've asked him to take over for me." She hesitated, her mind bolting. Mike nodded and silently mouthed the words, "You're doing fine."

For some unknown reason she felt like crying. "Simone," she said, forcing her voice to steady, "I'll miss you, and I hope you…" Her throat started to tighten. The thought of Simone alone with Reginald Fox was more than she could bear. "I hope you…enjoy the time off. Bye."

She hung up the phone and squeezed the receiver. *Dear God, what if something goes wrong?*

HE PULLED THE VAN *into the airport security parking lot and drove into his designated spot. When he switched off the ignition, he was still beaming. Tomorrow at this time he'd have her. He could barely contain himself with excitement.*

Finally, he'd mete out her punishment in slow, agonizing degrees, just like they'd done to Sonny.

And as a bonus, he'd outsmart that hot-dog boyfriend of hers, too. He felt the charge of adrenaline rush through his veins.

The fools. She and Landis actually believed that he'd fall for that trap. Landis must have somehow discovered the second bug. Hell, so what. He knew Landis was flying her to the Catskills and that's all he needed to know.

He was humming as he walked into the airport terminal, waved back at Maggie behind the security gate and climbed on the escalator that would take him to his office. All he had to do was check the past flight records that TALON-6 had filed. The reports would give him everything that he'd need to know about the various aircraft owned by them and their maintenance schedule.

That and a few phone calls would give him all he'd need to put his own plan into action.

Chapter Fifteen

It was a little past 6:00 p.m. by the time Mike and Liam had airlifted from the Crib's rooftop in the TALON-6 helicopter to the target destination in the Catskills. That night, Brianna had felt so worried about Mike after he'd gone that she hadn't fallen asleep until after 2:00 a.m. When she had, she'd dreamed that she was to meet Mike at a masquerade ball. From what she could remember through her nightmarish haze, a man in an evil-sorcerer's costume kept chasing her through the throngs of festive party-goers. She bolted through the lines of guests, desperately searching for Mike. When she finally spotted him, she rushed into his waiting arms. Then he ripped off his mask and the face of Reginald Fox glowered back at her.

She awoke out of breath, her heart pounding. Dear God, what would she do if anything were to happen to Mike?

You're experiencing acute anxiety, a normal reaction for what you're going through, she admonished herself sharply. She should have taken Bailey's advice and gone to bed early. But without Mike, the thought of spending a night alone, after what they'd had together these past few days, was torturous.

Instead, she'd spent the evening in the war room with Bailey. She'd wanted to help, to feel that she was doing something worthwhile. Bailey showed her how to log checkpoints on the perimeter area of her family estate in the Catskills. As she worked, Brianna was awed at TALON-6's specialized technology, and she was filled with admiration at Bailey's expertise as she coordinated orders between Mike, Liam and the other field agents with the aplomb of a four-star general.

The actuality of the mission, the exposure that Mike was undergoing, had turned the exciting hours of devising strategy into the reality of danger. The trap was set. There was no going back.

She'd lain awake until the pink rays of dawn filtered into the bedroom window, her mind hopelessly mired in recent memories of Mike. How she wished that just before he'd boarded the copter, when he'd gone into the bath to shave and change, she had joined him in the shower.

At the time, she didn't think she could bear another goodbye. But now, as she lay in the huge, empty bed, she longed for him. When she closed her eyes, she could envision his face, teasing, serious, passionate, that special crooked grin that made her heart melt. She smiled, remembering the sound of his rich baritone singing *their* song, and a profound yearning had her unconsciously reaching out for him.

Then reality jolted her back from her fantasizing. Dear God, he'd only been gone a few hours. What would it be like to say goodbye to him forever…again?

She shoved her hair back with her fingers and returned to her packing. With a quick glance around the bedroom, she felt reasonably sure that she'd left nothing behind… except her heart.

Her eyes blurred with tears as she snapped the lock on her suitcase and carried it into the hallway. She swiped at her damp cheeks when she heard Bailey's footfalls on the staircase leading from the war room.

"I just received word from Mike," Bailey said with a

smile. "He's got his men in the field and all positions have been set. Now all we have to do is wait for Liam to pick you up in the helicopter. Mike said that Liam will be here by one o'clock this afternoon."

Brianna glanced at her watch. "We have over two hours to wait." She had a feeling those two hours would feel as long as two lifetimes. "Mike said the yacht is moored not far away. I'll call you to let you know I've arrived."

"Okay, but you'll appear as a blip on my screen. There's an automatic tracker installed on the copter." She smiled. "Mike has more gadgets on it than *Star Wars*." She cocked her head and grinned with pride. "The Tiger is Mike's favorite chopper."

"His favorite?" Brianna was truly surprised. "How many does TALON-6 use?"

"We have four, but two are only used for out-of-the-country missions."

Brianna only smiled a response, not trusting her voice. Although she would have enjoyed to toss back a glib reply, the truth was, she was jealous of the cutting-edge technology that challenged him. How could she compete with a lifestyle fraught with danger and intrigue? Mike carved this life from nothing. But she was alien to it. She couldn't exist in his world and he couldn't exist in hers.

"Did you hear me, Brianna?"

Brianna shook away her daydreaming. "I'm sorry, Bailey, what did you say?"

"I said Liam called last night from the airport after he returned from piloting Mike to the Catskills. Have you heard from Mike this morning?"

"N-no. I—I asked him not to call." She swallowed against the tightness in her throat. "I told Mike I'd call him once I'm safely aboard the yacht. Liam mentioned that Mike needed to focus on the operations, and I respect that."

Bailey smiled. "I have a feeling that Mike will call you

later.'' She glanced at the suitcase. "Looks like you're all set. Do you need anything?''

"No, nothing that I can think of.'' Brianna shook out the stiffness in her neck and shoulders. "I've counseled women during the hours before they planned to leave their abusive relationships. I've seen how nervous and jittery they were. But I'm just now realizing how devastating it feels to think that another human being wants to harm you.'' She dragged a hand through her hair.

Bailey was silent for a moment, then she said, "Heed the words of your own counsel and remember, in a few hours you'll be safely on the TALON-6 yacht and this will be over.''

"Yes, that's what keeps me going.'' She smiled at Bailey. "I've really enjoyed our time together. When this is over, you'll have to bring your mom and stay at my aunt's estate for real.''

Bailey's eyes lit up. "We'd love that. Thanks.''

"I know you have other things more important than baby-sitting me,'' Brianna said, picking up her suitcase and heading toward the stairway.

"Hey, try not to worry.'' Just then the satellite phone rang. Bailey moved to get it. "It's for you, Brianna. Mike.''

Brianna picked up the receiver as Bailey discreetly turned and went down the stairs to the war room.

"Bria? I've only got a minute,'' Mike said, his voice loud over the din in the background. "But I needed to hear your voice.''

"Mike.'' Just the sound of his husky, deep voice sent a ripple of desire through her. "Where are you?''

"I'm in one of the police vans we're setting up with surveillance equipment. I'm installing some of my own gadgets. We're just about finished here.''

She knew he'd been working straight through since arriving last night. Besides dealing with all the red tape to bring in the proper authorities, Mike was supervising air, land and legal operations. She could hear the fatigue in his voice. "Everything is fine here, Mike," she said brightly, hoping to conceal her nervousness. "I'm all packed, just waiting for Liam to arrive."

"Hang in there, sweetheart. It won't be long now."

"I know."

"The ex-Special Forces woman who's acting as your decoy got to the hotel about two hours ago. She's been briefed and will be arriving at the estate around three this afternoon."

"Do you think Fox will believe it's me?"

"She's about your build and she's wearing a blond wig. Dressed in your clothes that I brought with me, she's a good match from far off. I don't think Fox will guess a thing."

"I hope nothing happens to her."

"Brianna, this is her job. She's the best at what she does. Now, do me a favor and stop worrying about everyone else and take care of yourself. Trust me."

"Oh, Mike, of course I trust you." *But you're not invincible, Mike. You're human, and you can get hurt just like anyone else.* For this one time she could pretend to be strong. He needed her to be strong. She didn't want to say anything that might take his mind off the operation. But if there were momentary thoughts that she could put up with a lifetime of waiting around for him to return from dangerous missions around the globe, this was bringing home the fact that she wasn't cut out for it. She'd grow to hate him for putting her through this kind of torture.

But it wasn't his fault. He'd carved out this life for himself and he thrived on it. This was her problem, her weakness.

"Bria, do you miss me?"

"No, I hardly noticed you were gone." She huffed with

a forced humor she didn't feel. "I think you know the answer to that," she said finally.

"Yeah…I know. I feel the same thing."

Phones were ringing and people were talking behind him, so she knew he couldn't speak freely. "I know we're going to catch Fox," she said with as much enthusiasm as she could muster.

"Count on it," he retorted. "And Bria…" The pause that spun on the line between them lengthened. "I love you. Don't forget that."

Her throat tightened with tears. She closed her eyes, forcing herself to be strong. "Keep safe."

She was trembling when she hung up the phone. She wanted to tell him what was in her heart but what was the use? Yes, he loved her. In his way, he did. But he'd hate her if she asked him to give up the dangerous life he loved. And in time she'd resent him, too, if she denied herself the children and stable home that children required and that she yearned for.

She stabbed at the tears that rolled down her cheeks. Damn, why did he have to call and remind her of how much she loved him? Yesterday, when they had stood on the Crib's rooftop before he lifted off, she had kissed him goodbye. She'd managed to be brave then. She'd do it now. Tears would do nothing but ruin her mascara.

MIKE HUNG UP the phone after talking with Brianna, battling for control. His stomach knotted at the thought that she might, once Fox was in jail, walk out of his life just as easily as she had before.

Damn, why couldn't Brianna say that she loved him? They both knew she did, whether she'd admit the truth or not.

She had showed him by their loving. So why couldn't she admit it?

Because she knows you have no future together. The truth jolted him like a cold shower. Hadn't she said that very thing? She wants a guy who needs her. A guy who won't get bored with diapers, Girl Scout-cookie drives and school soccer games.

Liam was right. Mike was almost obsessing about his ex-wife, and he needed to keep his thoughts on the mission. When this was all over, he'd talk to her. This time, he wouldn't let her get away without a fight.

If this was all over. He quelled the negative thought. Everything was going to work out. In another two hours she'd be safely aboard the TALON-6 yacht, at sea, away from any chance that Fox could get to her. When they finally picked him up, Mike would call her, and the captain would bring her back to the city. For now, he had enough to concentrate on to keep his mind on target. Those hairs on the back of his neck wouldn't let him shake the feeling that they'd overlooked something.

He usually never felt like this before a mission. Maybe Liam was right and Mike's concentration was thrown off by thoughts of Brianna. Hell, he hadn't thought of anything else since she'd walked back into his life.

Or was it the dread of her walking out of his life that was ripping him up? He turned from the console, snatched up his handheld computer and strode from the room.

AGAINST THE DIN of the airport maintenance hangar, a country music song, filled with words of heartbreak and faithless love, twanged from a portable radio. Reginald Fox glanced over his shoulder at the work crew supervisor's office cubicle. Perfect timing. The supervisor had stepped out for lunch and the few men working the helo arrival and departure areas were at the other side of the hangar runway.

Fox glanced at the security clipboard in his hand, then back at the flight schedule posted on the blackboard outside the maintenance office. Liam O'Shea would be picking up the TALON-6 helicopter at 1230 hours. He glanced at his watch and smiled. Perfect. He'd have just enough time.

He flipped through the pages of the maintenance log, scanning the name of the mechanic assigned to the TALON-6 copter. William Lennon. Fox strode past several choppers until he came to stall 18 where the army-green, Tiger HAP, air-to-air combat helicopter stood waiting. The insignia of an eagle claw gripping a world globe with a gold number 6 shone upon the sliding door.

Fox walked purposefully toward the uniformed man tightening a bolt on the tail rotor with a torque wrench.

"Hi, Lennon. I'm from security." He flipped his black ID-photo badge and held it up for the mechanic to see. "I'd like a word with you."

"Sure." Lennon tempered the bolt one more time, then slid down the side of the fuselage. "Let me turn down the music first," Lennon said, reaching for the small radio on the floor beside his lunch box. He grabbed a towel and wiped his hands as he lumbered toward Fox.

Fox glanced over his shoulder again. For the moment, no one was in this section of the hangar. "We've had a call from TALON-6, Lennon. They apparently couldn't get through to your boss before he went to lunch. They want you to move this chopper back over to taxiway alpha." Fox rubbed his hand against the shiny pylon, then made his way along the side of the tail boom. "The owner wants you to rev this up and check out a vibration they noticed in the cabin ventilator system. They said it starts at around 2500 rpm."

Lennon lifted the visor on his baseball cap as he screwed up his face. "That doesn't make any sense. There's nothing wrong with the ventilator system. I checked it out myself. Besides, the pilot just called me not more than ten minutes ago. He didn't mention any noise."

Fox shrugged. "You know how these big wheels are. They think they hear a noise and we little guys have to jump. Did you speak to Landis?" he asked with a note of authority.

"No, I spoke to O'Shea. He flew the copter in this morning. He's picking it up, too." Lennon cocked his head as Fox kept walking toward him.

"Something's fishy," Lennon continued. "O'Shea asked if the chopper would be ready on time. I told him I was all through and ready to taxi it up to the helicopter apron." He frowned. "Say, why is security checking on a regular maintenance job?"

Fox glanced around again, then when he saw the coast was clear, he lunged for the mechanic. For a thin, wiry man, Lennon put up quite a struggle. Before he had a chance to yell for help, Fox pulled a gun from his jacket and hit Lennon over the head. The mechanic slumped to the floor.

Without a wasted motion, Fox grabbed Lennon's shoulders and dragged the body to the workbench, then folded the mechanic's long legs and wedged the body under it. He then pulled two rolling tool chests up against the bench until Lennon's body was no longer visible.

Voices and laughter echoed from the far end of the hangar. Fox picked up Lennon's visored cap from the floor and yanked it over his head. He hurried back to the Tiger, slid open the door and climbed into the pilot's seat.

He felt a rush of exhilaration as his gaze scanned the intricate flight-display panel. This baby was loaded with everything, including a 30-mm gun turret and submunition rockets. He'd give anything to see Landis's face when he heard that Fox had stolen the chopper right out from under O'Shea's nose.

Just then he glanced at the navy-blue flight suit folded neatly in the copilot's seat. Everything laid out, nice and tidy, Fox thought derisively. Just like those ex-Special Forces hot dogs.

Within a few minutes, Fox had slipped into the flight suit, put on the helmet and flipped down the smoke-tinted sun shield over his face. He slid the clipboard under the seat just in case he needed any of the flight-data info if questioned by the tower before takeoff. He pulled on the flight gloves, then flipped on the starter switch. The engine hummed to life, and within seconds Fox coasted the chopper through the open hangar doors.

Adrenaline churned through his veins. He was almost there. Within minutes, he'd have the bitch. Just the two of them, alone. Then he'd show her what it was like for Sonny. She'd know, once and for all, what it was like to die a painful, lingering death.

BRIANNA STOOD on the rooftop of the Crib and leaned toward the wind, the blue silk scarf tying back her hair fluttering against her cheek. She glanced at her watch again, then up at the sky, her stomach in knots.

"Hope that storm holds off for another hour," Bailey said, her red hair ruffling around her face. She turned to face Brianna, shielding her eyes from the sun. "Wouldn't you rather wait inside? Liam won't take off without you," she said with a laugh.

"The invigorating breeze will do me good," Brianna said. "But there's no need for both of us to get windblown. Why don't you go in and call Mike. Tell him I'll be airborne within a few minutes."

"Mike told me to stay with you until liftoff."

"Well, you are with me," Brianna said, smiling. She raised her gaze skyward again. In the distance was a dark speck. As it grew larger, her excitement grew. When she was certain the object was a helicopter, she pointed in its direction. "Look, Bailey. I think I see him."

Bailey turned at the whomping sound before she saw the helicopter, then glanced at her watch. "He made great time. He's fifteen minutes early."

Brianna smiled as she zipped up her windbreaker, and reached for her suitcase. "I'll take that as a lucky sign."

The chopper hovered a few minutes before coming to rest at the heliport. Brianna gave Bailey a hug. "Thanks for everything, Bailey," she called into the wind. "I'll phone you when we arrive on the yacht."

"You'll love the TALON-6 yacht," Bailey shouted over the roar of the wind. "Lots of gadgets to keep you occupied. You won't be bored."

The gusts from the chopper's blades drowned out any further chance for conversation. Brianna turned and dashed across the rooftop toward the helicopter.

Bailey saw Liam wave from the cockpit, and she smiled and waved back. Brianna's windbreaker billowed, her scarf fluttered wildly as she forced herself against the gusts and made her way toward the chopper.

Only when Brianna climbed aboard and the passenger door slid shut did Bailey turn and head downstairs. With Brianna in the sky, she needed to contact the yacht captain and alert him that his cargo was on the way.

When she reached the rooftop doorway, she heard the phone ringing from inside. She smiled as her steps quickened down the stairs. No doubt it would be Mike, anxious to know if Brianna was airborne and finally en route to safety. She could hardly wait to give him the good news.

LIAM CHECKED the service order again. Yes, his memory wasn't failing him. Stall 18 was the assigned maintenance site for the Tiger. So where the hell was it?

And where was Lennon? Liam looked around, then noticed a lunch box sitting on the floor beside a radio. He peeked inside the mechanic's cubicle. A thermos-bottle cup was half-full of coffee. Cold coffee, he noticed. He lifted the lid of the lunch box. Inside was a corned beef on rye and a banana. Hell, if Lennon had gone on lunch break, he must not have been hungry. Besides, it wasn't like him to leave the site while on duty, especially when he'd received Liam's call a little over half an hour ago.

Something wasn't right.

Maybe Lennon had misunderstood and thought Liam would pick up the chopper on the taxiway. He whipped out his cell phone and punched in the number of the maintenance supervisor. Just then, Liam heard a groan. He looked around. Another groan and a faint tapping was coming from the next helo stall. He made a mad dash toward the sound, then rolled the two chests aside, only to see Lennon stuffed under the bench, barely conscious.

Fear and dread coursed through Liam as he punched in the numbers for the airport medic. When he'd reported to them what had happened, he dropped to one knee in front of Lennon. "What the hell happened, mate?" Liam asked, checking the mechanic for injuries.

Lennon rolled his eyes and groaned again. "A—a man…" He blinked several times, then opened his eyes again. His hand shot to the top of his head where a huge lump was already forming.

"Take it easy, buddy," Liam said. "You're going to be okay. Can you tell me what happened?"

"That son of a—" Lennon tried to sit up but Liam held him still.

"Easy. Try not to move until the medics arrive. I'm going to call security—"

"The son of a bitch *was* Security," Lennon managed to say.

For a moment, Liam stared at him, then something clicked.

"What's the name of the company who handles airport security?" he asked.

"Spender."

Liam swore. He punched in Bailey's number and prayed for a miracle.

"TALON-6," Bailey said, picking up the phone on the fourth ring.

"Bailey. Get Brianna off the rooftop and stay with her."

"Why? Didn't you just pick her up?" A feeling of fear raced through her.

"Listen carefully, Bailey. Fox stole the chopper and is on his way there. Get Brianna off the roof. Hurry. You don't have a minute to lose."

"It's too late." Bailey almost cried the words. "The chopper picked her up about five minutes ago. I—I thought it was you." Her throat constricted with fear and dread. "Oh God, Liam. What are we going to tell Mike?"

A pause hummed at the other end of the line. "That's not your problem, Bailey," Liam said solemnly. "That's my job."

MIKE'S PAGER WENT OFF just as he finished dispatching the location of his men to the sheriff. "That's all, men. I'll check back in an hour."

He glanced at the number on the display, then grabbed the phone and punched in the Crib's number. All through the meeting with the sheriff and deputies, Mike had been aware of the time. He'd wanted to grab the phone and call Brianna again, to hear the sound of her voice and know she was okay. But he also knew it was for his own selfish reasons. She had a lot on her mind, too. If she thought he was worried, it would do nothing for her peace of mind. Better that she thought this was a routine op, one that would be successful. But until Fox was caught and behind bars, he wouldn't sleep soundly.

He felt uneasy. The more men they had on board this op, the more things could go wrong.

"Mike?" Liam answered the phone on the first ring.

"About time you called." Mike glanced at his watch again. "You're running late, pal. Has she arrived on the yacht?" The slight pause on the other end caused the hair on the back of Mike's neck to rise. "Liam? What's wrong?"

"Fox overtook the maintenance mechanic at the airport. He left with the chopper before I got there."

Mike felt as though he was watching the scene play out from afar. "Where's Brianna?" he heard himself ask.

"Mike...I'm sorry."

"What the hell does that mean?"

"Brianna embarked the chopper, thinking it was me at the controls."

Mike felt as if a steel fist had punched him in the stomach. Bile rose to his throat. But he felt his nerves turn to ice as his feelings dropped back and logic took control. "Have you called the FAA?"

"Yes. They put out an all-points bulletin."

"Is Bailey tracking her?"

"Bailey says the Tiger is moving straight up the Hudson."

"Get on the phone and call the nearest airport from Kingston. Have whatever the hell can fly waiting for me when I get there. I'll ask the sheriff for an escort. I'm about twenty minutes out. Get back to me with the flight path on the Tiger."

"Roger."

"Liam," Mike said. "We don't have much time. If the Tiger gets behind these hills up here, we'll lose its signal."

BAILEY HAD BEEN RIGHT, Brianna thought as she adjusted the shoulder harness and clipped the seat belt around her waist. From her seat in back, she could see the colorfully lit instrument panel clearly. She flushed with pride, knowing that many of the gizmos were Mike's inventions, many of which, if Bailey was to be believed, were as sophisticated as the government's.

Liam brought in the power and she could feel the air build under the rotors as the Tiger slowly lifted off the roof.

The noise would make conversation difficult. Besides, Liam seemed deep in concentration as he manned the controls, listening to his headset.

She leaned back and tried to enjoy the clear view of the Manhattan skyline while the chopper accelerated across the Brooklyn Bridge and the East River. Below, Manhattan skyscrapers rushed beneath as they flew about five hundred feet above the tops of the buildings as they crossed over the city. Up ahead, she recognized the Hudson River and New Jersey. Strange, she thought. From what Mike had told her, the yacht was docked at one of the Hudson River piers at Twelfth Avenue. Why were they leaving Manhattan and heading north?

Maybe the approaching storm was causing Liam to change course? Maybe that was why he was so serious. Was the storm going to be that much of a problem on such a short flight?

Stop it, Brianna, she chided herself, and forced her attention on the view below.

After a while, she wondered if she should ask Liam. He'd remained so quiet, listening to his headset. Was something wrong? They were definitely taking a north, north-westerly direction. The Hudson was far on her right now. Aqua swimming pools and verdant square patches surrounding New Jersey homes scrolled beneath them.

She leaned forward and tapped Liam on the shoulder. ''I

thought the yacht was docked on Twelfth Street,'' she shouted above the noise.

As he turned to face her, a scream froze in her throat as she realized the pilot at the controls wasn't Liam. Through the tinted glass of his face mask, she recognized the sharp cheekbones, the deep-set eyes of Reginald Fox.

What have you done with Liam? screamed through her brain, but she couldn't get the words out.

''I see you're surprised.'' He lifted the tinted face shield, revealing the glittering hate shining from his eyes.

This is the man who threw Kristi down the stairs. The same man who wiled his way into Simone's life just to get close to her. Mike had said he could be capable of anything.

Brianna fought for control. Think. This man wasn't rational. She knew better than to say or do anything that would upset him further. Her instinct to help warred with her instinct for survival as she was filled with outrage for what he'd done.

The facts that Mike had learned about Fox raced through her mind. Ex-military, a rogue CIA operative, the father of a male batterer who'd been beaten to death in prison.

He turned back to the controls, his hand pulled up slightly on the control stick to the right of his seat. The helicopter pitched and rose. As they lifted, she could see the Hudson snake along the countryside below. From the slight angle of the sun, she could tell they were heading north.

He turned his head around and lifted his visor. ''Why don't you think about all the things I could do to you, bitch. Let's see. Maybe I'm going to throw you out the cargo door?'' His thin lips quirked. ''Yeah, I like that. I could count the times your body would bounce on the ground.'' He laughed as he pushed the control stick farther. She felt the thrust of the aircraft jerk as it lifted sharply in the wind.

"'Course, the higher we are when you fall, the longer your body will tumble, and the more time you'll have to think about the size of the mark you're going to make on this world." He laughed maniacally then, and she looked away, determined not to show him her fear.

He stopped laughing and she could feel him stare at her.

"Don't think I know you're not scared, bitch. But it's early. We've got a way to go, and plenty of time to play this game. You'll break in time. And where we're going, we'll have all the time in the world. And your cocky, oh-so-smart boyfriend won't ever be able to find you."

She leaned back in her seat, not wanting to upset him any further. He must have planned this all along. How did he know about the helicopter? He must have had another bug planted.

Her mind raced with questions, each one hitching her panic up a notch. He was going to kill her. He'd have to kill her. This time he'd made no move to disguise himself.

She was going to die.

No, dammit. She wasn't dead yet. She felt herself tremble and she fought against it. Think. Victims panic. Brianna Kent, you are no victim! What would Mike want her to do?

Mike. Dear God, what would Mike do if he knew that Fox had taken the chopper and she was with him? Tears sprang to her eyes as she thought of his anguish. She forced the tears away. No, she could fall apart later. Now she had to think.

He hadn't tied her up yet. That would probably come later, she thought with a chill. If she made it to the landing, she had to find some way to defend herself. She looked around for something to use as a weapon. If she tried to unlatch her seat belt, he'd sense the move and try to grab her. But he's got his hands full with the controls; there's a minimum he could do. But she can't fly this thing, she has to rely on him. Stalemate.

She glanced around but there was nothing loose that she could use as defense. He'd already thought of that.

The chopper banked slightly and they were heading in a decidedly northern route. To the left was a river, the Hudson. Below, orchards and farmland spread between small towns and villages. They were heading out of the city, toward the more rural areas.

She had to keep her wits. Certainly, by now, the airport knew the chopper had been stolen and the FAA would have them on radar.

No, that's why he's been flying so low since we left the city, she realized with another shot of panic. This man was no fool. But there must be something she could do. There must be.

Chapter Sixteen

Oh God, now what was Fox up to?

Brianna stiffened in her seat as she watched him. With his left hand on the control stick, he appeared to be fumbling with something in his lap. She waited, her senses on alert. Did he have a gun? Did he have a knife? Before she had another thought, his right arm swung around toward her. She felt a sharp sting in her thigh, and a sudden throb pulsated through her leg muscle.

When he pulled his hand back, she saw the hypodermic needle in his fingers.

"Now the fun begins," he said, turning back to the controls. "You'll feel a little woozy in a few minutes." She heard him chuckle. "Enjoy it, bitch. I've injected you with a lethal injection." She heard him laugh that maniacal laugh, and already her senses were being affected.

She tried to move her legs but found they felt leaden. Her throat felt dry and her eyes were getting heavy. She fought the feeling of lightheadedness, then she couldn't feel at all.

THE POUNDING WOKE her up. Her eyelids fluttered open. Darkness. What was that smell? Mothballs? Or a pine-smelling disinfectant? She tried to lift her head, but her head felt as heavy as a bowling ball and pain zigzagged across her brain.

Where was she? What happened? Then she remembered.

Her heart thudded as she tried to get her bearings. They weren't in the chopper. Her face was pressed against scratchy wool. A blanket. She was lying facedown on a cot.

She forced herself to try and turn over, but she couldn't move her body. Her head turned slightly and she tried to stare into the shadows. Gradually her pupils became accustomed to the lack of light. She blinked, forcing her brain to discern the shadowed objects in front of her.

Logs. The walls were logs. She glanced down at the floor, ignoring the shot of pain riveting her head at the mere motion. Bare plank lumber. She was in a log cabin. She tried to move her fingers and hands, but they were numb. She had feeling in her arms. Thank God, she wasn't tied up. She must try to escape.

Hope swelled in her chest. Her mind was clearing, then she wondered, where was Fox? Was he watching her from a dark corner, or maybe with a hidden camera? Why else wouldn't he tie her up and leave if she could escape?

Maybe he wanted her to try to run away. Yes, that was it. He was playing with her, like a cat with an injured bird.

An anger of which she never thought herself capable built inside her. No, don't lose control, Brianna. Think. Anger will only cloud your logic and give Fox the advantage.

She had to figure out where she was and what was going on before she dare escape. Was it dark outside or were the windows covered? She didn't want to lift herself from the cot in case he had her under surveillance.

She couldn't hear anything. But he was nearby. She could sense him. She tried to wiggle her fingers again but her arms and legs felt so heavy. Yes, she'd been drugged.

More than likely he'd give her another shot once he found her conscious.

Her only chance was not to let on that she was awake. Maybe when he came to give her another shot she could startle him and have the advantage. Just a few seconds, then one well-placed punch at his eyes or his larynx.

What had her instructor told her at her self-defense course? A sudden upward thrust with the heel of her hand directly at an assailant's nose could drive his nose bone into his brain.

Yes, she could do it. She must do it.

She lay there for what seemed like hours, forcing herself to remain awake. She flexed and pointed her fingers and toes, anything to start her circulation flowing and reduce the effect of the drug. Feeling was gradually returning in her legs and arms, and her fingers and hands tingled. A surge of hope and success elated her. Keep positive. You can do this.

"I see you're awake and ready to play again," Fox said menacingly.

She froze. The voice seemed to be coming from overhead. She remained still, refusing to show fear although her heart beat a wild tattoo in her chest.

Minutes passed. Why didn't he say something else? The minutes dragged on. Was he testing to see if she'd really been awake?

No, he liked playing games. Even if he had a camera on her, he had no idea *how* the drug had affected her. If she remained still, in time he'd have to physically check her vital signs. And when he did, she would make her move. That is, if he didn't kill her first.

But her professional guess was that he was bent on mentally torturing her. He'd proven that by the very first photographs he'd delivered to her. He didn't want her dead. Not yet, anyway.

They played the waiting game as minutes turned into what felt like hours. She had no idea how long. But she didn't care. Each minute would gain her time to recover from the drug.

What did prisoners of war do when they were being mentally tortured? Mathematics. Yes, that was it. They did numerical calculations in their heads to keep from thinking of where they were and what was happening to them. No. She'd think of Mike. She smiled to herself as she evoked the image of Mike's handsome face in her mind. Her throat tightened at the thought that she might never see him again.

The sound of a hinge creaked and the door opened. Facedown on the cot, her face was slightly turned toward the sound. Through lowered lids, she waited, watching through her lashes as the door opened then closed. She could see daylight. Then a flashlight beam swayed as footfalls lumbered toward her. He was making no attempt to be quiet.

She kept her shallow breaths even and steady. Food smells, garlic or onion, and Italian spices grew stronger as he came near. He reached out as if to take her pulse. She waited, her nerves tensed. When his fingers touched her left wrist, she drew herself up. Brandishing her right fist directly at him, she poked her fingernails at his eyes.

"Ugh!" he yelled, staggering back. The flashlight fell from his hand and danced across the floor.

Brianna lunged for the light. Her fingers gripped the handle as he hurtled himself at her like a wild man. Her fingers clenched the light's long handle, then she wielded it like a baseball bat, aiming at his larynx.

But he pivoted just in time, and she missed. When he lunged for her again, she spun around and thrust her size seven boot square into his groin.

She heard his low growl of pain, and she was filled with triumph as he stumbled to the floor. She wanted to bolt, but she forced herself to pound the flashlight on top of his head as hard as she could. He groaned again when the flashlight struck his skull.

Brianna flung the door open and made a mad dash across the small room toward the porch. Adrenaline coursed through her veins, forcing her heavy legs to move. She definitely wasn't herself. Throwing open the front door, she dived off the porch, stumbling to the ground. She rolled several times until she forced herself to her feet, then hobbled toward the woods.

Damn, her body felt leaden. She must get away. Dragging herself through the dense brush and trees, she refused to look back. How long she staggered, she had no idea. When she stopped to gulp air into her lungs, she gripped the trunk of a huge pine to prop herself up.

She waited, listening. So far, she was lucky. But the blow she'd given him would only stun him. She had only minutes to get a head start. But that would be enough.

By the slant of the sun, it would be dark soon. She couldn't rest. She had to keep going.

But where could she go? She was surrounded by thick woods.

If there had been a road by the cabin, she'd missed seeing it. Where was the helicopter? Had he parked it in a nearby clearing or on a road somewhere?

She had to get away. She raced through the pines and patches of tall ferns, when she realized that she had to get her bearings. If she didn't, she'd be running in circles and she'd end up back at the cabin with Fox.

Is that why Fox wasn't chasing her? He knew she'd circle back. Was this another one of his games?

Think, Brianna. Think.

Her hands were damp and sticky with pine pitch from a tree trunk. Her fingernails were jagged, filled with moss and lichen.

Moss and lichen. A feeling of elation filled her. Moss

and lichen grew thickest on the north side of objects. She glanced at the tree trunks ahead to get her sense of direction. She was facing south. Gazing up at the treetops, she tried to judge the sun's slant. But instead of shining over her right shoulder, the sun was at the nine o'clock position over her left shoulder. It wasn't dusk. It was morning! She must have been knocked out all night.

She'd have hours of daylight to chart a straight course. She remembered something from her childhood when she visited her aunt Nora and the Judge at their family estate. *If you're ever lost in the woods, walk around the right side of one tree, then the left side on the one ahead of it.* Yes, she'd walk in one direction.

Maybe she'd come across a road, a farmhouse, or hear a noise.

Or…spot a plane. Maybe, just maybe, Mike would find her. This seemed too good to be true. Tears of hope stung her eyes and she fought to keep going through the woods.

BAILEY LOOKED UP from the console where she had been tracking the Tiger helicopter's beam on Skywalker—the satellite tracking station—when Liam came through the door of the war room.

"Any sign of them?" he asked her.

She took off her headset and shook her head. "Not yet." She almost choked on the words. Never before had a mission taken on such a close-to-home feel. But in the short few days since she'd known Brianna, she'd felt a bond with Mike's ex-wife that was almost as close as a sister. Bailey fought back the unusual burst of sentiment. A mission was no place for emotion. She put her headset over her ears and scanned the screen. "I was sounding off Skywalker tracking the Tiger when I suddenly lost the signal. Still no luck." She looked back at Liam. "I'm afraid Fox has landed. If he's behind any one of those mountain peaks, I won't have much luck picking up the Tiger's signal.''

"Fox may be able to fly the Tiger, but he sure as hell doesn't understand all of Mike's technology. Fox won't know enough to turn everything off. Even when the copter is down, the sensors run off the batteries.''

"What is Mike's 10-20?''

"He's here,'' Bailey answered, pointing to the last known coordinates on the map of the Adirondack area that Mike had given her when he'd checked in ten minutes ago.

"He told me he was zeroing in on the last known location of the Tiger,'' she added, forcing a neutrality into her voice.

"How's he holding out?'' Liam's gaze remained on the screen.

"Like a rock. You know Mike.'' She turned and looked up into Liam's chiseled features. Her heart went out to him. She knew that he blamed himself for Fox stealing the Tiger and kidnapping Brianna. All the while they had tried to track Fox's erratic flight patterns through the mountains, Liam had remained uncommonly quiet. Usually under tense conditions, his quick wit and sense of humor were welcome stress relievers. Now, only the tight clench of his jaw gave any sign to his feelings.

"Don't beat yourself up, Liam. It's not your fault that we didn't know about Fox working for airport security.''

"If I had checked to find out what companies were clients of Spender, I would have known that Fox had access to the airport.'' He swore. "Damn. Fox had an office there!''

"No one can be expected to cover all the bases in such a short time, Liam.'' Bailey shook her head. "Two more days and we could have told Mike how much lint Fox had in his belly button.''

Liam chuckled. "God, you sounded just like your dad.''

"Thanks.'' She lifted her chin. "There's something else

Dad used to say. A man can only be expected to do his best with the facts at hand.''

''Ah, maybe that's how your old man told you, but the way I heard him tell it, it was a bit less sanitary.''

She laughed, feeling glad to see Liam smiling again.

''I'm going to call Mike,'' Liam said finally, picking up the console speaker. He pressed the button down. ''Mother Hen to Ranger N206. Mother Hen to Ranger N206. Come on back.''

Over the airwaves, the high-pitched whine of the Bell Ranger helicopter's turbine engines hummed in the background. ''Ranger N206 to Mother Hen. What's up?'' Mike said.

''I was wondering if you thought the Tiger might be between Mother Hen and your 10-20?'' Liam asked. ''Want me to come up there and help?''

''Negative, Mother Hen. I think the Tiger slipped past my 10-6 before I was able to reach its coordinates. The Tiger can hit to two hundred ten knots, don't forget. The Ranger I'm flying maxes at a hundred twenty. Anything new from Skywalker?''

''Negative.''

''Have Mother Hen use a crossing pattern, west to east. Then walk the beam north.'' Mike ordered.

''Roger.'' Liam paused. ''What's your 10-20 look like?''

''Extremely dense woods. From the forest ranger's report, there aren't any cabins around the region where we last received a signal. My guess from the speed and direction of the Tiger's flight path is that the Tiger continued through the Catskills heading toward the Adirondacks. My hunch is that he's landed there somewhere.'' Mike lifted the cyclic control stick, and the Ranger copter lifted over the treetops. ''Mother Hen, I want you to call all the airfields, small airports, both private and commercial, that are fifty miles each side of the Tiger's last known flight path.

Ask them if there were any visual sightings of the Tiger or
if anyone heard it. Give them a description. After all, the
Tiger looks military and would get attention if anyone saw
it.''

"Roger. Anything else?''

"Negative. I'll be flying a roving orbit, northward. I'll
call back in ten minutes. Out!''

Liam looked at Bailey who was already following
Mike's change in orders. "Go to it, Bailey. You heard the
man.''

BRIANNA SHOOK HER HEAD and fought back another wave
of nausea. Was this the result of the drug Fox had given
her? Then she realized she hadn't eaten in over a day. She
lowered her head between her knees and waited for the
dizziness to pass. Dear God, she must remember to pace
herself and not overexert.

From the sun's slant, she calculated that about three
hours had passed since she'd escaped. So far she'd seen no
sign of Fox. A sense of exhilaration filled her. So far, she'd
successfully eluded him. Now, all she had to do was stay
alive until she ran across some sign of civilization.

She took several more steps, but it was no use. Her legs
were too wobbly to stand. Her knee was bleeding from
slipping and stumbling down the side of the ravine. Her
arms and hands were scraped and bruised from the rocks
at the base. She forced herself to keep going. Twigs cracked
underneath the spongy forest floor as she trampled ahead,
willing one foot in front of the other. Up ahead was a large
boulder. She would make it that far, then rest for a few
minutes.

Her lungs burned as she drew in a breath. When she
finally reached the boulder, she thought she heard something. Her senses quickened as she flattened herself against
the cold granite and listened. Yes, she heard something. A

whirring. No, it wasn't a helicopter. It was a rushing sound. Water. She heard water running.

With a renewed sense of energy, she forced herself to keep lumbering toward the sound. She parted the foliage. There, less than twenty feet away was a wide stream. Branches slapped at her as she hurried to the bank. Water. Her mouth was so dry she could hardly swallow. Her boot slid and she almost tumbled headfirst, but she caught herself just in time. When she was almost to the shore, she peeked through the limbs. Maybe it's a wide feeder stream or small branch of a river. Maybe it leads to the Hudson?

She took a gulp of air before she collapsed.

BRIANNA OPENED HER EYES, instantly awake. The sun was still shining. Good, she hadn't lost very much precious daylight.

She pulled back the hair that had come loose from her ponytail and fallen into her face and looked around. She must have fallen asleep. Insect bites covered her body. She managed to get to her feet, every muscle aching in protest. Lumps and bumps covered her face, swollen from insect bites. Her arms and legs were scratched and bruised from the slapping branches. But she was grateful to be alive. She was a survivor. She would find help. Someone would come by. She had to believe.

She would follow the shore. Trees and undergrowth were dense enough to provide cover, in case Fox managed to somehow track her. That thought propelled her to move. How long had she slept?

Several hours by the sun's position. She'd have a few more hours of daylight. This time of year it didn't get dark until almost 9:00 p.m. But here in the mountains, the darkness would come suddenly. By then she would be safe. She needed to believe that.

WAS SHE SEEING THINGS? Brianna blinked. No, it was real. The white-shingled, weather-beaten cottage looked uninhabited. No smoke drifted from the chimney. No telephone or electrical wires led to the building. The porch and steps were mounded with dried leaves and debris. She moved to the edge of the clearing and looked around. Several black shutters hung by their broken hinges. The white paint on the porch trim was peeling. She crept to the front window and peered inside. White sheets covered the furniture. Her heart sank.

Maybe they had an old compass, a C.B. radio? A map?

A small shed loomed in the distance. Maybe she could find a bike, or a motorcycle, something. Her heart raced as she dashed toward the outbuilding.

There, inside the shack, was an old, beat-up aluminum canoe and a paddle. Her breath quickened as she picked up a rock and broke the door pane.

A short while later, Brianna was paddling with the current downstream. The craft was light, and to be safe, she took a few extra minutes to place several large rocks in the canoe bow. Although the wind wasn't blowing now, and the water was calm, the canoe would be too light to manage if the weather changed or the current got rough. She might be in this canoe for days.

She would survive, she repeated again and again. She must.

While she paddled, she assessed her wounds. She had a nasty gash on her forearm. But of all the cuts and bruises, the gash on her right knee was the worst. She whipped off her head scarf and wrapped it around her knee. Her right boot heel had snapped off when she'd fallen. Maybe if she removed the other boot, she could break that heel, too. At least she would hobble evenly.

When she tugged off her left boot, she noticed a thin, transparent, plastic-coated bracelet circling her ankle. A silver bead, no bigger than a small pea, was threaded on a wire inside the plastic.

Fear surged through her. Fox must have put this on her while she was unconscious. A shiver slid down her spine. Now she knew why he hadn't followed her.

He didn't have to. She tugged and yanked until the wire cut her flesh, but she still couldn't remove it.

Fox was probably watching her with his scope right now. He knew her every move. The cry of anguish she heard was her own.

AN OWL HOOTED somewhere downriver. It would be dark in a few hours. Maybe, if the moon was full, she could keep paddling. She'd move all night if she had to. The only way she could escape was to reach help before Fox caught up with her. And he would. The bastard had this planned all along.

She used her anger as fuel to paddle. She'd be damned if she'd be bested by a psychopath like Fox. Her shoulders ached as she jabbed the wooden paddle into the water. The canoe hit a rock and the loud bang echoed in her ears as she righted herself. Damn, the river was widening but getting rockier. She would manage, she said to herself. She would manage somehow.

In the distance she heard it. The low *whop, whop, whop,* of a copter. Her heart leaped into her throat as she glanced around for cover. *Maybe it was Mike.* No, Mike had no idea where she was.

She gripped the paddle as her gaze searched in vain. Both sides of the bank were gravel with poor vegetation. If she beached the canoe, would she have time to hide in the woods?

What was the use? He'd find her as long as she was wearing that damn tracker bracelet.

The *whop whop whop* sound grew louder. She glanced

up to see the tops of the trees rock and sway from the wind gusts as the Tiger's rotors hammered down on the pines.

"You did very well, bitch. I never thought you'd get this far," Fox said over the loudspeaker.

She clenched her right hand on the top of the canoe's gunwale while gripping the paddle with her left hand, fighting to steady herself. But the wind rush from the copter's rotors was pushing the craft toward the opposite shore.

"Steady as she goes," Fox said with a laugh. "Let's see how well you can swim." He lowered the craft until the wind rush from the rotors flipped over the canoe, despite the rocks she had placed in the bow for ballast.

Wind and water beat at her, but she didn't let go of her grip of the paddle. The river wasn't deep. Although surprisingly cold, the water came up only to her hips. With the help of the current, she tipped the canoe right side up, then hung on to its side. She was a strong swimmer, but her legs were so tired the frigid water was already causing them to cramp. What did Fox plan to do next? Shoot her, like a fish in a tank?

She glanced up at him. She couldn't see through his face shield but she could sense the bastard was laughing at her.

"That's not swimming," he called out to her. He brought the chopper even closer. This time the helicopter skids were barely four feet over her head. The thunderous roar was like a freight train; she could feel its vibrations ramming through her. The turbulence of the wind force and the water caused her to stumble facedown in the water. Squeezing her eyes shut, she surfaced and fought for air.

Dear God, was he going to kill her by setting the copter on top of her?

The blast from the chopper blades was deafening and she felt as if the force was sucking the air from her lungs. Waves of water blinded her. All she knew was to hold on to the paddle for dear life. Right now, it felt like her only link to sanity.

When she opened her eyes to look for the canoe, her hope sank as she saw the wind rush from the rotors lift the craft like a long silver kite into the air. It bounced and banged downstream, coming finally to rest among the rocks and driftwood along the shore.

She stumbled to her feet. The cold water was causing her legs to cramp. She couldn't remain in the river like a sitting duck. Clutching the paddle, she turned her back on the wind and let its thrust push her after the canoe.

Trees waved and bent nearly double by the turbulence as she fought her way toward shore. She gripped a tree and pulled herself into the underbrush, then darted a glance over her shoulder to see what Fox would do next.

Suddenly she realized this powerful rush wasn't caused by just one helicopter. There were two. Was she seeing double? With her eyes continually filling with water and debris from the wind force, she couldn't be sure. Shielding her eyes with one hand, she peered through the slits between her fingers. She couldn't believe what she saw. Another helicopter, a smaller craft, hovered over Fox.

From the cockpit of the Tiger, Fox was craning his neck for a glimpse of what was causing him to sway and buck. The abrupt movement bounced Fox against the instrument panel. As she watched, the Tiger suddenly lurched forward and was brought to land farther upstream in the shallows. What was going on?

She wiped the sand from her eyes with the hem of her T-shirt and looked at the second helicopter.

Mike! Dear God, was she dreaming? It *was* Mike! He was piloting the smaller helicopter, but somehow he appeared to be also controlling Fox in the Tiger.

''Drop your weapon, Fox,'' she heard Mike say from the second chopper. ''Climb out and lie facedown, spread eagle, on the shoreline. The Forest Service airboats will be here any minute. You're surrounded. Fox, you know the drill. I'd love nothing better than for you to give me the excuse to finish you off for good.''

The door slid open and Fox jumped into the stream with a splash. Where he landed, the water was barely to his shins. Instead of giving up, he drew a gun and fired at Mike's chopper's engine. When he saw that he'd missed, he darted into the woods farther downstream near where she had entered the woods. Fox fired several more shots at Mike again. The forest was too dense to see Fox, but from the sound of the blasts, she knew Fox had to be close.

Why isn't Mike returning Fox's fire? Then it dawned on her. She's directly behind Fox in the line of fire. Mike couldn't shoot because he was afraid he'd hit her.

What was Fox trying to do? Was he planning on over-taking her and use her as a hostage to protect himself from Mike?

Once Mike saw Fox heading for the woods, he immediately moved his chopper downstream and landed in the shallows, now drawing Fox's attention away from Brianna.

Oh, Mike. She realized that his concentration was mired by her. She must do something to help.

Suddenly, another shot fired from her left. She ducked into some bushes. She couldn't see Fox, but she heard him. A branch cracked. Yes, he was looking for her.

She inched around to see where Fox had moved. Peeking between two leafy branches, she spotted him crouched behind a huge uprooted pine. He'd removed his helmet, and in profile, he seemed even more frightening. He changed clips in his handgun, then sharply drew up the gun with both hands and trained it on Mike.

She gripped the handle of the canoe paddle with both hands and crept back, then circled behind Fox.

The sporadic gunfire and Fox's yelling at Mike seemed

to shield any noise she made as she sneaked behind Fox. When she was within several feet of his blind side, she swung the canoe paddle with all her might. "Game's over, mister. You lose."

Fox turned toward her just in time to catch the edge of the paddle right in his Adam's apple. Stunned, he fell to his knees, choking. Instinctively, his gun hand swung around from his right side just when her second swing with the paddle landed edgewise across his wrist, breaking it. The gun flipped harmlessly to the ground.

Fox hunched over on all fours. Her third blow whacked him on the back of the neck. He collapsed, facedown in the weeds.

She dropped the paddle and stood there, dazed. Suddenly the woods seemed still. The wind had died down and the helicopter rush was gone. Mike? Where was Mike?

Maybe Fox had landed a lucky hit when she was circling back to overtake Fox. Her chest constricted with fear. Please God, no. I couldn't bear it if something—

"Brianna!"

She whirled around and gasped as she leaped into Mike's arms.

Chapter Seventeen

Brianna leaned back in her office chair and glowered at the pile of letters that needed to be signed, the phone messages that needed to be returned and the stack of reports that needed to be written. Her muscles still ached from the ordeal three days ago. The stitches on her knee itched and her bruised elbow hurt like hell. But she had to face getting back to her life. And work was her life.

Some life. Never had she felt more miserable, empty and alone. Well, she better get used to it.

With a deep sigh, she shoved the reports to one side and cradled her head in her arms on the desktop. *Why hadn't Mike called?* It had been three days since he walked out of her apartment with an ''I'll see you.''

What the hell did that mean? When would he see her?

He'd been so loving, so attentive when he carried her to the Field Service airboat and held her during their flight back to New York. She couldn't have felt more cherished if he'd wrapped her in cotton wool. After their ordeal, all she wanted was to be held, be loved, as only Mike could love her. He'd remained glued to her side at the hospital when she'd been hydrated with IV fluids and the gash on her knee was sutured. He'd remained overnight by her side, then demanded to stay with her until Saturday, when Nora arrived, insisting on caring for her.

Brianna was surprised when Nora mentioned that Mike had called her. He'd asked Nora if she would come to New York and take care of Brianna. Brianna still felt the sting of disappointment. She'd been enjoying the time with Mike, and she thought he had, too. It seemed that they couldn't get enough of each other. But once Nora arrived, Mike left, and she was damned if she'd beg him to stay.

What did you expect him to do, after you practically told him all along that you never wanted to see him again once the stalker was caught?

She mentally shook herself. *Get to work, Brianna,* she commanded sharply. Get on with your life. Mike is out of the picture, just the way you wanted it.

She limped out of her chair and took a seat on the leather couch, propping her throbbing knee on the hassock. She closed her eyes and forced herself to relax.

She should be counting her blessings. Fox was in jail, awaiting a trial date. From what Mike had said, Fox would be sent away for a long time. Simone had taken the news well. Although devastated that David Malden was the man stalking Brianna, Simone had said she'd realized that the man she knew as David Malden wasn't her type long before. He was a companion and they had enjoyed the Broadway shows.

Mike was safe and no one else had been harmed, thanks to Mike and the TALON-6 team, who'd also performed a magnificent job. If Mike hadn't been the person hired to apprehend Fox, who knows what might have happened? If she'd left the matter to the authorities, the outcome could have been very different.

Mike. Yes, she was more than grateful. She owed him her life. And now he was gone.

The door opened as Simone rapped gently then tipped her head inside. "I don't want to disturb you, but…"

"Come in. You're not interrupting anything." She rubbed her temples. "I seem to be woolgathering."

"You're not woolgathering, you're exhausted from your ordeal. I thought the doctor told you to take some time off." Simone studied her with the same motherly attention that Aunt Nora did.

"Please don't mother hen me, Simone. I've had all of that I can stand from Nora."

Simone's mouth quirked. "You're a terrible patient, Doctor," she teased. She took a seat across from Brianna. "Did you see the message I put on your desk from Kristi McFarland?"

Brianna looked up. "Yes, I see that she took my advice and went to stay with her parents." She smiled, so relieved.

"Kristi was disappointed not to have spoken with you directly, but I told her you'd call her when you returned to the office."

"Thanks, Simone. I'll wait and call her in a few days. When my head clears."

Simone smiled in sympathy. "If you've got a few minutes, I've been meaning to speak to you."

Brianna swallowed and felt the pang of empathy for her friend. She paused, hoping to somehow say the right words to comfort her. "I'm so sorry that Reginald Fox involved you in all of this."

She waved her hand. "I'm just thankful that you're all right and that he's in jail." She shook her head. "I don't know what I would have done if—"

Brianna reached out and patted her hand. "Simone, it's you I'm worried about."

She shrugged. "I'm not as foolish as you might think. Several things that David, er, I mean Reginald Fox said about his past didn't ring true." She pursed her lips. "I was foolish enough to think that he was lying to try to impress me, but now I see that he was only trying to get close to me so he could get to you.''

''You were smarter than he thought you were.''

''Oh, he was charming and attentive when he wanted to be, but his moods could be so changeable. I thought it was because he was afraid to trust. But now I understand why.'' She glanced away, fingering the top button of her blue cardigan. ''The night before he stole the helicopter, I told him that I didn't think we should see each other again.''

''How did he take it?''

''Not very well. But we were at a restaurant, so when he pressed me for more of an explanation than I was willing to give, I left. I wanted you to know that. I knew you'd be concerned for my feelings.''

Brianna felt a wave of relief and admiration for her secretary. ''Oh, Simone. I just want what is best for you. I believe you'll meet the right one when it's time.''

Simone smiled. ''Well, I think I might have already done just that. A widower whom I've known through my church, asked me out. I've always admired him. He's very good-looking, and I guess he's finally able to get on with his life.'' She smiled shyly. ''He's a banker. Just to be on the safe side, I asked Mike to run a check on him before I go out with him again.''

Brianna laughed. ''That doesn't sound very romantic, but I think it's a good idea.''

''So did Mike.''

Surprised, Brianna asked, ''When did you speak to him?''

''Last night. I'd called him several days ago and left a message on his answering machine. He's been out of town.''

Brianna pushed down a flutter of resentment. He left town and didn't tell her? But why should he? They weren't joined at the hip. ''I'm really not interested, Simone.''

Brianna struggled to her feet. "If you'll excuse me, I'd better sign those letters so they can go out in the morning mail."

Simone hesitated, as though wanting to say something, but thought better of it. She rose and left the room, closing the door with a soft click.

Try as she might, Brianna couldn't concentrate. Her head pounded. She felt so tired and unlike herself. Picking up the Dictaphone receiver, she opened the first report. Before she said two words, Simone knocked on the door again.

Brianna glanced up. "What is it, Simone?"

"Your new client is here, Dr. Kent."

Brianna stifled a feeling of irritation. "New client?" She took a deep breath. What was the matter with Simone? Her secretary had strict orders not to book any appointments for the next few days. She quirked her mouth. "See if you can reschedule the client with Larry. I'm not up to seeing clients just yet."

"I'm afraid this client won't take no for an answer."

Brianna frowned, her irritation growing. "Why not? Who is it?"

Simone smiled, then stepped aside as Mike came through the door. The secretary's smile widened as she discreetly shut the door and went back to her desk.

Brianna felt the air rush out of her lungs. "Michael," she said, her voice breathy. *Dear God, not another goodbye. She couldn't stand to see him walk out of her life again.* "I thought we'd said everything to each other, Mike. I don't think—"

"I'm here as a client. Didn't Simone tell you?"

"Well, yes…" She looked up at him. "A client?"

"Yes, Doctor." He pulled up a seat in front of her desk and sat down. "You see, I'm having a problem with my love life."

She studied him, noting the serious look in his eyes. "Your love life?"

He nodded, then paused, as though thinking carefully before he spoke. "I'm divorced. The biggest mistake of my life. You see, we were young. Very young. I was head over heels in love with her, but I had no idea how to tell her so. Oh, I showed her." He shook his head and grinned. "We had no trouble in *that* department." He stopped, his blue eyes studying her, and she found it difficult to maintain a professional demeanor.

"Mike, I don't see the point to all this." If he was playing games, she needed to put a stop to it.

"I messed up, big time, Doc." He paused. "It's all right if I call you Doc, isn't it?"

She leaned back. "Do whatever makes you comfortable, Mr. Landis," she said, then quickly added, "within reason, of course."

"Of course." He grinned. "I made lots of mistakes, and now she doesn't believe that I've changed. She—"

"Enough, Mike. Okay, I get the picture." She threw down her pen. "Look, the trouble is with me, not you. I can't be the stay-at-home wife, waiting and wondering if I'm going to see your face flash on the TV news as the latest casualty in some covert operation somewhere."

She stood and folded her hands as she paced back and forth. "Most of my clients come from broken homes. Single parents trying to raise their kids. I want a family, but I want a husband and a father for my kids. A guy who will come home every night. I'm just not the kind who can sit by and worry to death, Mike. In time I'd resent you. And you'd resent me if I asked you to give up the life you've made for yourself."

"You don't have to ask me, Bria." He stood and moved beside her. "I'm here to tell you that I'm taking over the New York operations."

Warily, she lifted an eyebrow.

"Bailey will be graduating and studying for her bar exams. Then she wants to travel. Maybe foreign law. Besides, I've got other plans and I won't have time for globe-trotting."

"Other plans?"

"Yeah. I want to build a house. Lots of rooms for all the babies you want to have. I've just come back from scouting out properties." He put his arms around her. "We can commute on the train each morning to our offices, if you want, or maybe we can drive in together. But I'm more than happy to settle down, Brianna. That is, with you."

"You're saying that now, but—"

"Bria," he said, cupping her chin. "I lost you once because I was a fool. When Liam called me and said that Fox had taken off with you aboard the Tiger, I thought my life was over. Something inside me died, and I knew that the only way I'd be whole again would be to get you back." His voice strained with emotion, and she felt tears sting her eyes as she silently listened.

"I prayed that if I got another chance," Mike said, "I'd spend my life showing you how much you mean to me. Then when I saw you alive in the streambed with Fox in the Tiger hovering over you, I thought, maybe, just maybe, we had a chance. I prayed to God that if He would spare you, I would vow to make it up to you in any way I know how."

"Oh, Mike. What makes you think you won't want to fly off when the next intriguing case comes along?"

"I can mastermind the operations from New York. TALON-6 has five other operatives. Plus we can always hire freelancers from Clancy's Pub." He held her fingers in his large warm hand. "I won't leave you, Bria. I can't leave you. Say you'll marry me."

Her throat tightened. "Oh, Mike…"

"I won't take no for an answer."

She closed her eyes and wiped the tears of happiness from them. "Marrying me will mean big changes in your life," she teased.

"Like what?"

"Well, for a start, I might buy a complete set of dinnerware, glassware and silverware for those empty kitchen cabinets at your apartment at the Crib."

"Hmm. Let's compromise. Paper plates?"

She laughed. "Okay, we'll compromise. I'll start with a coffeemaker and four cups and saucers."

"We'll go shopping right now. As soon as we call Bailey. The TALON-6 yacht is docked, champagne in the cooler, and Bailey, Liam's sisters and Aunt Nora have been making arrangements for an engagement party all day."

"Party? Why not a wedding? Aunt Nora is still in town. Wait until she hears we're getting married."

"Ah, Nora already knows. She was part of my backup plan. That's why I asked her to come into the city. If you'd turned me down, I was going to have her plead my case."

"You wouldn't."

"All's fair in love and war."

"You're pretty sure I'll say yes."

His face sobered. "No, I'll never take you for granted, honey. But I know that if you marry me, I'll never let you regret it."

"Oh, Mike, of course I'll marry you." He kissed her, and as their kiss deepened, Brianna knew that she and Mike were still two different personalities. But if they loved each other enough to be willing to work through their differences, then who could ask for anything more?

HARLEQUIN®
INTRIGUE®
presents
~~NIGHTHAWK ISLAND~~
by award-winning author
RITA HERRON

Strange things are happening on Nighthawk Island...government projects kept under wraps...secret medical experiments. Is it for good—or for evil? What mysteries lie beyond the mist?

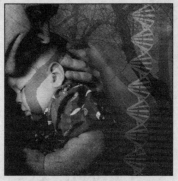

The series continues with
THE CRADLE MISSION

Can a loving nurse and a hardened cop help save a child from being Nighthawk Island's latest project? Find out in May 2003.

Available at your favorite retail outlet.

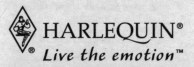

HARLEQUIN®
Live the emotion™

Visit us at www.eHarlequin.com   HISSNWI

Bestselling Author

TAYLOR SMITH

On a cold winter night, someone comes looking for Grace Meade
and the key she holds to a thirty-five-year-old mystery. She is
tortured and killed, and her house is set ablaze. Incredibly,
the prime suspect is her own daughter, Jillian Meade, a woman
wanted in connection with two other murders of women Grace
knew during the war. And FBI Special Agent Alex Cruz has to find
Jillian before her past destroys her for good.

DEADLY GRACE

A "first-rate political thriller."
—*Booklist*

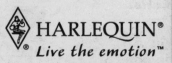

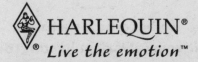